I'll Call You

HOME

SHARON L.
CLARK

I'LL CALL YOU HOME
Copyright © 2025 by Sharon L. Clark

ISBN: 979-8-88653-432-0

Published by Satin Romance
An Imprint of Melange Books, LLC
White Bear Lake, MN 55110
www.satinromance.com

Published in the United States of America.

Cover Design by Caroline Andrus

Dedicated to the teachers who pushed, challenged, and inspired me through the years.

This is all your fault.

ONE
CHARLOTTE

The heels of Charlotte Trevino's shoes clicked loudly on the tile floor of the hospital, keeping time with her racing heart. Less than 24 hours ago she'd gotten a call that made everything else stand still: her father had been injured and was in the hospital. She dropped everything and took the first flight from her current home in San Francisco to her childhood home in Texas. It had been a few years since she'd been back and the guilt of not being there for her dad had her stomach in knots.

When she finally reached the room number her brother had texted her, the door was wide open, and she barreled in. Her larger-than-life dad looked so small, hooked up to a variety of beeping machines, his arm in a sling, and she couldn't stop the tears that sprang to her eyes. "Dad."

He was sitting up in the bed, his wavy white hair longer than she remembered, and his brown eyes popped wide when he saw her. "Charlie-girl! What are you doing here?"

"Where else would I be?" She kissed his cheek. "How are you feeling?"

"Charlotte, what the hell?" Her brother Brandon walked in carrying a fresh cup of coffee and a newspaper. "I would have driven to the airport to pick you up if you'd have told me you were coming."

She waved him off but wrapped her arms around his waist for a hug. Being barely 5'5" when Brandon was 6', it was all she could manage. "I didn't want to put anything more on your plate, so I just rented a car. It's no big deal."

Brandon shook his head. "Of course you did. Still wasn't necessary. Can't you just let people do things for you?"

"When I'm fully capable of doing them myself? Not on your life." She smiled at her dad. "Wonder where I learned that?"

Arthur Trevino chuckled and wagged a finger at his daughter. "Ya got me there, Charlotte Rose. Stubborn as a mule—and I proudly take full responsibility."

Perching on the edge of the bed, Charlotte held his hand and looked up at Brandon. "So, who's going to tell me what happened?"

The two men shared a look she couldn't read, and she narrowed her eyes. "All right. What's going on?"

"Go ahead, Dad, tell her." Brandon crossed his arms. "This is all you, old man."

"Quiet, you." Arthur patted his daughter's hand and shrugged. "I was out for a ride around the property at the end of the day and something spooked the horse just as we were getting back to the paddock. Threw me on my ass."

"On your head, more like." Brandon nudged Arthur, trying to lighten the mood, but Charlotte wasn't fooled. His smile didn't reach his eyes, pinched at the edges from lack of sleep and an over-abundance of worry. "Old graceful here ended up dislocating his shoulder and bruising a few ribs. But they're not sure his heart didn't do a little dance, too."

She'd been so busy planning her flight and lining up a substitute to cover her kindergarten classes, that Charlotte hadn't allowed herself to be scared—and it seemed that moment was when her entire system decided to jump in with both feet. "Your...heart? Seriously? Like a heart attack or what?"

"Nothing like that. Your brother is just being melodramatic." Arthur narrowed his eyes. "It was nothing, barely a blip."

Tears blurred her vision, and she was having trouble catching her breath. If she hadn't already been sitting on the edge of Arthur's bed, her knees might have gone soft under her. Instead, she squeezed her dad's hand and tried to sniffle back all the what-ifs that flooded her brain.

"Damn it, Dad. You're barely into your sixties and I expect you to be around for at least another twenty years, you hear me? You've got to be more careful."

Throwing his hands in the air, Brandon scoffed. "That is exactly what I've been telling him. It's time to step back and think about retiring."

With a snort at his son, Arthur patted Charlotte's knee. "Oh, come on now darlin', you know I'm far too stubborn to go anywhere just yet. You'll see—give me a couple weeks and I'll be up turning cartwheels!"

Just then, the nurse came in to take some vitals and give him some medication, so Charlotte dragged her brother into the hall.

"Tell me the truth, Bran. How bad was it? I know he's not telling me everything."

He ran his hand through his shaggy dark hair and leaned against the wall. "Not gonna lie, Char, I was pretty scared. He thinks the injuries are the most concerning part of all of this, but I really think he was lucky he didn't have a full heart attack. If Doc Angus hadn't still been there to call the ambulance, well...I don't know. But he's in the best heart hospital in southern Texas and they said he should recover just fine. He has some artery build-up but not enough that he needs surgery. Which is a good thing because the old man's cranky enough that he has to take it easy and relinquish a lot of his duties."

"Yeah, well, he's gonna have to rest, probably longer than a couple weeks." She tapped a finger against her chin and paced the hallway. "Maybe we can give Hank and Calvin some more responsibilities and convince Milo to come out after school, too."

It quickly became obvious that Brandon was trying not to meet her eye, so Charlotte laid her hand his arm. "What? I'll find out one way or another, so just spill it."

"We had to let Calvin go about six months ago. Chores and duties were redistributed then, mostly between Hank and me, so we're already stretched pretty thin."

"Oh, no." Charlotte had always liked Calvin. He was around her age and had always been quick with a smile or a joke. They'd taken him on as a ranch hand during her senior year of high school and he'd been around every time she came home, keeping her company while they worked. Maybe he wasn't the most reliable employee and had been a little mouthy at times, but he was good with the animals. In fact, Cal was the one who had helped her break the rowdiest colts once they were old enough. "I'll miss seeing him around the ranch. What happened?"

Brandon shrugged. "Oh, you know how he was. It just got to the point where he was late more often than not, was getting into arguments with Hank and Dad, wasn't getting shit done. So when money got tight and we realized we had to let someone go, he made the most sense. Turns out he has a rich uncle who offered him a job up near San Antonio. It's been rough, but it was best for everyone, all around."

Gaping at him, Charlotte tried to make sense of what he was saying. "Wait—back up. What do you mean when money got tight? T & M Ranch has always been able to take care of their employees."

There had to be some mistake. But before she could ask any more questions, the nurse slipped by and Brandon scrambled to get back in the room. Charlotte could only follow, compiling a mental list of questions for her brother once they were home. But for the moment, she just wanted to relish the time with her little family.

––––––

When Arthur started yawning and having trouble keeping his eyes open, Charlotte and Brandon reluctantly left him to rest. The whirlwind of the last twenty-four hours was starting to take its toll on her, so she left her brother to run his errands in Seguin, and she started on the long drive home.

T & M Ranch was situated a quarter mile off the highway and Charlotte was glad it was still light out. Coming up the tree-lined drive and seeing the yard open up in front of her was a sight that never got old.

On her left, the two-story farmhouse was the first thing that came into view, and she was inundated with a flood of memories: Sitting on the covered porch, repotting plants with her mother, or learning how to tie knots with her dad. Her bedroom was on the second floor, just over the porch awning and she grinned thinking about the many times she'd snuck out and shimmied down the trellis. While she never got caught, Charlotte was pretty sure her dad knew what she was up to and stayed awake most nights until she came home.

She parked in front of the house and just sat with her hands gripping the steering wheel, lost in some other memories that weren't all that great. Like the day she came home from school and found her father, eyes red, waiting to tell her that her mother had passed. She thought he was joking, just trying to scare her, even though he would never be that mean. Instead, he sat her down on those front steps and tried to explain to 14-year-old Charlotte that Rose Murray Trevino had suffered an aneurysm while hanging out the laundry and hadn't known what was happening, hadn't suffered at all. Her heart hurt staring at those steps, seeing in her mind's eye the day of the funeral and all the black-clad, well-meaning folks who had come out from Zearing to pay their respects and share their useless platitudes.

"She's in a better place, dear."

"At least she didn't suffer."

"Everything happens for a reason."

There were many, many comments about how she was the spitting image of darling Rose Murray. Charlotte knew she was her mom's carbon copy—which only made it more painful to look in the mirror. Her dad and Brandon were tough. They're ranchers, and men, and they refused to cry in front of anyone, even Charlotte. Because of that, they didn't want to see her cry, either. So she suffered alone.

Well, almost alone.

Charlotte slid out of the rental car and climbed those familiar steps to sit on the hanging porch swing. The months following her mother's death had been dark, nothing was good, nothing made her happy.

She had a sneaking suspicion that Jason Archer was the only reason she'd kept going that summer.

They had been on their first date just two weeks before Rose died and were a very young and very new couple. Helping someone deal with a death isn't something many 15-year-old boys would take on willingly or with such care. But Jason was something else.

Charlotte tucked her legs under her as she sat, a sad smile on her lips. She did everything she could to push him away: refusing his phone calls, sitting silent and sullen anytime he came over to see her, and then turning around to seduce him the next minute. Her cheeks burned in the fading light. Not her proudest moment, that was certain. After years of therapy, she knew it was a desperate attempt to feel something, anything, good again.

But Jason had been the voice of reason, careful and kind, holding her in his arms while she cried. Or he'd stand as her scapegoat and let her scream and yell out her frustrations. Jason had a calmness about him that was nearly the opposite of Charlotte's own hot temper. By the time they graduated high school, he could soothe her dark moods with a gentle hand barely grazing the back of her neck. She could almost feel it; the memory was so strong.

Shaking herself, Charlotte jumped up from the swing and stomped back to the car. Jason wasn't part of her life anymore and hadn't been for nearly eight years. After graduation he made it perfectly clear to her that he didn't want her around. Well, by god, she wasn't. A fantastic scholarship to City College of San Francisco and the creation of a life with her new best friend, Katie, had kept her mostly on the Coast ever since. When she did make it back to her hometown, she did everything she could not to run into Jason.

Unfortunately, she wasn't always successful. At least once every time she was in town, they ran into each other. And it always took her breath away.

The first time wasn't as much of a surprise as it was a punch in the gut. She'd only been home for a day and was already feeling pretty low. Things weren't going as she'd thought at school, and she was really homesick, and then when she spotted Jason walking on the other side of the street, an arm around a woman she didn't recognize, well...it was hard.

Dragging her suitcase into the house, Charlotte left it in her old bedroom, which was nearly unrecognizable. It was a neutral guest bedroom now, beige and pale green instead of the bright yellows and blues she had decorated it in. Back in the kitchen she poured herself some iced tea and returned to the porch swing to watch the night take over the sky.

Her mind wandered back to Jason as the deep blue of twilight crept over the vast Texas sky. It was the exact color of his eyes, hovering somewhere between blue and violet. Again, such a contrast to her own light brown eyes. He always called her his golden-eyed goddess which would make her blush. Even remembering it now brought the heat into her cheeks.

What the hell was she doing? Jumping up from the porch swing again, she paced the boards under her feet. She hadn't thought this much about Jason in years. It had to be the familiarity of being home, all the memories bombarding her at once in her agitation. Yeah, that was all it was. Having her dad in the hospital brought all those old feelings back and it was natural for her to think about the time she spent with Jason. But he was a topic she needed to banish from her mind. Hell, she didn't even know if he was still around Zearing. Probably took off for San Antonio or Austin to start a new life.

He'd probably forgotten all about her.

TWO
JASON

"Come on, Ma. You have to eat."

Elizabeth Archer scowled and pushed the spoon away. "Jimmy, you know I can't eat this stuff! Where's some of that divine apple cobbler I made just yesterday? Bring that to me and I'll eat it all."

"Ma, it's Jason, not Jimmy." His heart fell. "Dad's been gone for a long time."

The older woman sat back in her chair to get a better look at the young man trying to feed her a bite of roasted chicken. "Jason, you say? I don't know any Jason, although you do look familiar."

Jason Archer rubbed his forehead, a headache quickly settling in right behind his eyes. It had been nearly a week since his mother had been this bad. Most days she was perfectly lucid, playing cards with him after dinner and asking him about his job at the investment firm where he worked with his uncle. But not tonight. What set her off? Was there something about the weather, or what she was eating, or watching on television that would send her back decades? He'd likely never know. Dementia was a devilish disease that stole the people you love one memory at a time.

"I promise I'll try to bring you apple cobbler tomorrow. But for today, you need to eat something." He tried to smile but it was obvious she was losing weight, and the nurses were concerned they'd have to feed her intravenously before too long. "The kitchen made this especially for you. It would be rude to not eat at least some of it, wouldn't it?"

Elizabeth's forehead crinkled and she eyeballed the forkful of food for a second. Then she rolled her eyes and took the utensil out of his hand. "Fine. I wouldn't want to hurt the cook's feelings. But I want to see some cobbler tomorrow or I'm going to town for dinner."

Once that was settled, his mother tucked into the meal as though there'd never been a question about eating it. She made pleasant conversation, laughing and smiling, but Jason knew she wasn't quite herself. And it broke his heart.

A young nurse stopped into the room to remove the plate and Elizabeth's eyes lit up. "Oh, hello darling! Have you met my husband, Jimmy?"

Jason winced and stood to shake the pretty blonde's hand. "Hi, sorry. I'm Jason, her son."

"Not a problem. We get that a lot. I'm Veronica, although she likes to call me Charlotte, for some reason."

Breath catching in his throat, he glanced back at his mother before turning to Veronica and lowering his voice. "Charlotte? Are you sure that was the name?"

"Yes, yes, Jimmy, dear, this is Charlotte. She goes to school with our son and is the sweetest little thing you're ever gonna meet." Elizabeth leaned forward and lowered her voice to a whisper. "I do believe they'll be married one day, but don't tell our boy that. He's far too young to be thinking about such things."

Veronica laughed and picked up the tray. "Don't you worry, Mrs. Archer, your secret is safe with us." Then she winked at Jason and backed out of the room.

His mouth hung open as he stared at his mother. How the

hell did she remember Charlotte, but couldn't remember his name from day to day? The nurse didn't look a thing like Charlotte, quite the opposite. Where Veronica was tall and athletic and blonde with shining light blue eyes, Charlotte was a tiny little thing with a personality as big as Texas. She wore her brown curls shaggy, always blowing her bangs out of her eyes. And those eyes...such a light shade of brown he'd never seen anywhere else. Like molten gold.

When Elizabeth started yawning, Jason knew that was his cue. "All right, Ma, I gotta go. It's time for your shows and I've got some chores to get done at home."

He leaned in and kissed her cheek, and she laid a hand on his shoulder. "I do appreciate you coming to see me, Jason."

Startled at the sound of his name, his eyes filled with tears, and he didn't know what to say. Instead, he just squeezed her hand and kissed her forehead one more time. "'Night, Ma."

On the quick drive home, Jason found himself lost in memories. There were plenty of reasons for him to remember Charlotte—they'd pretty much grown up together, leaning on each other as they changed from fifteen-year-old babies into young adults. They had shared so much it would be impossible for him to forget her. Every memory he had from those formative years included her. Even now he could picture her smile and the way her eyes lit up when she laughed—or when she was pissed beyond all reason. She was such a spitfire, the antithesis to his boring, mundane existence. The moment they met he was smitten.

Jason parked in front of the ranch-style home where he'd grown up. An only child, he had been close to both of his parents and spent almost all of his free time with them until he hit high school. Football is king in Texas and, although he wasn't very good at it, he joined the team right away his freshman year. Made his dad so proud to see him decked out in his pads and jersey.

After he'd changed out of his suit and tie, donning a more

appropriate pair of jeans and t-shirt, he padded into the kitchen and felt a weight slide off his shoulders. Here was where he felt most at home. Working with his hands, mixing the right flavors and creating dishes that made people happy, experimenting with new ingredients. It had been one of the ways he and his dad had grown so close when he was a teen.

He let his mind wander while he chopped some onions and rosemary and started boiling water for rice. Being on the football team had made his parents happy, and he didn't hate it, but it wasn't where his heart was.

Until Charlotte joined the cheerleading team and was at every single game.

Such a high school cliché, the football player and the cheer-leader, but it was just so natural for them to end up together. There were plenty of shared bus rides to neighboring towns, and they were frequently practicing on the field at the same time after school, so it was easy to get to know her. Charlotte was one of those people who shined so bright you were drawn into her orbit, full of excitement and life—the penultimate cheerleader.

And then her mom died, and she was suddenly adrift.

Ever since that day, there had been a bit of a shadow hanging over her. It took a few months before she let herself be happy again, to laugh at jokes and get excited about, well, anything. But boy, when she was happy, it was like the sun was only shining on you.

Jason shook himself and got back to work. There was no point in thinking about Charlotte. She'd made her choice, and it was the right choice. If she'd known that Jimmy Archer was sick that summer after graduation, she'd never have left. He couldn't regret keeping that information from her, knowing that she'd resent him after a few years if she'd stayed. Every day after giving up her scholarship would have been spent blaming him for missing her chance at an exciting, fulfilling life. She'd been gone for almost eight years, and they'd only spoken a handful of times when she was in town, always with disastrous results. It was obvious she'd forgotten all about him, so he was going to have to work harder on forgetting her.

Wiping his hands on the towel over his shoulder, he chuckled. Forgetting Charlotte Trevino was a feat easier said than done.

THREE
CHARLOTTE

W aking up in the bedroom that used to be hers but looked nothing like she remembered, Charlotte didn't want to get out from under the covers. A layer of exhaustion was still wrapped around her, and it wasn't hard to figure out why. The last few days had left her head spinning.

She had just returned to San Francisco after visiting her best friend, Katie Parker—soon to be Katie Collins—in Iowa and helping her with the grand opening of her new trauma center. It had only been a little more than a year since Katie had survived a terrifying ordeal at the hands of someone she'd known and trusted. In true Katie fashion, she decided to use everything she learned in her own trauma recovery to help others. It seemed that no sooner had Charlotte settled into her San Francisco routine and gotten back into the kindergarten classroom she so loved, than she got a terse, late-night phone call from her brother telling her their dad was in the hospital. After that, she'd been up all night making flight arrangements, putting together lesson plans for her substitute, and just trying to keep from throwing up. Once she'd eaten and gotten herself settled the night before, she'd nearly passed out. Judging by how stiff her shoulder was, she hadn't moved at all during the night.

A quick shower helped bring her back to herself and she made her way downstairs to the sunny yellow kitchen. Brandon was already there making breakfast and grinned over his shoulder at her.

"Morning, sleepyhead. Boy, you're out of practice for ranch life, aren't you? I've already been out watering and feeding the horses today while you were catching up on your much-needed beauty sleep."

Covering her mouth with the back of her hand, she swatted at her chuckling brother on her way to the coffee. "Give me a break, will ya? With the time difference and every-thing I am gonna need a couple days, at least, to get my groove back."

He set a plate of bacon, eggs, and toast in front of her and kissed the top of her head. "I'm just teasing you. Things are under control for now. But I wouldn't say no if you wanted to come out and help exercise the crowd when you're done."

A slow smile spread over Charlotte's face. It had been a while since she'd been home, which meant it had been a while since she'd gotten to ride. Living on a horse ranch, Charlotte had essentially grown up in the saddle. She was barrel racing by the time she was ten and training the horses before she was fifteen. When she was younger there had been no getting out of her share of the chores. Cleaning out the stables and putting down fresh straw, watering and feeding the horses, helping out with anything that was asked of her. But training and riding were as much a part of her as her golden-brown eyes, and she'd missed this life after she left for school.

"I think that can be arranged."

Looking around for something to read while she ate, Char-lotte pawed through the pile of mail on the kitchen table. There were catalogs, junk mail envelopes, and various bills and statements. One piece of mail caught her eye, though, and she frowned as she picked up the red-stamped notice from the bank.

"Hey, now," Brandon tugged the paper from her hand. "Why don't you finish eating so we can get to the horses? They get antsy, you know, then they're impossible."

"What was that, Bran? It looked important."

Keeping his back to her, Brandon shrugged. "It's nothing for you to worry about. Dad and I are working on it."

She jumped from her chair and snatched the paper from him, scooting to the other side of the kitchen before he even knew what hit him. "Don't give me that. Just let me look at it." As she skimmed the page, her eyes grew wider, and her mouth dropped open.

"Bran, this isn't nothing." She waved the paper at him. "This says we could lose the ranch, do you realize that?"

Her brother hung his head and leaned back against the counter. "I'm aware, Char. We all are. And I told you we're working on it."

Charlotte's brain was kicking into overdrive, firing on all cylinders. "Okay, we need a plan. I need to know how much we're behind, exactly, we need to take inventory and sell off what we can, then we—"

Now it was Brandon's turn to rip the paper away and he shoved it into a drawer, out of sight. "We will. We're working on some options. But we—" He pointed from Charlotte to himself and back. "Right now, *we* need to take care of the day-to-day life around here. Finish. Eating."

She grimaced at the way he still treated her like a child. "Fine. But we're not done talking about this."

"Oh, I'm well aware." Her brother rolled his eyes and nudged her with his elbow. "I know you better than to think you'd ever walk away from a fight."

When she was done eating and had helped clean up the kitchen, she grabbed her old pair of boots that were still in the mud room and piled her shaggy brown curls on top of her head. She nearly skipped out to the modern, climate-controlled stable where she'd spent most of her childhood. Almost every stall was occupied, and she frowned.

"Bran, haven't we been able to get our horses out to the cattle ranchers? Aren't we selling as many?"

Her brother kept his head down and held some hay out to the Quarter Horse closest to him. "Oh, I don't know. We're doing all right, I guess. We've started taking in some boarders, that's all. We're one of the top breeders in central Texas, but we needed a little extra help. I told you we're working on it."

The frown deepened as Charlotte made her way down the row. The Quarter Horses and Appaloosas were friendly and beautiful. She could tell that Dr. Angus had been keeping everyone healthy and happy on the ranch. But the fact that they weren't making ends meet through their regular business of breeding and selling the finest horses any Texas cowboy had seen was concerning.

Brandon sidled up next to her and slung his arm around her shoulders. "Now, don't you get all worried and making plans, Charlotte Rose. It's fine. I mean, there are challenges, of course, but who doesn't have a bad year every now and again?"

"What other challenges, Brandon?"

He ignored her question and led her to a stall where a beautiful pinto mare, glossy chestnut except for a white and brown dapple pattern on her rump, was already saddled. "I knew you'd want to get back to the hospital as soon as possible, so I had Milo help me trot most of these horses out for a bit. I didn't get to Bess here, so can you please run her for me?"

"You're avoiding the question. But you're not wrong about me being anxious to get back to Dad." She poked a finger into his chest, backing him against the wall. "You're gonna tell me what's going on, make no mistake."

He shot her a toothy grin and steered her toward Bess. "Oh, I know you're right. But let's table it for now."

Hitching herself into the saddle, Charlotte felt an immediate thrill shoot through her. Oh yes, this was where she was supposed to be. Nowhere on earth had she ever felt so comfortable, so exactly where she belonged. There was a building knot of excitement in the middle of her chest, and she could sense that Bess was just as anxious as she was to get out there and stretch her legs.

She led the horse out to the paddock and cantered her around for a few laps. It was important to her for Bess to feel comfortable with Charlotte on her back and she needed a minute to take stock of Bess's temperament and movements. Once she felt they were on the same page, she walked Bess to the head of the trail that wound through the entire property. It was mostly cleared of low-hanging branches, and it was a favorite place of hers to train the horses for the types of terrain they'd be working.

"Get up, now," she clucked at Bess, and they started the climb up the rocky hillside. Charlotte was pleased at how sure-footed the mare was and impressed at the speed she was climbing. But her heart was really racing in anticipation of hitting the other side. There was wide-open pasture at the bottom of this hill, perfect for flat-out running, and then another path that wound through trees and fields and back around to the stable. Charlotte couldn't wait to feel the wind in her hair and lose herself in the rhythm of Bess's hoofbeats.

Leaning forward, she lowered her voice so only the horse could hear her. "Ready, girl?" The whinnied reply was all she needed and as soon as they cleared the ridge, she kicked her heels against the horse's flanks and whooped. "Hyah!"

She leaned into the wind as they flew down the hill, exhilaration bubbling up inside her. Laughing and squealing, she couldn't remember the last time she'd felt so free. The powerful animal was taking advantage of the free rein Charlotte was giving her and was barreling along an invisible, twisting path toward the line of trees in the distance that marked the edge of the Trevino property. Just before the tree line lay a trail that wound around the field and back toward the stable and Charlotte was disappointed when it came into view, and she had to slow Bess down to a trot. The horse snorted and shook her head in protest.

Once Charlotte had caught her breath, she leaned forward and patted Bess's neck. "I know, darlin', I know. If only we could just run and run and never stop, right? I understand, believe me."

The sun was warm on Charlotte's back as the pair made their way back toward the house. She was anxious to see her dad and to bring him home, but it had always been hard to drag her away from her horses. Today would be no exception. A heaviness settled in her chest when she slid from the saddle and led Bess to the trough for a well-deserved drink. After removing Bess's tack and rubbing her down, she left her in her stall with a kiss on her nose.

"Thank you, Bess."

———

Arthur was able to come home a couple days after his accident, with strict instructions to take it easy, to rest, and to not do anything more strenuous than take out the garbage. He scoffed at the doctor but took the printout, anyway, trying to fold it up and shove it in his back pocket. But Charlotte snatched it away from him and added it to the folder of paperwork and information she'd been gathering.

"We need this, Dad. I know for a fact you're gonna try to convince us that the doctor didn't say these things, so this is my proof." Leveling him with a strict glare, she laid a hand on his arm. "Don't try to pull any funny business once we're home, either. I've got your number, old man."

He scrunched his forehead like he was trying to look angry but then laughed and kissed her cheek. "Whatever you say, Charlie-girl. Let's just get outta here."

Brandon had stayed at the ranch to take care of the morning routine, but he was sitting on the porch when Charlotte and Arthur pulled into the yard.

"There you are! Finally sprung him, huh?"

"He's free as a bird—well, relatively." Charlotte followed her dad to the swing and snuggled into his good side. "I will be keeping an eye on him to make sure he's following the doctor's orders, including no strain to the shoulder for at least two weeks. I can't in good conscience leave you two here without knowing that he's going to be alright."

Arthur rested his cheek on his daughter's head and they all just enjoyed the warmth of the Texas spring for a few minutes. Then Arthur cleared his throat.

"So, how are things going around here, Bran? Have we had any more...visitors?"

Straightening up from where he'd been leaning against one of the porch beams, Brandon stared into his glass of tea and shrugged. "Nope. No one in the last couple of days. It's all been quiet."

Charlotte narrowed her eyes. Her brother was acting weird, and her dad knew why. But the question was what were they hiding?

"Been getting a lot of random visitors out this way, have you?"

No one replied right away or even looked at her. She pushed herself up to glare at both of them.

"All right, you two. Spill it."

Brandon exchanged a look with their dad then shrugged. "It's not a big deal. We're handling it."

God, she was getting tired of hearing that. She opened her mouth to protest but just then a voice rang out across the paddock from the direction of the stable. "Well, lookie here! Is that my Charlotte home for a visit? Get over here, girl!"

Walking across the yard was an older woman with gray-streaked brown hair pulled back into a ponytail, straight bangs covering her forehead above a pair of warm green eyes.

"Dr. Angus!" Charlotte jumped up and closed the distance between them, throwing herself into the woman's arms. "Oh, I missed you."

The doctor laughed and squeezed Charlotte tight. "Oh, sweet-pea, you are a sight for sore eyes! Let me get a good look at you!"

Charlotte's cheeks were starting to hurt from smiling so much but that was okay. Dr. Janelle Angus had been like a second mother to her growing up. The veterinarian was a staple in the region and had been helping out with the Trevinos' horses for a decade, at least. But after Rose passed away, Janelle was a comforting female presence for Charlotte at a time when she had none.

Dr. Angus held Charlotte at arms' length and beamed proudly. "You don't look a bit different. Still that fresh-faced, tough little beauty I remembered. How long are you in town?"

"Not sure yet." She looped her arm with the older woman's, and they strolled back to the porch where Arthur and Brandon were sitting. "I just came out to lend a hand while he recovers. Maybe six weeks?"

Her smile warmed Charlotte's heart. "Well darlin' we'll be glad to have you."

"Hello, Janelle. How're the patients today?"

Arthur started to stand when Dr. Angus reached the porch, but she waved him down and sat next to him instead. "Better'n you, I'd guess." She patted his knee and grinned at him. "Coming along just great, Arthur. There are two colts and one filly in there that are just about ready to start their training, and your mare Ginny is looking like she'll be ready to give birth in the next couple of months."

They continued to make small talk for a while, and it didn't take long for Charlotte to notice that something was up with her dad and the doctor. His arm was laid out along the back of the swing, just behind her shoulders. More than once, she laid a hand on his knee or his arm, or she'd lean into him when she laughed. Brandon either didn't notice or it was common enough that he didn't think anything of it. Charlotte smiled to herself. In all the time since her mom passed, she hadn't seen nor heard anything about her dad dating anyone, not in more than a decade. This was a good pairing, as far as she was concerned.

They all heard the sound of crunching gravel and turned to watch a big white dually pickup tear up the driveway, and Charlotte felt the atmosphere prickle with tension immediately.

"Who's that?" No one answered her, but her dad was on his feet and planted at the bottom of the stairs by the time the pickup's door was even open.

"I told you before, we aren't interested." Her dad was glaring at the stranger who emerged, while Brandon stood behind him with arms crossed. "So just get back in your truck and head on out of here.".

The approaching man wore an impeccable white cowboy hat that looked like it cost more than Charlotte's car. Smiling under a steel-gray mustache, he had his hands folded in front of him, the sun glinting off his diamond rings and the gold bolo tie around his neck.

"Come on now, Trevino, listen to reason. You can't keep running this ranch by yourself and we both know it's not making any money. This is a fair offer, and you need to consider it seriously." Just then he caught sight of Charlotte coming down the steps and his grin widened. "Well, now, who is this little filly? I don't believe I've had the pleasure. I know I'd remember a beauty like you."

Brandon took a step, opening his mouth to defend her, but

Charlotte grabbed his arm to stop him. Being the little sister, and nearly six inches shorter than Bran, she knew it was in his nature to protect her. But also because she was the little sister, she'd learned to stand her ground and fight her own battles. Crossing her arms, she glared at the stranger. "I believe my father said he wasn't interested. It's time for you to go."

She saw the skin around the man's eyes tighten slightly, but the smile stayed wide and bright. "You must be Charlotte." He bowed slightly, never taking his eyes off her. "Charmed. But why don't you just run along now and let us men handle this."

Dr Angus let out a low whistle and muttered, "Now you've done it."

Pressing her lips together, Charlotte breathed deep through her nose before responding. "No, I don't believe I will. Why don't *you* run along before I call the sheriff and have you dragged off for trespassing?"

He slapped his thighs like she'd told him the funniest joke then wagged a finger at her. "You are quite the delight, Miss Charlotte. So much fire in such a little package!"

"Don't be fooled by my size. A rattlesnake is small, but you sure don't want to tangle with one."

Brandon snorted from behind her and Charlotte saw the corner of her dad's mouth twitch. However, the smile on the stranger's face froze and he narrowed his eyes quickly before pulling an envelope out of his jacket pocket.

"Well, little rattlesnake, look this over and see if you can talk some sense into your stubborn old man, here." Smoothing his mustache, he let his gaze rest on each of them in turn. "T & M Ranch is on its last leg, and you all know it. You can sell it to me, pay off your debts, and have a nice pile of cash to retire on. Or you can take your chances that the bank won't repossess the land and leave you swinging in the wind."

Stepping forward, Charlotte snatched the envelope out of his hand. Then he tipped his hat and backed away. "I know you'll make the wise decision. I hope to hear from you soon, Trevino family."

"Don't hold your breath." She was clenching her teeth so hard she thought she heard one crack.

He climbed back into his truck and sped down their driveway, kicking up dirt and gravel all the way. No one moved until he was completely out of sight, then it was as if they let out the breath they were collectively holding. Charlotte opened the paperwork he'd handed her before Brandon could grab it out of her grasp.

"So, what's all this and who the hell was that? God, he made my skin crawl."

Reaching over her shoulder, Brandon took the paperwork out of her hands and carried it back to the porch, leafing through the pages as he walked. Arthur rubbed a hand down his face, looking exhausted and sad.

"That, darlin', was Gerard Chancellor. He's some bigwig tycoon from San Antonio who's been working his way through the families all around Zearing, buying up land like it was going out of style."

"You're kidding. And people are just selling to him?"

Brandon lifted one shoulder. "A lot of people are. You know it's not easy maintaining a family-run ranch these days. So far out of the ten or so families with property outside Zearing, there are about six of us who haven't sold. But I don't know how much longer we can hold out."

Charlotte's throat was suddenly very dry, and she narrowed her eyes. "What does that mean, exactly?"

"Things haven't been going too smoothly lately. We're hemorrhaging a lot of money and haven't been able to make it up." Arthur readjusted his sling with a grimace. "Chancellor owns our mortgage now and he's putting the squeeze on us to pay. We've held him off so far, but can't keep this place running forever, not with the way our income has been dropping recently."

Charlotte's mouth fell open. "Is the ranch really in trouble? We're still selling horses, aren't we?" At the look her dad and brother exchanged, her heart dropped to her stomach, and she knew the answer before either of them spoke.

Arthur lowered himself onto the porch swing and patted the seat next to him. "Come sit, Charlie-girl." With his good arm around her shoulders, he sighed. "Things have been rough the last couple of years, I won't lie. The ranch is…a little in arrears to the bank, but I've been certain things would pick back up any day now."

"A little in arrears?" Brandon raked his hands through his hair. "We are at least ten thousand dollars behind and getting further in debt every month. It has been almost three months since we've made a full payment. Chancellor's been breathin' down our necks, reminding us he could call in our mortgage at any time. He could repossess, and we could lose everything. And that is why I think we need to seriously consider his offer. Now."

"Brandon." Arthur leveled a stern glare at his son.

"Right. Sorry." He scratched at the stubble on his neck and sighed heavily, his jaw clenched tight. "Anyway, I've got plans tonight so I'm gonna go clean up." Then he was gone through the front door, taking the stairs two at a time.

Arthur patted Charlotte's shoulder in time with the swing, his expression placid. "Don't mind him. He gets a little anxious about losing the ranch and would rather we sell it, at least got something for it all. He just doesn't want to see your old man in financial straits once I retire."

"Is he right, Dad? Could we lose the ranch?" Charlotte chewed her lip, already knowing the answer in the way her dad's shoulders slumped at her question. She nodded. "What are our options? Can we talk to anyone at the bank? Can we sell off any equipment we don't necessarily need or cut expenses some other way? There has to be something we can do."

He pulled her close and kissed the top of her head. "Ah, my Charlotte. Always trying to fix the impossible, so much like your mother. I don't want you to worry about any of this, sweet girl. You've got your life in California to be thinking about. We'll figure this out, we always do."

Then he disappeared into the house, leaving Charlotte alone on the porch, eyes stinging with tears.

FOUR
JASON

Loosening his tie and unbuttoning the top button of his dress shirt, Jason took a long pull from his bottle of beer.

"Been a rough week, man?" His friend Mitch leaned both elbows on the high-top table and cocked an eyebrow. "I mean, it's only Wednesday, but you've got that look."

"That obvious?" He smiled then scrubbed a hand down his face. "My mom's been in a bad place lately and it just sucks to see her like that."

Nodding and making his curls bounce, Mitch's eyebrows drew together. "Sorry to hear it. She's such a sweet lady and I know how much she means to you. But you're doing the best you can, bro. She's lucky to have you."

"Yeah, I know she'll be okay. But she calls me Jimmy more and more often." Jason shrugged. "And my uncle has a new hot client who's taking up all his time so I'm having to pick up the slack around the office. This may be my last night out for a while."

Working for his uncle had its advantages: Jason was able to set his own schedule and enjoyed a fair amount of autonomy. But he'd *earned* the big office, his stellar reputation, and his better-than-decent salary. He'd also earned his uncle's trust, landing him the most important projects and a spot as Jed's second-in-command.

Being a financial analyst was not the career he'd envisioned for himself at the end of high school. Shit, he hadn't even known what a financial analyst did. But when his father died and his mother started showing signs of early-onset dementia, Uncle Jed took him in, paying him far more than he was worth to run errands and help with anything the other financial advisors needed. When Jay showed an aptitude for numbers and data analysis, Jed paid for him to go to a local college to learn the ropes, and over the years Jason had proven himself again and again.

"When are you gonna quit that job and find a culinary program, m'man? Little by little, it's sucking your soul dry."

"It's not that bad. I don't hate it, you know. And I'm pretty damn good at it." The two tapped the necks of their bottles together in acknowledgment. "I can't afford my mom's care without that soul-sucking job, so I'm happy to stay as long as I need to."

Mitch shook his head in admiration. "You're a hell of a good man, Jason Archer."

"Excuse me?" A timid female voice interrupted their conversation, and they turned to find a pretty brunette standing near them.

Standing up straighter, Mitch gave her his full attention. "Well, hello there. How can we help you, Miss?" He was trying to catch her eye, but she was focused only on Jason.

She twirled a strand of her long hair around a finger and smiled at him with a lip trapped between her teeth. "I saw you over here and couldn't take my eyes off you. If I didn't come talk to you, I knew I'd regret it for the rest of my life."

"Oh yeah?" Jason returned her smile then took a drink. "And why's that?"

Her flirty demeanor faltered for a split second, but she recovered quickly and laid a hand on his arm. "Because you could just be the love of my life." Squaring her shoulders, she tossed her hair and lifted her chin. "I'm Kelcie, by the way."

"Nice to meet you, Kelcie. Have you met Mitch?" Jason directed her attention across the table. "He owns his own business and smells like sandalwood and dreams. Mitch, why don't you ask Kelcie to dance while I get next round."

Confused, she looked back and forth between the two men, but Mitch held out his hand and flashed his brightest grin. "What d'you say, Miss Kelcie? I've got a mean two-step that'll take your breath away."

She hesitated for just a moment before slipping her hand in his with a shrug. "Sure, why not? Show me what you got, Mitch."

Waggling his eyebrows at Jason over her head, he led her to the dance floor and had her smiling and laughing before they had gone more than ten feet. Jason chuckled and shook his head. No matter what anyone else thought, his best friend was full of fun and had charm for days. Women frequently approached them to talk to Jason, but they inevitably ended up giving Mitch their numbers.

And that was perfectly okay with Jason.

When the song ended, he watched his friend take his cell back from Kelcie who then pushed up on her toes to kiss his cheek. They parted ways, Mitchell giving her a wink while she walked backwards with a wave.

"Damn, Mitch. Your game is on point." Jason handed him a fresh beer and laughed. "I've never seen anyone win over so many hearts in such a short time."

"They'd all rather be with you. Don't deny it." Mitch pointed at him to stop his protest. "I will never understand why you refuse to talk to any of them. Kelcie was an absolute delight. *And* she used to be a gymnast." He winked over the lip of his bottle before tipping it back.

Looking out into the crowd, Jason just shrugged. "I'm fine. Not really looking to settle down."

Mitch watched him for a moment, pressing his lips in a thin line. "I'm not suggesting that you propose to someone tonight. But in all the time I've known you, you've gone out on like five dates. I know I'm stellar company, but what gives?"

"Nothing. I don't know." But that wasn't technically true. He had a pretty good idea why he didn't pursue anything with the women he'd met.

Mitch narrowed his eyes. "It's that Charlotte you've told me about, isn't it?"

After taking a long drink, Jason scratched at the stubble on his chin. "She was my first love and things didn't end well between us. But you know how it is."

"Nah, bro, I don't." Shaking his head, Mitch leaned his elbows on the table. "To be honest, I don't think a lot of people do."

"What do you mean? Everyone has a first love, falls for someone hard when they're young. This is no different."

"This is one hundred percent different, m'man, and you know it." He perked up and waved at Kelcie who was waiting for him by the dance floor. "Yes, most people have a first love. However, most people do not have a first love that outshines everyone else to the extent that they can't move on. Even after nearly a decade."

It was true he'd hardly spoken to Charlotte since she left for San Francisco after graduation, but it was also true that no one had ever lived up to her. He could see her in his mind, golden eyes flashing as she gave him a piece of her mind, see her laughing at something he said, her head thrown back. And no matter how much he fought it he could easily picture her rosy cheeks and slightly parted lips, eyes full of love and desire when he kissed her.

"If you'd met her, you'd know that letting her go was so much harder than it sounds. She's funny, whip-smart, full of life, and has the biggest heart you'll find on this or any other planet. That's what I want, *she* is what I want, and I can't have her. I fucked that up long ago."

Mitch stared at him for a moment, chewing the inside of his lip, then drained his beer.

"Look, Jay, I say this out of love, but you gotta shit or get off the pot." Slapping a hand on Jason's shoulder as he made his way toward his new date, Mitch leaned close. "Find a way to fix things, bro. Put this to bed or make a move, but something has to change. You deserve to be happy."

Knowing Mitch would fend for himself the rest of the night, likely letting Kelcie take him home, Jason decided to head back to his own house. Now that he was actively thinking about Charlotte, he just wanted to wallow: wallow in his stupidity for sending her away, wallow in the cowardice that kept him from calling her or apologizing when he saw her in town.

He hadn't shared a civil word with Charlotte Trevino for almost a decade, but he always knew when she was back to see her family. And while she looked different and grown-up, he could still see the same girl he'd fallen in love with at fifteen.

And the woman who continued to hold his heart.

FIVE
CHARLOTTE

"Charlotte, sweetie, why don't you take a ride with me into town." Dr. Angus strolled out of her little exam room and office area, tucking her hair under her cowboy hat.

Ride into town? Charlotte hadn't been into Zearing since she got home. Hell, she'd barely spent any time in town in years. It was no secret to her why, either. When you return to a small town that you spent your whole life in, it's nearly impossible not to run into people you knew. And there was at least one person she didn't want to run into.

Janelle Angus leaned against the door of the stall Charlotte was sweeping and crossed her arms. "It'll be good for you to get away from the ranch for a bit. Plus, I think we both could use a little girl time."

Brushing her hands off on her jeans, Charlotte relented. "Okay, I'll come along. You know I can't say no to you."

The radio played a classic country tune and the wind from the open windows whipped Charlotte's hair around. Ever since Chancellor's visit to the ranch a couple days before, she'd been in a funk. The ranch was in jeopardy of falling out of family hands for the first time ever, her dad and brother

I'LL CALL YOU HOME

were possibly going to be evicted, and she had no idea how to fix things. She sighed.

"Okay, now, that was a heavy sigh—too heavy for a beautiful day like this. What's on your mind, Char?"

She rolled her eyes and turned the radio down. "What am I supposed to do? I'm expected back in San Francisco in a few weeks and I can't just leave, knowing that the ranch is in trouble. How could I live with myself? I have to do something, Doc."

Reaching out to pat her hand, Janelle smiled. "You can't fix everything, darlin'. Arthur and Bran have been working the books and have let a couple part-timers go to save money, so they're trying. You have your life to live. You know your dad wouldn't want you to give up everything you've worked for."

"I know. Ugh, I know. He was adamant that I leave town for school and wouldn't let me even think about sticking around to help out after graduation." She frowned. "Not that I had much else to stay for."

They rounded the last curve in the highway and Zearing came into view. It wasn't a big town, not by any stretch of the imagination. It was a city of maybe three thousand people, a kind of bedroom community to the San Antonio area. Dr. Angus pulled her truck into the square, where the shops and restaurants surrounded the courthouse, and a flood of memories overtook Charlotte. It punched her in the gut in a way that took her breath away.

There had been a few noticeable improvements, like the new sidewalks and awnings on most of the brick-faced buildings, a couple of new shops and improved street lighting. The Greenbriar Restaurant was still there, right next to the dance studio that Charlotte had taken lessons at when she was eight. She wondered if Mrs. Damstrom was still leading the classes or if it had been passed down to her daughter. The Jackalope looked just the same, the windows dark and posters for upcoming and

33

long past concerts waving around on the sign out front. She had to look away when they reached Francie's, though. That one was a little too painful just then. Of course, the only spot available on the block was right in front of the little diner.

"We can grab some lunch here when I'm done at the general store, if you'd like." Janelle's eyebrows were drawn in as she looked at Charlotte. "Or we can walk down to the Greenbriar, instead."

Her concern was sweet but also annoying to Charlotte. Was it that obvious that her heart hurt being there? The sadness made way for irritation at the fact that all these years later she was still so affected by the place. Taking a deep breath, she offered the older woman a reassuring smile. "Yeah, sure. Whatever is fine with me. Does Mr. Scutter still run the store? He's gotta be a hundred years old by now."

Looping her arm with Charlotte's, the doctor chuckled. "Oh, no. He retired a few years ago, and only after receiving an exceptionally generous offer from a random stranger out of Florida."

"What? You're joking."

"Not in the slightest. Scutter had put the shop on the market, hoping a local family would take it over and run it just the way he had, while also knowing that a box store would likely come in and build their own behemoth, buying his shop just to kill the competition." She pulled them to a stop in front of a refreshed version of the General Store from Charlotte's childhood. "Instead, Mitchell Drew saw the posting online and called Scutter directly with an offer he couldn't refuse. Rumor has it he paid nearly three times its worth and insisted on keeping everything the same, as long as he could add an ice cream freezer."

The big picture windows carried the name Scutter General Store in huge green paint, and it looked like the green and white striped awning had been replaced. "An ice cream freezer, huh? Interesting." Janelle pushed the door open and the bell that hung above jangled.

"Be right with you!" A disembodied voice called from the back of the building as the two women strolled inside.

"It's Dr. Angus, Mitch. Take your time."

Janelle patted Charlotte's arm and made a beeline for the wall of gloves and boots. While she was perusing the work gear, Charlotte wandered the aisles. Just like when she was growing up, you could get nearly anything here. There was a small drugstore, clothing, groceries, and minor hardware items. She could see a gardening area with seed packets and fertilizer, and even kitschy items like magnets and keychains bearing the name of the town. But the ice cream counter was what really caught her eye, white and chrome and glinting with sweet promise along the wall next to the cash register.

She approached and grinned at the tubs of ice cream behind the glass partition. There were only four of them, but they were as varied as they could be: bubble gum, vanilla, orange sherbet, and rocky road.

"A little bit of everything, to appeal to any taste."

Charlotte jumped at the closeness of the voice that sounded right behind her. She spun around and was met with a pair of bright blue eyes above the biggest smile she'd ever seen.

"Sorry, sorry! I didn't mean to scare you!" He held up his hands and took a few steps back. "Man, my ninja skills must be on point today."

With a hand on her chest over her racing heart, Charlotte laughed. "Don't you worry about it. Guess I'm just a little on edge."

He ran his hand through his mass of red curls and shrugged. "I didn't make the best first impression, did I? I'm Mitchell Drew, owner and proprietor of Scutter's General Store. Can I get you some ice cream, Miss...?"

She opened her mouth to introduce herself but instead, a voice from the door made the words lodge in her throat.

"Well, well, Charlotte Trevino. Didn't think I'd see you again."

Oh shit. Turning slowly on her heel, she could barely breathe, knowing she'd see a face she hadn't forgotten in all the time since she left Zearing. And when her eyes found his, her knees went soft and she had to brace herself on the ice cream case.

There he was, Jason Archer: the One Who Got Away. And holy shit he looked good. *So* good. His face had filled out, squaring his jaw and chiseling his cheekbones out of the roundness she'd left behind. His eyes were still the same midnight-blue she saw in her dreams and had never seen on anyone else. He was dressed in a gray suit with a burgundy tie loosened at the neck, his dark hair shorter than she remembered, but long enough that it curled around his ears. Damn, this was a good look on him. So good, she had to bite her lips to keep from telling him exactly how good.

"Hello Jason. And why would you be surprised to see me? Zearing is a small town, I come back now and again to see my family, and the last time I checked it was a free country so I'm just as entitled to be here as you are."

The corner of his mouth twitched, and he narrowed his eyes. "Same old Charlotte."

"Hold up—this is Charlotte? *The* Charlotte?" Mitch tipped his head her way with a broad smile. "It is definitely my pleasure to finally meet you after hearing so much from this guy."

Jason's cheeks flushed bright pink, and he pressed his lips together, making Charlotte immediately suspicious. "You've been talking about me? What did you tell him? Let me guess—you've painted me as some kind of villain. Of course you have." When he shook his head and looked away without denying it, she was surprised at the pain in her chest.

She had no idea what she had done to deserve not just his dismissal but his apparent hatred. Over the years, she'd racked her brain, sifting through memories, trying to pinpoint the moment his love for her ended. When he'd sent her away it had broken her heart. She'd be damned if she'd show him that ever again.

Lifting her chin and adopting a benign, pleasant expression, she turned away from Jason and smiled at the new store owner. "Mitchell Drew, it was so nice to meet you. I'll be sure to stop in for some of that ice cream before I go back to San Francisco. Janelle, I think I'll wait for you outside."

Without another glance at Jason, she turned on her heel and walked calmly past him to the sidewalk. Once outside, however, her façade fell away and she leaned back against the brick building, her face in her hands.

This wasn't the first time she'd run into him, and it wouldn't be the last. But it seemed that instead of time healing her wounds, it only poured salt into them.

"So, you're not sticking around?"

Charlotte jumped at Jason's voice and spun around to face him. "What?"

He stood watching her with his arms folded, a light breeze rustling his hair. "Can't say I'm surprised that you're reverting to your old trick of running away."

"What's that supposed to mean?"

"Oh, come on, Charlotte. The last time we saw each other, you refused to talk to me." When she tried to argue, the lift of his eyebrow silenced her. "If I remember correctly, you turned on your heel and stomped off mid-sentence, almost exactly like today."

He wasn't wrong. And that only served to piss Charlotte off more. The last time they'd seen each other had been two years ago. Walking out of the butcher's up Main Street, she hadn't been looking where she was going and had literally run into him.

· · ·

The impact was hard enough that she grabbed onto his shoulders to keep from falling over while his hands wrapped around her waist. When their eyes met, Charlotte suddenly couldn't remember how to breathe. So many warring emotions raced through her looking into those eyes she'd spent years memorizing: anger, pain, and somehow—

Still—affection.

"Charlotte." His tone was all surprise and awe as he looked down at her. His fingers flexed once, twice, drawing her just a little closer.

She was so stunned that for a moment, just a brief moment, she didn't resist. It would be so easy to just lean into him, to let him wrap his arms around her and tell her how sorry he was—

And that's when she snapped out of it. She pushed his hands away, stepping back to put some much-needed distance between them. "Let me go, Jason."

He dragged his fingers through his thick hair with a heavy sigh. "Charlotte. Please. Can we talk?"

"I cannot possibly express to you, in any number of words, how much I would rather do literally anything else." She tried to step around him, but he blocked her way.

Hands up in surrender, he tilted his head. "I just need you to listen. Just for a minute, okay?"

What the hell made him think he deserved any amount of her time? "No."

"Char—"

She rounded on him, feeling her anger emanating from every pore. "You know what? No. Just no. You don't get to…to—" But the words failed her, she was still so hurt and angry that she just couldn't be near him anymore.

So, she closed her mouth and pushed past him, leaving him on the sidewalk, watching her walk away.

Shaking away the memory, Charlotte narrowed her eyes. "So?"

"It's just that I'm shocked you're here in the first place and NOT surprised that you high-tailed it out of there so you didn't have to talk to me." The corner of his mouth lifted into a smirk. "What could have brought big-city Charlotte back to hob-nob with us rubes?"

Fury bubbled up in her chest and she could only stare. "What the hell are you talking about? I'm not 'big-city'. I'm the same person who grew up around here and, if you remember correctly, you're the one who chased *me* away."

The color drained out of his cheeks, and he shuffled his feet on the sidewalk. "Yeah, well..." Jason cleared his throat, and his gaze flicked up to her face without actually meeting her eyes. "So you're not home for long?"

"No, Jason." God, why did he have to look at her like that, half pissed off and half hopeful? "I'm just here to help out while my dad recovers."

He frowned. "Recovers? From what? What happened to him?"

"Not that it's any of your business," she snapped, glaring at him. "But he got thrown and dislocated his shoulder, broke a couple ribs. He just needs an extra set of hands."

"Shit. I'm sorry Charlotte." He raised a hand like he was going to touch her, but when she flinched involuntarily, he seemed to think better of it. "Tell him I hope he heals quickly, and I hope you'll let me know if he needs anything. Or if you do."

Clenching her fists, she narrowed her eyes. "Don't start acting like you care about my family—or me—now. It's a little late for that."

"I do care, Charlotte." Jason's voice was low and rough, his jaw clenched. He swiped a hand through his hair. "After everything we've been through together and despite what you may think, I'm not a monster."

"What I think?" Hands on her hips, her eyes wide, she scoffed. "I think you've been talking shit about me, that's what

39

I think. I have never spread a disparaging word about you, Jason Archer. But, judging by your friend's reaction, I doubt you can say the same. You gave up the right to give a shit about me when you—well, you just don't get to anymore."

The door jangled behind her and Dr. Angus stepped out of the general store, laying a hand on Charlotte's shoulder. "Let's go Charlotte. It's nice to see you, Jason. Tell your mama hello."

Keeping her hand on Charlotte's back, she steered her down the sidewalk and back to the truck before she could say anything else. Charlotte kept her arms crossed and couldn't stop herself from peeking over her shoulder repeatedly. Jason was standing just where they left him, shaking his head while Mitch kept up a one-sided, animated conversation.

"Want something to eat? I think you need to decompress."

Charlotte shook her head and leaned back on the truck with a huff. "I don't want to eat. I just want to get out of here. What the hell is he playing at? He broke up with me when we were kids and has barely spoken to me in years, but he's acting like I'm the one in the wrong. I will never understand him."

Gently grasping her elbow and pulling her toward the diner, Janelle grinned. "Food, now. We can talk about what just happened. Or not. But I'm hungry and short of stealing my truck you're stuck with me."

Francie's Diner looked and smelled exactly as Charlotte remembered. The sparkly green vinyl seats, chrome accents on the counter and the stools, even the jukebox against the back wall. Breathing deeply after they were seated, she felt herself relaxing even as her stomach rumbled.

"I was never able to find any place as good as Francie's in San Francisco. Made me crazy. I probably ate at every diner in the Bay Area, but nothing even came close. Why do you think that is? I mean, San Francisco attracts the best of the best chefs and foodies in the world. How the hell could Francie's, in this one-horse town in the middle of nowhere, serve the best food I've ever eaten?"

Janelle grinned behind her menu. "Come on, Char. I'm sure you know the answer to that question. What could make the simple, greasy fare here taste better than anything else?"

Casting her gaze around the restaurant, Charlotte's heart was filled with a warmth that radiated through her whole body. She knew. Of course, she knew.

"Okay, fine, that was a rhetorical question. I know that the good memories I have of this place are tied into the food. There was no emotional connection to any of the other places. Is that what you want me to say?"

"Oh my god! Charlotte Trevino? Is that you?"

The waitress standing next to the table looked shocked and thrilled at the same time. Her orange hair was thinner but still piled up in curls on top of her head, and she was wearing the same pink retro waitress dress that Charlotte remembered— although it was a bit snug.

"Hi Francie! What the heck are you still doing here? I thought you would've retired and run away to Cabo by now." Charlotte slid out of the booth and was wrapped in a hug so tight she could barely breathe. When she was finally released, she was touched to see tears building in the older woman's eyes.

"Oh wow, sweet thing, you don't look a day different than I remembered you! Still just as pretty as a picture. Things haven't been the same around here since you and Jason stopped coming in here."

Charlotte winced but offered a warm smile to Francie. "I was just telling Dr. Angus here that I've never found a place that could hold a candle to this one. Still the best food I've ever had."

"What'll you have today, dear? The usual? For you, too, Janelle?"

"You can't possibly remember what I used to order. It's been eight years."

Walking away with a wink, Francie called over her shoulder, "You'd be surprised what I remember, darlin'. Just you wait and see."

Charlotte was starting to think that coming back to town was a huge mistake. Shredding a napkin on the table, she frowned. She thought she'd put all of this behind her but with every step today she'd twisted the knife in her heart a little further. What the hell was wrong with her? She wasn't a moon-eyed teenager anymore. Her heart had been broken so long ago, she'd moved past that pain—hadn't she?

Jason Archer. Charlotte frowned at the paper placemat on the table. Five minutes and she'd fallen back into her old, confused feelings for him. When she left for San Francisco without him, it had broken her heart. She begged Jason to come with her as they'd planned, but he refused. Not only that, he made it very clear he wanted her to leave and couldn't wait for her to go. Their last conversation played out in her mind as the silence stretched across the table.

"There's still time for you to come with me, you know." Charlotte *wound her fingers with Jason's and smiled up at him. "I could use a little piece of Texas out there on the West coast. You got accepted into the culinary program, just like you always dreamed of. Don't you want to see what's out there?"*

But Jason wouldn't even meet her eyes. He pulled his hand free and shrugged. "I don't need to go gallivanting around the country, Charlotte. Home is good enough for me, and I'm perfectly happy to go to the community college and work the farm with my dad. What's wrong with that? When did you become such a snob?"

His words stung, but Charlotte had never been one to just give up. "I'm not being a snob. It's not like you can't come back. We'll be back for holidays and summers, even after we graduate, maybe we could move back here. I just…" She blew her hair out of her eyes and tried to get him to look at her. *"I just want you with me. Don't you want to be together?"*

That got him to look at her, but she regretted it immediately because those weren't his eyes, the eyes of her favorite person. His gaze was so cold she took a step back. "It's all about you, isn't it, Charlotte? You never stop to think about anyone else. Have you even considered that my life is here? That I don't want to move away from everything and everyone I know—that I love?"

"I thought you loved me." Her voice was barely audible.

"Yeah, well." He shoved past her and walked out of the barn, but not before firing one more shot over his shoulder. *"Things change, don't they?"*

Blinking rapidly to keep the tears from falling, Charlotte dropped her head into her hands.

"Well, that was eventful, wasn't it?"

Forgetting that she wasn't at the table alone, the voice surprised her. "Sorry, Doc. I guess I just got lost in my head for a minute there."

"Don't you worry about it. Are you feeling okay? You nearly blew a gasket back there."

"What? No, I didn't." She drummed her fingers on the table. "Okay, fine, I lost my temper a little. He just knows how to push my buttons."

"What buttons? I still don't know what he said that set you off."

Francie reappeared and set a plate in front of Charlotte. "Bacon cheeseburger, fries, and a chocolate milkshake." She tapped a finger against her temple. "Steel trap, darlin'. If you need anything else, just holler."

She stared at the food in front of her, amazed at the woman's memory. Popping a fry in her mouth, she scowled at Janelle. "What do you mean, you don't know what he said?

He was rude and accused me of being snooty and thinking I'm better than everyone else. He doesn't know the first thing about me anymore and I can't believe he'd assume that he does. He broke up with me and made it very clear that he had no use for me. What I do or don't do, whether I leave tomorrow or stay forever is none of his business."

Dr. Angus held up her hands in surrender. "Okay, okay. Let's just eat. This little trip into town wasn't supposed to upset you, I wanted to give you a break and let you relax. I guess I failed miserably."

"It's not your fault. And I'm sorry, I'm ruining the whole day." She sighed. Well, Jason ruined the day, but she didn't say so to Janelle. She hefted the burger and took a big bite. "Oh, wow, that is still one damned great burger."

The two women ate their meals and chatted about everything and nothing. Charlotte told Janelle all about San Francisco and Katie and her teaching job, and about how she also missed the horses and the quiet mornings at her childhood home in the country.

"First thing, there is traffic and ferry horns and trolly bells and just the sounds of a big city. I miss just listening to the noise of the cicadas and crickets and frogs. You sure don't get much of that where I live."

The doctor dropped her wadded napkin onto the plate and folded her hands under her chin with her elbows on the table. "Well, then, being home should do you some good. And that's kind of what I wanted to talk to you about today."

Charlotte chuckled. "What? Are you going to try to convince me to move back here? To come back to work at the ranch and take it over so Dad can retire?"

Eyes wide, Janelle leaned back in the booth. "Well, no. That's not really what I was thinking, but it seems you were."

Charlotte blanched and immediately started to backtrack. "No, I wasn't. Not really. I mean, it's just a thought, I couldn't really do that." She slurped up the rest of her milkshake, keeping her eyes locked to the bottom of the empty glass. "Besides, Bran has that all under control, doesn't he? He's the logical choice to take over."

"Mm. You'd think so, wouldn't you? But I don't think Bran's heart is in it the way Arthur's—or yours—is. You know he wants to run away from home, too, right?"

Charlotte frowned. "I didn't run away from home, you know that."

"I know, poor choice of words. Brandon hasn't had a chance to live his own life, only what's expected of him. And you said yourself that you've missed the quiet and the work on the ranch. Maybe just a year? Take a sabbatical and give yourself a little peace." She stopped and cocked her head as she regarded Charlotte. "Never mind, that's an awful lot to ask of you. It may just be time for Arthur to retire and for Brandon to really focus on his band and try to make something of Texas Drawl."

"And sell the ranch? Not on your life."

Janelle raised an eyebrow over the lip of her glass as she took a drink but said nothing.

"For a veterinarian you're pretty good at psychology." Charlotte wagged a finger at her friend. "I won't say absolutely not at this point, but I'm not selling my place on the coast just yet, either. I'll buy lunch and then we'd better get back and make sure Milo and Brandon have everything under control."

SIX
JASON

Jason watched Charlotte get herded down the sidewalk and let out a long breath. Jesus, he was so stunned and thrilled to see her that he almost forgot about her hair-trigger temper. He didn't mean to accuse her of anything—what the hell had he even said? To be honest, he was just so shocked to see her in front of him that he bungled the whole thing.

"Dude. That's crazy! I thought you said she never came back here, had left Zearing for good!" Mitch had followed them all out and looked just as shocked as Jason felt. "Did I make things worse? Man, I'm sorry. I've heard you talk about her so often that *that* adorable little creature was not what I was expecting. But I totally see why you never got over her."

Jason frowned at the sidewalk and ran his hand through his hair. Nope, he sure hadn't gotten over Charlotte. Glancing up the street, he saw her head into Francie's and his heart gave a little jolt. That was their place. For four years, they were there after Friday football games, on most Saturday nights, and anytime they could get away from chores and homework. Francie's was where he'd asked her out for the first time. He'd taken her there on their first date, for every dance and Homecoming and Prom they went to. After her mom died, he'd brought her milkshakes and burgers when she couldn't muster the energy to leave the house.

He broke up with her there, too, and hadn't set foot in the place since.

Clapping a hand on his friend's shoulder, Jason grinned. "Nah, Mitch, you didn't do anything. You know there's a lot of history between us and she doesn't even know all of it. But shit—have I really talked about her that much?"

Mitch's curls bobbed as he nodded. "Uh, yeah, a little. I was beginning to think she was a figment of your imagination, bro. So, what are you gonna do now that she's back in town?"

"She's not back in town, not really. Char is here to take care of her dad and then she'll leave again and that'll be that." He stared down the street to where she disappeared. "Besides, she doesn't want anything to do with me. She hates me."

The loud snort and guffaw that came from Mitch made Jason jump. "What the hell, man?"

"You're joking, right? You don't really think she hates you, do you?" He shook his head at Jason's bewildered look. "Ain't nobody get that bent out of shape over their past with someone they want nothing to do with. Mark my words, bro: that woman still feels squishy things for you."

Words eluded him as Jason looked from Mitch to the restaurant down the street and back at Mitch. There was no way he was right. Was there? He wouldn't blame Charlotte if she secretly burned him in effigy every weekend, but was it possible that she still had feelings - positive, romantic feelings for him?

Before he could ponder the question further, his phone rang. "Hey Mitch, I've got to take this. I'll call you later."

"Right on, m'man."

"Hey Uncle Jed. What's up?" When Jason and Libby floundered, rudderless, after Jimmy's death, it was hard to know what to do or where to go from there. Libby's health issues became more pronounced, Jason had no plan and no money. He didn't even have Charlotte to encourage him through the darkness. Jimmy's brother Jed took Jason under his wing, hiring him on at his investment firm to run errands and help out the other financial analysts, showing him the ropes along the way. When he realized that Jason had an aptitude for numbers and data, he insisted on paying for community college, giving him a prestigious title and a comfortable salary to continue working for the firm after he graduated. Jason didn't know where he and his mom would be without Jed, and he hoped to never have to find out.

"Hey kid. You on your way back with lunch yet? I'm about starved, here."

Jay laughed. "I think you'll survive long enough for me to get there. I'm on my way. Anything else you need?"

"Nah. Just get back with the food before I start eating the interns."

"Hey, want to come have dinner with mom and me tonight? Thinking I'll grab some ribs and cobbler she's been asking for. We could make a night of it."

There was a pause, then Jed cleared his throat. "Sorry kid, I already have something going on tonight. Next time, right?"

Before he could answer, Jed had hung up. Jason shook his head and frowned. His uncle had been a little absent as of late, ducking out of dinners and locking himself in the office for half the day. What the hell was going on with him? Once he got back to the office, he'd try to pry some information out of him.

His phone buzzed with a notification that his lunch order was ready to pick up, but he didn't move. He'd seen Charlotte and Doc Angus go inside Francie's, but they hadn't come back out yet. And he didn't want to take the chance of really getting on Char's bad side.

Or did he?

Leaning on the hood of his truck, he watched the front of

the diner, wanting to catch a glimpse of her again. He hadn't been prepared to run into her. Why didn't Brandon let him know she was in town? They'd just talked a few days ago and he hadn't even told him about Arthur. Next time they got together, he'd have to have a word with him.

He and Charlotte had always been opposites. Some might say he was boring: steady, quiet, aloof. But Charlotte? You would never suffer a dull moment with her. There was a spark inside her, one that would turn into a blaze of fury if given the right fuel. She was always kind, always fun, always ready to lend a hand or make a plan or save the day. It was easy to get drawn into her orbit, and hard to let her go once you were there.

Chewing on the corner of his mouth, he let his mind wander back to the days before he ruined everything between them by deciding he knew what was best for Charlotte better than she did.

Weekends, after all the chores were done and the sun was hanging low in the sky, Charlotte would come over to his house. They'd have a glass of sweet tea with his mom before running off to the gazebo on the back edge of the Archer property. How many afternoons had they laid on the benches, talking about anything and everything? He'd lay with his head in her lap, listening to her talk about one of the books she'd read or some new place she just HAD to visit. Closing his eyes, he could still feel her fingers trailing through his hair.

"Are you falling asleep on me, Jason Archer?"

His eyes popped open, trying to focus on the face frowning down at him. "Never. But if it would make you feel better to repeat what you just said, I won't mind."

That made her laugh, and that was his favorite sound in the world.

"I don't think you hear a thing I say. You nod and smile, but nothing actually sticks, does it?"

He shook his head. "I hear everything you say, Char." She scoffed but he needed her to know he was serious. Sitting up so he could see her face better, he caught her hand and pressed it flat against his chest. "You talk about cheerleading, and I hear how self-conscious you are about what people see when they look at you. You talk about how boring and tedious your homework is, but I hear your frustration at not being challenged, about wanting to learn everything. You talk about things you remember from when you were little, and I hear how much you miss your mom."

When she looked at him, tears pooling in the corners of her caramel eyes, his chest squeezed. "I may not be great at listening all the time, but I always hear you, Charlotte. Always."

From down the street he heard door chimes and looked up to see Dr. Angus and Charlotte talking as they came down the sidewalk toward him. She hadn't seen him yet, so he ducked further behind the truck where he could still see through the window. That familiar heaviness rolled through his heart while he watched her.

The memory was fresh from the spring right before graduation. Right before he lied to her face and sent her away thinking that he didn't love her anymore.

Right before he let go of the best thing in his life.

SEVEN
CHARLOTTE

"You all right, Charlie-girl? You've hardly said a word all night."

Pulled from her thoughts about what to do to save her homestead and her family's legacy, she shrugged.

Brandon snorted. "Probably sitting there plotting her escape."

"I am not." She scraped her plate into the garbage and tried not to chuck it at his head. "But we do need to talk about the bank and Chancellor and what to do next."

Nobody responded or even looked up at her, as though they hadn't heard her. More than the fact that they were denying there was a problem, being ignored made her see red. Spinning back around, she threw her hands in the air. "What the hell, you guys? I wish you would've called me, told me what was going on. I would've been on the first plane."

"And done what, exactly?" Her brother shook his head. "You can't save everyone, Charlotte, no matter how much smarter and better than the rest of us you think you are."

The words hit her like a slap in the face. "I never said I was smarter or better, Bran. I just want to help. This is my home, too."

"No. It hasn't been your home since you ran off eight years ago." His voice was low and heavy. "You took off to live your life, leaving the rest of us here to manage the ranch. Your 'home' is in San Francisco now."

"Now hold on just a minute—"

"Enough." The tone of the one word from Arthur startled her enough she swallowed her words. He looked at each of them in turn, giving his son an eyebrow lift, then he waved his daughter over. "Come here and sit, darlin'."

She crossed her arms and glared at her brother but sat down anyway. Turning to her dad, she laid her hand on his. "What happened?"

Stroking his beard, he sighed heavily. "I didn't call you because I didn't want you to worry. It was only one thing at first, a dip in sales of our Quarter Horses. Things like that happen sometimes, so I figured I could just make it up in the next few months. Then some suit from San Antonio showed up and offered to buy us out, the whole property, the stables, the horses, everything, and I sent him packin'. Not so sure that was the right choice, now."

Brandon cleared his throat and leaned back in his chair, crossing his arms and staring at the floor. "After that, we had a string of bad luck that we just couldn't get in front of."

"What kind of bad luck?"

"Oh, you know. The truck broke down, there were problems with the septic tank, things that needed taking care of and cost money. One thing led to another, we got a little behind then a lot behind and…here we are."

Sighing, Charlotte leaned her elbows on the table. "Okay, fine. I get it. But now what? We could sell some of our equipment, an acre or two, to the neighboring farms. Would that help, do you think?"

"Don't you think we already thought of that?" Brandon shook his head. "We've sold what we can but no one's buying so that didn't give us much. Not nearly enough."

"Bran—"

"I can't do this right now, Char. I'm goin' into town. The band has a show coming up and we need to practice." He dropped his plate in the sink, then paused on his way out the door. "It's great you want to help, I just think it's too little too late."

"That was fun." Charlotte watched her brother's taillights disappear and shook her head. "Good to know his band is still doing well. I just wish he wasn't so pissed at me about leaving."

"He's not pissed about you leaving. He's pissed that he stayed. Music is where his heart lies, I've known it for a very long time. His band is getting bigger gigs and living both lives is wearing on him right now. But he'll be fine, darlin', just give him a minute. Now, I don't wanna talk about money and the bank and our troubles anymore." He took his daughter's hand and smiled broadly. "It's good havin' you home, Charlie-girl. Despite the circumstances."

Her shoulders relaxed and she smiled. "It's good being home, Dad. Sorry. I just wasn't expecting any of this. I promise I'll help however I can. There's no way we're losing the ranch, not after all the generations who fought to get us here. How long has it been in the family, anyway?"

"We certainly owe a debt of gratitude to a long family line." Arthur leaned back in his chair and scratched at his neck. "Your great-grandfather's family was already in the area, up from Mexico, in the mid- to late 1800s, but it wasn't until the big oil boom in 1901 or so that your great-grandmother Eleanor came to Texas. Miguel Trevino fell for her, hard, the moment he saw her, and they wed, despite her family being absolutely against it. They had come south for the oil, but Miguel's family was well-established here, with a parcel of land twice the size it is now. With everyone drilling and looking to strike it rich, the once-lucrative ranching industry was left wide open. Miguel and Eleanor saw the opportunity and they took it. There's been a Trevino running this ranch ever since."

As his voice trailed off, all the playfulness died out and they fell into silence. Charlotte stared at her hand in his, wishing to take every ounce of his worry and despair off his shoulders, letting it wash over her, instead. The way the light in his eyes had dimmed while he talked about the dying legacy that was now his responsibility broke her heart. But her dad didn't need her pity right then, he needed reassurances and love. So she plastered a smile on her face and bounced out of her chair to kiss his cheek.

"And there always will be, Dad. We'll figure this out. For right now, though, you go on up to bed and get some rest. I've got these dishes, and I'll hit the hay soon enough."

He frowned as he pushed out of his chair. "Are you sure? You're my guest, you shouldn't be waiting on me. I don't mind cleaning up." Out of nowhere his jaw nearly unhinged with an enormous yawn.

"With only one good arm?" Her eyebrows lifted. "Don't you argue with me," she laughed. "Get on up to bed and I'll see you in the morning, old man."

———

There was something soothing about the mindless task of washing dishes. Charlotte stood at the sink with her hands in the warm soapy water, letting the silence of the house settle around her. The sun had already gone down and not even the faint orange glow of dusk remained. Bran was still out with his band and Arthur was upstairs, sleeping peacefully. Letting her mind wander a little, she went over the events of the day and shook her head. It had been a shit-show, there was no doubt about that.

If she hadn't been sure whether Brandon resented her for going away to college, she was positive now. He made it sound like she ran away to put her life at T & M Ranch in the rearview mirror, trying to pretend like she hadn't had some of her best and worst days right there. But that wasn't even close to the truth. She wanted to stay, tried to convince her dad to let her wait a little longer or let her go to the local community college first. But he would have none of that. He insisted that she follow through on her plans, that she take advantage of the scholarships and opportunities her hard work had awarded her.

And then, when Jason called things off, she actually came home and unpacked her bags, moping for the next few days before she was confronted by Arthur, Dr. Angus, and even Brandon, telling her she had to go, that they'd MAKE her go if they had to carry her onto the plane themselves. Shaking her head, she smiled at the memory.

After drying another glass and putting it away, she slung the towel over her shoulder and turned back to the sink. She'd been fighting it, but her encounter with Jason earlier in the day was not going to be ignored and kept pushing its way to the front of her mind. God, he looked good. The wiry teen who had been her best friend and first love had upgraded to a breathtaking man. She'd avoided asking about him over the years for fear of wanting–no, needing–to know more about what he was doing, how he was, if he was dating or married or still in town. It had been tough, but she hadn't even tried to look him up on social media. He had made it perfectly clear that he didn't want anything to do with her, so she was not about to give him the satisfaction of knowing that she still thought about him. A lot.

Butterflies flitted around in her stomach for the whole week before their first date. When the night finally came, he'd been so sweet and awkward. Holding the door for her at the restaurant, he ended up getting stuck as several appreciative, but clueless, families slipped past him, unaware that he had somewhere to be. Too timid to cut in front of anyone or to let the door swing shut, he stood there, sweating in a near-panic until Charlotte came back to get him.

She thought about their first kiss–under the bleachers after the homecoming football game–and the thousands that followed. Warm and tentative, his lips brushed over hers like a sigh, cupping her face in one hand while the other pressed flat against the small of her back. After the first kiss, she couldn't get enough.

Having a boyfriend who lived on the other side of the Trevino property—and who was very good at sneaking out of his house at night—was an exceptionally lucky break for Charlotte. Most nights, they would meet up under cover of darkness out behind the old barn. She wanted to meet him halfway, in an old lean-to where extra hay was stored, where they could have even more privacy, but Jason wouldn't hear of it. He tried to tell her he was worried about her walking alone in the dark, which never made sense to Charlotte. Who would try to hurt her on her own property? But as long as he came over and they got to talk and laugh and drown in each other's kisses, she only pretended to mind.

Right now, all she could think about was the grown version of Jason she'd seen earlier: his expensive suit and midnight eyes, the lock of dark hair that flopped over one eye, the curve of his soft lips. The years had definitely been kind to him, and he seemed to be thriving. What had he seen when he looked at her? The darkness outside, paired with the kitchen lights behind her, had turned the kitchen window into a mirror and Charlotte gazed at her reflection, trying to see herself through his eyes.

How was she different now from the girl who'd loved him? Where his face had filled out, hers had slimmed down. She combed her fingers through her choppy bangs, trying to be objective as she looked at her reflection. Fresh-faced, hair loose around her face and over her shoulders, she was surprised at the young woman she saw there. They weren't children anymore, she knew that, but she'd never taken the time to appreciate the changes. Sure there were laugh lines that crinkled at the corners of her eyes, but those eyes were wiser and kinder than she'd been as a kid. She didn't have on any makeup and found that she truly preferred her look without it. Besides, who had the time to fuss with that now, especially when you spent your days with a room full of six-year-olds who couldn't care less?

A creak in the hall behind her caught her attention and she turned toward the sound. Had her dad come downstairs, looking for pain meds or something? She poked her head through the doorway, but there was no one there. The house was probably settling, cooling down after the warm day and contracting around itself. She listened for another moment, just to be sure Arthur wasn't puttering around in need of help, but all was silent again.

Returning to the task at hand, she put the last of the dishes in the rack to dry and pulled the stopper to release the dirty water. When she glanced at her reflection in the dark window, movement caught her eye. She spun around, expecting to catch her dad or her brother skulking around behind her, but once again there was no one there. Turning back to the glass, she leaned closer. She had seen something, she was sure of it; could one of the horses have gotten out?

Charlotte tilted her head, trying to get a different perspective, and what she saw sent an icy finger of fear skittering down her spine.

Just on the other side of the glass, a finger's width away, was a dark figure, face obscured by a blue bandanna. His eyes were dark and hollow in the haunting light from the kitchen that illuminated only partial features, but she could feel the menace emanating from them regardless.

With a gasp, Charlotte stumbled backwards, knocking over a chair and nearly going down with it. She scrambled for purchase against the table, her gaze torn away for no more than a split second. But it was long enough that when she looked back to the window, the man was gone.

———

Charlotte didn't get much sleep that night.

Once the shock of seeing someone watching her through the window had passed, she grabbed the baseball bat near the door and bolted into the yard to track the bastard down. She'd barely stepped off the porch when the headlights of Brandon's truck swept over her. He was out of the truck in an instant.

"What the hell are you doing, Char? What's with the bat?"

She didn't answer but stormed around the corner to the spot she'd seen the menacing figure, Brandon following in her wake. "Someone was here, Bran."

"You're not making any sense. Someone who?" He pulled in front of her and grabbed the weapon from her hand. "Take a breath and explain."

Reaching for the bat she glared at him. "I don't know who. There was a man outside the kitchen window, watching me. If you'd get out of my way, I could still catch up to him."

Brandon was quiet for a minute, scanning as far as the light allowed before grabbing Charlotte's shoulder and steering her toward the house. "Get inside, Char."

"The hell I will!" She made another grab for the bat, but he held it out of reach. "Dammit Bran, I'm pissed, and I want to have a word with whoever it is, so get out of my way."

With a hand on her back, he walked with her to the porch. "I'm not joking. Go back inside and let me handle this."

"I'm not scared."

"Jesus, Charlotte Rose–you should be!"

He tried to pull the front door open, but she slapped her hand on it and leaned against it, narrowing her eyes. "What's going on, Brandon? What aren't you telling me?" She watched his eyes shift to the side and above her, looking anywhere but into her eyes, and a wave of cold raced through her veins. "You know who it was."

With another furtive glance, he pulled her inside with him and locked the door. "No, I don't know who it was. Not really. But shady shit's been going on for a little while now."

Charlotte wrapped her arms around herself as she paced, trying to hide the way her hands were shaking now that the adrenaline had worn off. "You need to tell me the whole story, Bran. I need to know what the hell is really going on around here."

Hours later, the sun started to lighten the sky, and she knew there would be no more sleep for her. Pulling her hair up into a ponytail, she snuck downstairs to make some coffee, figuring she'd get a jump on the chores. Her brain seemed to work better when her body was preoccupied with something else, anyway. And this morning there was an awful lot for her to work out.

The talk with Bran had dragged into the wee hours of the morning and she still couldn't believe half of it. It all sounded like a soap opera instead of real life: mysterious breakdowns and supply problems, phantom cell phone calls with no one on the other end, lights being left on and equipment ending up on the other side of the ranch from where it belonged. He said he had an idea who it was, but he wouldn't give her any other information. Said he didn't need her running off half-cocked when he didn't have any proof. But she'd figure it out.

Frowning at her feet as she strolled toward the stable, Charlotte pushed the family's troubles aside. Of course, that left room for the irritation about seeing Jason to wash over her. It would have been one thing if she'd been prepared to see him; she could have protected herself a little better. It galled her to no end that she had reacted to him the way she did. And that he knew it. What the hell was he playing at? What was he hoping to gain by looking so good and being charming and sweet and reminding her of how he used to kiss her and touch her just right—

Nope. Charlotte shook her head and pulled her shoulders back. Not diving down that rabbit hole today. He'd made it clear that none of those old feelings existed for him anymore. If she didn't want to end up in a fistfight, she'd just have to make sure she and Jason didn't see each other before she returned to San Francisco.

Brandon went out to the far pasture as soon as he was up, and she wasn't sure he'd even gone to bed last night. He was still kind of mad at her when they decided to table the talk. She couldn't really blame him. It was going to take a little time for him to get used to her being around again. Taking over was never in her plan, no matter what he thought. But she'd definitely thrown everyone off their routine. He'd come around eventually.

Arthur came outside with his work clothes on, his arm in the sling, and started to make his way toward the stables. Charlotte ran to head him off.

"Whoa! Where do you think you're going?"

He smiled and patted her hand as she pressed it against his chest. "There's work to be done, Charlie-girl, and it ain't gonna do itself."

Looping her arm with his good one, she steered him to the rocker on the porch, shaking her head. "You know you have to take it easy, Dad. At least for a few weeks." When he started to protest, she held up her hand and continued. "It's under control. I've been up working this morning, Milo was here, Bran is out in the field. We will pick up the slack and get things taken care of. You. Sit."

He grumbled and pouted but stayed seated. Charlotte sat on the top step, wrapping her arms around her legs. "Is there a chance I can take a look at the books this afternoon, Dad? I just want to see where income has dropped off, or what expenses have gone up, see if there's an easy fix to get things set right."

"I don't see why not." He shrugged. "I still think it's just a bad season and a spell of bad luck. We'll get it turned around soon enough. But that won't happen as long as Chancellor's nippin' at our heels."

Charlotte frowned and debated telling her dad about the trespasser the night before. It seemed he hadn't heard her arguing with Brandon or yelling outside about the man looking in the window. For now, she figured it could wait. There hadn't been any damage done, just some asshole trying to scare her. Arthur needed to relax and recuperate. He didn't need this stress. Sticking to the money and things that he could control and understand was the best course of action for today.

"Dad, I refuse to believe that there's nothing else we can do besides sell or default. Once I get a look at the numbers, I should be able to help you come up with a plan to get in the black again. And no matter what Bran says, this has nothing to do with me wanting to save everyone. This is my legacy, too, and keeping it is important to me."

Arthur smiled down at his daughter, but it never reached his eyes. The sadness he wore was enough to make Charlotte's heart hurt, too, and she knew that the first thing that needed to change around the ranch was her. It wasn't going to be easy, and she knew her brother wasn't going to be overly pleased with her decision, but she knew deep in her gut that she was where she needed to be.

Charlotte was moving home.

EIGHT
JASON

"Hey Jay, come into my office for a quick minute."

Looking up from his desk, Jason barely caught sight of his uncle before he retreated and pulled the door shut without waiting for a response. That was how he operated but Jason couldn't say he was used to it, even after all the time he'd worked for Jed.

The portfolio he was working on was coming together nicely but he still had a little more research to do. It was like solving a puzzle sometimes. He gathered as much information as possible about a certain financial trend, looked at previous years and all the variables, and made well-informed predictions. And he was good at it.

This career choice never crossed his mind growing up. In fact, he'd been enrolled in culinary school in San Francisco right after graduation, with dreams of opening his own restaurant one day. God, what a fantastic adventure he and Charlotte had planned out. Their schools were walking distance apart so they'd still get to see each other every day. The plan was to live on their respective campuses for the first year and then find a little place together. At eighteen, he knew he was going to marry that girl one day. Laughing under his breath, he pictured her face when she told him he would. He'd been thinking about it for a year already, knowing they needed to experience the world a little first, and he loved that she thought it was her idea.

His smile melted away, thinking about how none of that worked out. At all. Even the best-laid plans get screwed up by unforeseen bullshit.

When his dad got sick, he went over every possible scenario, every choice he could make, and he knew there really was only one. His mom disagreed with him, convinced that she'd be fine and that his dad would beat the pancreatic cancer that had just reared its head. But he knew she was wrong, could see it in his dad's face and the way he moved. He knew it was too late, and that Jimmy Archer was already fading away.

Trying to wrestle those memories back into their box in the back of his mind, Jason shook his head. There was no changing the past, he knew that. And he was exceptionally grateful to his uncle for taking him in and recognizing his knack for numbers and data. He didn't know where he'd be without Jed. And he hoped he'd never have to find out. He stared at his screen and the spreadsheets he'd been poring over and sighed. This project was a little more challenging than he'd expected, and progress was slow. Most likely, that was what Jed wanted to see him about. He'd dropped this project in Jason's lap at the beginning of the week with very vague instructions and a fairly tight deadline.

After rapping his knuckles on Jed's open walnut door, Jason stepped inside. "What's up?"

"Hey, kid. Come on in. Shut the door behind you."

"That doesn't sound good." He chuckled but did as he was told then stood with his hands in his pockets, waiting while Jed finished what he was doing. Glancing around the familiar room, his heart squeezed and swelled looking at the pictures scattered around on the shelves: Jed with Jason's parents at their wedding, the four of them at his high school graduation, the three of them at his dad's funeral, and then just Jed and him at Jason's college graduation. He'd been there for some of the most important and difficult times in his life, and he loved him like a second father.

Jed finally looked up with a bright smile. "What're you doing? Come in, sit down."

Relaxing into the leather chair directly across the desk, Jason loosened his tie and started rolling the sleeves of his shirt. "Everything all right?"

"Of course. I just realized I hadn't checked in with you for a while. Been a little buried."

"Anything I can help with?"

With a wave of his hand, Jed brushed away the offer. "Nah, I'm a tough old bull. I can manage. How are things going, Jay?"

"Fine. Good." He shrugged. "I'm almost done with the portfolio for the Ortiz family, if you want to take a look."

"I'm not talking about work, kid." Leaning forward on his elbows, he tipped his head to the side. "I hear an old friend's in town."

The blood rushed to Jason's face, and he busied himself with picking invisible lint from his tie. "Charlotte? Yeah. Her dad got hurt so she's back for a little while to help out on their ranch."

"Mhmm." Jed waggled his eyebrows. "Any sparks between you two? Think there's any possibility of rekindling that little flame?"

"Doubtful, judging by the way she jumped down my throat when I ran into her. You know things didn't end well between us." Jason cleared his throat. "Besides, she's not sticking around for long. She'll be heading back to the coast soon."

Jed didn't say anything for a beat. "Is that right? I mean, Arthur's probably ready to retire and his son doesn't strike me as the full-time rancher type. A lot of folks around here are selling and moving on. Maybe she'll wax nostalgic and want to come back for good and put down roots. Think that's a possibility?"

"I don't really know, I don't really know her anymore. But I can't imagine she'd allow her dad to sell the place. It means too much to her." Or, more accurately, means *everything* to her. It's her childhood, her home base, the only place she still feels close to her mom. Frowning, Jason scratched at his neck. "What's with all the questions about Charlotte? I don't think you've ever asked me about her before."

"Are you sure?" Jed's brows drew together. "I swear I have. Doesn't matter. Always looking for ways for friends and neighbors to make some money. And I'm looking out for you too, kid. You're not getting any younger."

Shaking his head, Jason laughed. "Yeah, look who's talking."

"I'll have you know that I've a very hot date lined up for this weekend out in Seguin. Met her online." His eyebrows shot up. "Can you even believe that? What a world we live in."

"Scoundrel."

Jason expected a bigger reaction than just a snort from his uncle. This was a running joke between them since the opposite was true; Jed was a good man who treated his dates exceptionally well. In fact, he was usually the one whose heart was broken. Taking the opportunity to really look at Jed, it was suddenly clear that something was going on. His shoulders were bunched around his ears, hands fidgeting with the things on his desk, and there were dark circles under his eyes. Jason's stomach dropped.

"Everything okay with you, Jed?" *Please don't be sick.*

He looked in Jason's eyes, brow furrowed and opened his mouth like he was going to say something. But then he closed it again and shrugged.

"Sure, kid. Everything's good, I'm just not sleeping well. There's an old owl that's taken up residence right outside my bedroom window. Can you believe that shit?" He laughed and shook his head.

Jason didn't laugh with him. His heart rate ticked up, his chest shrinking and threatening to choke him. Leaning forward, he laid a hand on the desk. "You'd tell me if something was wrong, wouldn't you? If you were in trouble or sick?"

When realization hit him, Jed's eyes opened wide, and he sat back in his chair. "Oh Jay, you know I would. But I'm not sick, I promise. And I would never keep that from you, especially after everything you all went through with Jimmy. I'm healthy as a horse, don't you worry."

Jason didn't move right away, and Jed's expression softened. "You're not getting rid of me that easy."

Out in the hall, Jason put his hands on his hips and frowned. In all the time he'd worked there, he'd never seen his uncle look so—what?—tired? Beaten down? Haunted?

Back in his own office, he ran his hands down his face. Jesus, he needed to take a step back. He was jumping to conclusions and projecting his own fears onto Jed. Jason's dad was the one who lied and hid things from him until it was too late to do anything. That didn't mean that Jed would do the same.

After a few deep breaths, his heart was feeling normal again. The anxiety wasn't completely gone and would probably settle on his chest for the next couple of days. But at least it was manageable enough that he could get back to work. Besides, this was Jed. He'd been a straight-shooter with Jason since he was a kid, and there was no reason to think anything had changed. He would trust Jed with his life.

NINE
CHARLOTTE

The next few days were a whirlwind for Charlotte, full of phone calls and online forms and disappointing conversations. Her principal wasn't overly thrilled that Charlotte was leaving, but at least the sub that was running her classes for the time being was excellent and was willing to stay on longer, maybe even permanently.

In San Francisco, she'd shared a house with four other teachers, and they were heartbroken to hear that she wasn't coming back anytime soon. But at least Charlotte knew she could trust them to look after her belongings until she could come pack them up and move them to Texas.

After wrapping up the last items on her to-do list, Charlotte sat back in the chair and stared at the computer screen in front of her. What had she just done? Had she really just uprooted her whole life to return to her childhood home? Yes. Yes, she had.

And part of her was secretly thrilled.

She'd always been a good student, organized, and a natural leader. Training horses made her happy in a way she hadn't known anywhere else, but after her mother passed, it seemed her dad was hell-bent on sending her away. Not in a way that made her feel unloved, but he was determined that she would have a different life, that she would meet and exceed all expectations she had for herself. He encouraged her to take advanced classes every chance she got and helped her fill out a multitude of college applications and scholarship entries. After that, it didn't matter what she said. She was going away to college.

Brandon wasn't a bad student, but he didn't seem to care as much about learning. He did what he had to do to get by. It was like that on the ranch, too. But when it came to making music, he had boundless energy and ideas and drive. And Bran was talented. He won a couple of local contests and even had a band scraped together that played in taverns as far away as Austin. But when Charlotte left, he stayed. Chewing on her thumbnail, she knew there was some serious underlying resentment toward her that was bound to come out sooner rather than later.

When she told her family she was going to stay, her announcement was met with mixed results.

"You've got to be shittin' me," Brandon snarled. He refused to look at her, only stared down into his dinner, shaking his head every once in a while.

"You know I'd love to have you here, Charlie, but there's really no need to give up everything you've worked for. We'll manage. We always do." Arthur patted her hand with an indulgent smile.

"I *want* to be here, Dad. I was due for a change, anyway. You know me, I'm never satisfied to sit in one place." Bran snorted but she ignored him. "This is my home, too, and even if I only stay until you're back on your feet, I'm glad to do it. Texas is a big place and I'm sure I can find a teaching position somewhere close by. And that's the bottom line; I want to be close by. Not just for emergencies but for holidays and birthdays, for the fourth of July and the State Fair, for the rodeos and Brandon's shows. California's great, but it's got nothing on Texas."

Finally, Brandon nodded and sighed. "Fine. We could use you. We haven't had a trainer as good as you in years. Maybe you could teach Milo and me a thing or two."

Once she had a chance to sit down in the office and look over the accounts, it became apparent that things were possibly worse than any of them had realized. Their main source of income had been sales of their Quarter Horses to cowhands all across the state. But in the last year, sales didn't just slow down, they dropped off. Just stopped all together, even the operations that had used T&M Ranch for decades had suddenly stopped coming around. When Charlotte started making phone calls to see if there was a problem with their stock, she was met with apology after apology.

"Oh, no, there's nothing wrong with your horses. They've always been the best we've ever had. It's just that—" Invariably the person on the other end of the line would hesitate as though they were afraid to say anything more. "Well, there's a new outfit in the area, Chancellor Quarter Horses, came calling."

Blood rushed loud through her ears, and she had to fight to keep her voice even. "Did you say Chancellor? Gerard Chancellor?" *That son of a bitch.*

"Yeah, that's the guy. Their horses were real good, too, and they were considerably less expensive. What with last year being a little rough on the cattle industry, we decided to try them out and so far, so good. It's nothing personal, Miss Charlotte. But everyone's a little strapped right now and no one's in a position to look a gift horse in the mouth, as it were."

After the third similar phone call, Charlotte was beyond livid. Her dad came inside, and she told him the news.

"Well, that low-down, rotten, dirty bastard! I knew there was something shady about him the second he stepped foot on our property." Pacing the small office space, Arthur continued to mumble under his breath. "Undermining me when I wouldn't sell him my land, huh? Playing dirty, sneaking around behind my back, stealing my loyal clients to force my hand. When I get my hands on Chancellor he'll wish he'd never heard my name."

The color of his face was concerning to Charlotte so she snapped the computer off and turned her dad toward the door leading outside. "All right, we need some fresh air. We can't do anything right now, so let's just take a quick walk and try to get your blood pressure out of the combustion range."

He grumbled and swore all the way around the outside of the buildings, but by the time they'd reached the stable he seemed to have run out of steam. Strolling down the length of the stalls, petting each horse and speaking softly, Arthur was wearing a broad grin by the time each animal had been visited.

Throwing an arm around her shoulders, he pulled Charlotte against him and kissed the top of her head. "Thank you, darlin'. I guess I was just thrown off a bit. To learn that we're being systematically pushed out of the industry we've been a part of for more than a century by some slick-talking billionaire, well...I just wasn't expecting that."

Sitting on the porch steps, looking out over the property, Charlotte sighed. "You know, dad, we're going to have to find a way to adapt. I'm not talking about giving up the horses," she sputtered when Arthur slapped his palm against his thighs. "I'm just saying that there has to be a way to expand what we do. Boarding, yes, breeding, yes, but what other opportunities lie here?"

Neither spoke for several moments, lost in their own thoughts. Charlotte's gaze fell on the paddock and memories of her first riding lessons filled her mind. Buttercup was the first horse she rode, a gorgeous Palomino, gentle as you'd ever hope to meet. Her mother had been so patient with her, teaching her not only technique and how to keep herself and the horse safe, but also explaining everything she knew about Quarter Horses and what made them special. Tears sprang to her eyes. She hadn't missed her mom this much in a long time. As though he could sense her sadness, her dad wrapped his arm around her shoulders and pulled her close.

"Your mom would've been real proud of you, Charlie. You know that, right?"

"I know." She leaned her head on his shoulder and swiped at her wet cheeks. "It's been so long but there are just moments that hit me out of nowhere. Why would looking at the paddock right now make me think of her?"

She felt more than heard Arthur chuckle. "That's your mom, for ya. She's probably trying to tell you something. What, I couldn't fathom a guess. But I feel her sometimes. I hope you do, too."

He kissed her head and retreated into the house. Charlotte sat on the step, letting the tears come, now, and looked out over the grounds. Maybe she was trying to say something, trying to point her daughter in the right direction. Closing her eyes, she took a deep breath and tried to calm her mind. Wasn't that how this mumbo-jumbo was done? Communing with nature and whatnot?

After a few moments of deep breathing and relaxation, an image popped into her mind. It was like the memory of her mom teaching her to ride in the paddock, except it wasn't her mom holding the reins, it was her. Clear as day, she could see herself coaching a little girl around the yard, and the girl was laughing. A smile crept over her face, and she wiped away one last tear.

"Thanks, Mom."

TEN
JASON

"That must be some daydream to earn a grin like that."

While he knew that Charlotte was home from California, he wasn't expecting to find her sitting on her front porch, the lowering sun painting streaks of gold in her hair. And he certainly wasn't expecting the way his body reacted to her upturned face, eyes closed, mouth curved sweetly. Holy hell, he wanted to press his lips to the corner of that mouth and bury his hands in her hair and hear her whisper his name.

But he was pretty sure he'd destroyed that possibility when he pushed her away all those years ago.

Her eyes flew open, and she struggled to focus on him, but when she did his heart thumped against his ribs. Hard. The breeze ruffled her bangs, her sun-warmed cheeks were rosy, and her golden eyes traveled over him, head to toe. Even in the warm Texas day, it sent a shiver down his spine.

"What the hell are you doing here?" Charlotte scrambled to her feet and narrowed her eyes. "Are you lost or something?"

"Nooo." He dragged out the syllable. "I'm here on a social call."

She snorted at that and pushed past him, striding toward the stable. "Who says I want to see you?"

His lips twitched and he followed her at a leisurely pace. "Who says I'm here to see you? Other people live here, you know. You aren't the queen." Why did he want to push her buttons so badly? If he was a smart man, he'd just walk away and get on with the reason he was there. But damn it, she was just too much fun. He'd missed that in his life.

Charlotte narrowed her eyes. "What's that supposed to mean, Jay? Are you here to take my horse out for a little rendezvous? Or maybe you and my dad are going shopping for matching shoes and handbags?"

"Maybe we are. It's a free country." What was it about her that got his blood racing and made him want to keep provoking her?

"Not on this ranch, it's not."

He ran his hand through his hair and sighed. "It doesn't have to be like this, Char. We were friends, once. I'd like us to be friends again."

Right. Friends. *Friendship* was not exactly the interaction he was imagining at the moment. For a second, he was distracted by flashes of Charlotte pressed against the stable wall with her legs wrapped around his waist and hands buried in his hair, while he kissed her senseless. He nearly groaned at the vision. Shit. *Get it together, Archer.*

"Friends, huh?" Charlotte regarded him with narrowed eyes, biting the inside of her cheek like she always did when she was trying to work something out. She cocked her head. "Okay friend. What do you know about this new horse breeder in the area, some big deal from San Antonio?"

He shoved his hands in his pockets and shrugged. "I don't remember hearing anything. Why?"

"Apparently, they've been contacting all of our clients and undercutting us. I called every number on our list, and they all told the same story: This city-slicker showed up on their property one day, promising them the sun and the moon for pennies and they couldn't say no."

73

SHARON L. CLARK

"What? That's bullshit. I haven't heard anything, but I can ask around." He stepped closer and smiled down at her. Her head fell back, the anger gone from her eyes, and damn if his heart didn't skip a little. "There. Was that so hard?"

He knew every inch of that face and it made his chest ache. It was the same face he'd dreamed about over the years. When she left for college, it had broken his heart, even though he knew it was the best thing for her. She just couldn't understand why he backed out at the last minute, why he didn't want to escape Zearing with her and see the world. They'd talked about it a lot over the years. If he was right, there was still a map tucked away somewhere in her bedroom that had all the places they were going to visit marked with red dots. How often had they laid out in the field, under the stars, long after curfew to make plans for their life together? His stomach twisted knowing that he could never make up for the pain he'd caused her so long ago.

"Whatever." She pushed at his chest and tried to scowl, but he could see the tug at the corners of her soft, pink lips.

"Seriously Char, I was worried you would spontaneously combust from being nice–no, not even nice–from being *cordial* to me. Oh, wait!" He leaned closer, cupping her chin and examining her face and her eyes. "We're not out of the woods yet. I can see the smoke building back there, and I expect it to come out of your ears any second now."

She laughed with him and the sound warmed him from head to toe. Jesus, had he ever wanted so badly to kiss someone as he did in that moment? Her eyes twinkled and she hadn't pulled away yet: was it possible she was feeling the same thing? Man, he hoped she was. Because he was drowning in not only nostalgia but all the years of missing her, all the years of regret for lying to her and letting her believe that he had stopped loving her. Because that was the furthest thing from the truth.

The truth was, he had never stopped loving her and being around her now was just as painful as his penance should be.

Their laughter died away, and Jason found that he was stroking her cheek with his thumb and leaning closer as her breath hitched. "Charlotte…"

"There you are!"

Jumping back, Jason shoved his hands in his pockets and turned toward the voice. Brandon was loping across the yard, shaking his head with a good-natured grin. "Gross, you two are disgusting. Get away from my sister, you degenerate. And you—" he pointed a finger at Charlotte, "—quit trying to seduce my friends."

Slapping his finger away, she glared. "Screw you. I was not seducing anyone. And since when are you two friends? The last I knew you barely tolerated each other. What gives?"

"Haven't you heard?" Brandon wrapped an arm around Jason's neck, pulling him into a headlock. "We have this kind of frenemies thing going on. We're both too lazy to actually fight, so we decided to hang out instead. You ready?"

Jason nodded and pointed to his truck. "Yeah, the rods are in the back, and I have a cooler and bait and all that." He turned his eyes to Charlotte, who was shaking her head, one corner of her mouth tilted up as she walked backwards toward the stables.

"You two deserve each other."

He watched her go, her ponytail swinging, her jeans hugging every curve, and her eyes locked on his. She was so ridiculously adorable.

"I'll be there in a second, Brandon. Char, wait up." He jogged after her, blocking her path when she turned to disappear through the door. "Let me take you out."

She pulled up short, brows drawn down and lips pressed together. "What? Why the hell would I do that?"

"Because I'm irresistible and you know you want to." She scoffed and rolled her eyes. "Look, I just want to talk, to catch up. Let me welcome you back to town properly with a nice meal and a couple of beers."

Maneuvering past him, Charlotte shook her head. "You're insane."

"Why? Because the person who was my best friend for all my teenage years is back in town and I want to get to know her again?"

Charlotte turned and frowned at him, but didn't respond right away. They *had* been best friends long before they started dating, that part was absolutely true. And he figured that ship had sailed when he walked away from their planned life together, had walked away from her. Looking in her eyes now, he knew that eight years had been a very long time—but not long enough to keep his heart from speeding up when she smiled at him.

"I don't know, Jay. Do you think that's a good idea? I'm not sure I trust your motives here."

"My motives?" His lips curved as he stepped closer, and her golden eyes widened, burning into him. Brushing her bangs back, he lowered his voice to make sure only she could hear him. "You used to like my motives. Quite a lot, actually."

She swallowed hard, but Charlotte held her ground. Jesus, was that intoxicating scent coming from her? It was like fresh-cut grass and oranges and wildflowers, and he wanted to bury his face in her hair and take a deep breath. But he needed to cool his jets a little; there was no way she was going to let him touch her like that, to dive back into that level of intimacy. No, he'd have to work hard to earn that privilege.

She was glaring up at him, but her lips twitched anyway. "That doesn't even make any sense." There wasn't any venom in her words, but a hint of laughter that made his stomach feel like it was full of pop rocks.

He took her easy smile as acceptance and leaned in to press his lips to her cheek. "I'll pick you up tomorrow night at six."

"For fuck's sake, are we going fishing or are you going to

make out first?" Brandon stuck his head out of the truck window and sighed theatrically. "Come on Jay, quit sniffing around my sister and let's get out of here."

Sauntering out of the stable, he grinned and waggled his eyebrows. "I know you're a big-city girl now Char, but you better be ready to get your Texas on."

He knew she was watching him walk away, and it sent a thrill through him. But as he reached his truck and started to climb in, Charlotte ran out to the yard to yell after him, "I might be ready, and I might be waiting with my shotgun. You'll just have to take your chances!"

Waving out the window as he drove away, he knew he was setting himself up for a mess of trouble. And he couldn't be more thrilled about it.

ELEVEN
CHARLOTTE

What an asshole.

Who the hell did he think he was? She never agreed to go out with him. That was a crazy idea.

But she also hadn't expressly said no, either.

She was still fuming by the time she was in the house, done with the routine of locking down the stables. Pacing, she played with the pros and cons of going out with Jason tomorrow.

It was a horrible idea. He didn't deserve her time or attention. He'd made that decision when he broke her heart.

But damn it, she wanted to be around him. And she hated how badly she really wanted to. For years she'd fantasized about what she would do or what she'd say to him if she had the chance. The sad truth of it was that she'd always envisioned him chasing after her, wanting her and wooing her.

Of course she'd never give in to him, it would just be nice to have that power over him for a change. In her dreams, he'd pursued her with sweet words and even sweeter kisses, taken her out for dinners and dancing, laid her down on a blanket out under the vast Texas sky.

Nope. No way was she going down that road, not even in her imagination. Besides, she had been only eighteen the last time Jason had kissed her and there was a really good chance that she'd romanticized it, building it up to some toe-curling nonsense from a romance novel.

Right?

She needed to clean something. This nervous energy building up inside her at the thought of Jason's hands and lips on her was going to make her catch fire if she didn't distract herself.

Because she knew she was lying to herself.

The memories were clear and visceral and her skin tingled thinking about those nights deep in the pasture or up in the hay loft. Fumbling, laughing, melting into each other in a way she'd never felt with anyone else.

She frowned as she scrubbed the sink. There was no way she could go out with him tomorrow. Not when she was getting hot and bothered thinking about how much they had learned and how much hotter sex with Jason would be now as adults.

Fuck.

Tossing the sponge in the sink, she thought a nice hot bubble bath sounded perfect right then. Her dad was out with Dr Angus, Bran was still out with Jason, and she could really use a little private time to release this mounting stress. She didn't need Jason for that, although thinking about him would definitely help her along.

She was about to flip off the kitchen light and climb the stairs when a strange sound caught her attention. Was that an alarm? It was high and tinny, bleating every few seconds. Oh hell no. She needed to find that and turn it off immediately.

After checking that it wasn't her own cell, she started opening drawers, sticking her head into different rooms trying to track it down. The sound was still going and getting louder as she approached the back of the house. Was it coming from the mud room? What the hell would be making that kind of a sound in there?

She turned on the light and scanned the room. There were coats hanging on hooks, boots lined up neatly in front of the bench, and only a couple pairs of gloves laying on the shelf. Reaching into pockets, she started by searching the coats, but it didn't take long for her to finally recognize where the sound was coming from.

But it couldn't be. That hadn't made a sound in more than a decade.

Her gaze fell on the old rotary phone perched on the wall next to the back door and her skin prickled. No way. There was no way that phone was ringing. They'd disconnected it long ago—hadn't they? Maybe they just stopped using it when they stopped using the barn or when cell phones became more common. And even if they hadn't, it wasn't connected to an outside line, not susceptible to telemarketers or wrong numbers. It was only connected to another phone way out in the old barn, which wasn't used at all anymore.

With trembling hands, she lifted the receiver and put it to her ear. "Hello?"

It didn't seem that there was anyone there at first but then Charlotte heard the unmistakable sound of breathing, low and heavy and definitely male.

"Who the hell is this?" Her voice was low and tight, and she hoped that it didn't sound as terrified as she felt. "Answer me, asshole, or you'll regret it."

There was a dark, quiet chuckle on the other end of the line that sent a chill through her veins. Then the line went dead.

Looking out the back window into the partial light of dusk, she stared hard at the barn in the distance. She didn't see any movement, there were no lights visible, nothing seemed out of the ordinary.

But just because she didn't see anyone didn't mean there

was no one there. After the trespasser who'd scared her in the kitchen window, she wasn't about to take any chances.

Grabbing the keys from the bowl in the kitchen, she ran outside to the Gator. Before she reached it, though, the stench of gasoline assailed her, and her stomach twisted at the growing puddle underneath the little vehicle.

"Son of a bitch!"

She spotted a crowbar in the bed of the Gator so she grabbed it before she started running toward the barn. If there was someone repeatedly trespassing on the ranch, she was not about to let them frighten her into letting them get away with it. She halfway hoped it was the same asshole who'd been watching her the other night–she had a few choice words for him.

Slowing her pace as she drew closer, she kept her eyes on the building, watching for any sign of movement in the windows or near the doors. The shadows were growing quickly, hiding details and blurring any clarity. It was hard to tell if her eyes were playing tricks on her in the ghostly light, or if that was movement to her left. Still keeping a wide berth, she arced to the side to get a better look at the set of doors there. Squinting and blinking repeatedly, she reduced her speed further, unsure if that was a figure lurking in the semi-darkness.

She held the crowbar low as she drew closer, her ragged breathing loud to her own ears, her gaze locked on the spot she expected to see movement and rush her at any moment. Once her eyes adjusted to the gloom and she was almost on top of the entrance, she realized what she thought was a menacing presence was nothing more than a partially open door, shifting on its hinges. The entire latch set, including the padlock that had kept the door secure had been pried away from the door and lay uselessly on the ground, the lock still engaged.

Approaching cautiously, Charlotte tried to quiet her breath, afraid whoever was out here could hear her heart racing. She slowly reached out and wrapped her fingers around the edge of the door, keeping her makeshift weapon at the ready. Then she yanked it open, bracing herself for the rush of an attack.

But none came.

The barn was silent and empty, no lights on, no phantom movement in the depths of the building. Charlotte walked farther in, trying to keep her eye on the door behind her and the shadowy nooks and crannies in front of her.

"Hello?" Her voice sounded flat and dulled when it came back to her, but there was no other sound. There hadn't been any animals or straw in there for years, but the scent still lingered. Most of the horse stalls had been removed and she had a clear view all the way to the end, where she knew the old telephone was. Standing directly across from the phone where it was mounted under a small window, her stomach lurched.

The handset swung slightly, dangling by the cord over a scattered collection of cigarette butts and sunflower seeds.

Someone had been here.

Someone had broken in and stood right here at the window with an unobscured view of the house and the paddock and the stables. Goosebumps broke out over her whole body, standing where he had stood for who knows how long, realizing that he could see everything going on at the ranch.

A sudden noise above her made Charlotte jump and cower before she realized it was just the flight of a bird who'd been nesting in the rafters. Even though she wasn't under attack by some unknown assailant, the hair on the back of her neck stood on end. Staying here alone was a very bad idea. The sun had almost completely disappeared below the horizon and the path back to the house was even darker and she still had no idea if whoever had been here was still lying in wait.

She sure as hell was not going to stay there and wait for him to come back.

Pausing at the door, she scanned the path back to the house and took several deep breaths. Then she took off at a sprint, feeling eyes on her back the whole way, the mounting certainty that someone was right behind her, reaching for her and about to take her down. But she kept her eyes trained on the light of the porch, nothing else existed but that light and the sanctuary it offered. Tears tightened her throat, fear squeezing her lungs until she thought her chest was going to burst.

She broke into the circle of light shining from the porch, every nerve ending on high alert, but she skidded to a stop just feet from her sanctuary. Someone was blocking out the light spilling through the open door.

"Charlotte?" At the sound of her brother's voice, the crowbar fell from her hand. She barreled toward him and collapsed in his arms. "What's wrong? Are you okay?"

Words wouldn't come at first, but she clung to him as she tried to catch her breath. Brandon held her tight, the alarm in his voice nearly matching hers.

"What happened? Did that guy come back? Did he threaten you?"

"No. I mean, I don't know if it was the same person, but someone was here." She pushed out of her brother's arms, lowering her voice. "In the barn. The phone in the mud room was ringing, Brandon. I picked it up and someone was there."

"And you went down there by yourself?" He scowled at her. "Charlotte, you could have been hurt. What were you thinking?"

"I was thinking I was pissed off and that I wasn't going to let someone scare me in my own house, that's what. No one was around when I got there, but they had been. And for a while it seems." She scrubbed her hands through her hair and shrugged away from Brandon's hand on her shoulder. "They cut the fuel line on the Gator, too."

Brandon glared toward the barn, lips pressed into a tight line. "Let's go inside and call the sheriff. This is bigger than we can handle on our own."

TWELVE
JASON

The next morning, Jason couldn't wipe the smile off his face. God, he'd missed that fire. Charlotte was the only woman—hell, the only person who could make him feel so alive. He shook his head. All this time and she still managed to make his heart race.

He pulled into the parking lot at work and realized that he needed to come up with a plan for their date. The invitation had been spontaneous and now, seeing that he hadn't thought things through, he started to sweat. Pulling his phone out of his pocket, he dialed quickly.

"Yell-o?"

"Mitch, I need your help."

There was a slight pause then Mitch drawled, "Oh-ho, really? What the hell have you gotten yourself into, m'man? Must be something pretty bad if you're calling me to get you out of it."

"It's bad. I mean, it's good—great, even—but I am woefully underprepared. What the hell is there to do on a Tuesday night in Zearing?"

"Depends on what you're looking for. Are you looking for

a solo mission, a group outing, somewhere to take a girl, or somewhere to take a girl that you like?"

"Somewhere to take Charlotte Trevino."

Mitch let out a low whistle and Jason heard him shift the phone around. "Well, that is a problem, isn't it? I'll have to think about it. Give me an hour."

Jason rolled his eyes, knowing already that this was a very bad idea. Things involving Mitchell Drew usually were. But the two men had been close since the day Mitch rolled into town and despite being an odd soul and an acquired taste, he had become Jason's ride or die and could always be counted on when he was needed.

Settling into work, Jason kept his head down, trying to push Charlotte out of his head but having little success. He'd thought about her off and on for years but now that she was back in town and within reach...she was all he could think about. The numbers on the pages in front of him swam around and made no sense.

Somehow, he lost track of the time and was surprised when he looked at his watch and it was already noon. How many times had he read the same column without registering what he was looking at? "This is hopeless." Pushing the charts away, he buried his head in his hands.

"Knock, knock, amigo."

Snapping his gaze to the doorway, he was relieved to see Mitch standing there wearing a big grin. "Hey man, what are you doing here? I thought you were going to call."

"No way, this is far too important. Requires a face-to-face meetup and—" He held up two brown paper bags and grinned. "Sabroso Tacos!"

Sitting at the shaded picnic tables in back of the building, they dug into their tacos, Jason letting out a groan after the first bite.

"Damn, these are so good. Would it be bad if I ate these every day, for every meal?"

"Well, only in the sense that your arteries would close up and drop your subsequent 600-pound carcass faster than a tornado."

After a couple more bites, Jason grinned. "Worth it."

They finished lunch and sat back to relax for a moment, but inside Jason was a bundle of nerves and excitement.

"This is dumb, isn't it? Trying to reconnect with her? It's a really bad idea, right?"

"Relax, bro. It's only a bad idea if it doesn't work." Mitch paused for a moment, watching Jason with furrowed brows. "So what happened between you two, anyway? I can't quite get a read. Do you hate each other? Love each other? Just want to bang it out and get it out of your system?"

"Fuuuuck." Jason rubbed his forehead and groaned. "All of the above, maybe? I think she wants to hate me but every once in a while, I see something in her eyes that makes me think she still has feelings for me."

"Oh yeah, she has feelings for you. Strong feelings." Mitch winked. "Whether they are romantic or homicidal remains to be seen."

———

Just like every other Wednesday night, Jason hopped in his truck after work and drove forty minutes to the next town and the senior care facility where his mother lived.

"Hey there, Jason. Right on time, as always."

"Hey Jill." He stopped to sign in at the receptionist desk and smiled. "How is she today? Is it a good day?"

The nurse grimaced and waggled her hand side to side. "It's touch and go, to be honest. She's in her room, if you want to just go on back."

He nodded, but couldn't quite muster a smile. Walking down the hall, he tried to prepare himself for what he might find. When she was having a good day, she was the same funny, sweet, doting mother she'd always been. The bad days were getting worse and more frequent, though. Those were hard on Jason. Would she recognize him today? Or would she think he was a stranger barging into her room to hurt her? Maybe she'd know his name, but she could just as easily think he was his father. Dementia was a heartless thief.

Rapping his knuckles against the door frame, he stuck his head into the room with a smile. "Hey, Ma."

The woman who looked up from the needlepoint in her lap was a shadow of the woman who'd raised him. Her brown hair was streaked with silver and was twisted into a messy knot at the back of her head. Her skin was pale now that she wasn't spending most of her days outside, and she'd lost weight. Again.

"Oh, hello darling. Come on in!"

With a sigh of relief, Jason approached and kissed Elizabeth Archer's cheek. "What're you working on? It looks beautiful."

She held up the half-finished project depicting a beautiful and vibrant sunset. "Do you like it, sweetheart? It's nothing too spectacular. Just a pretty little thing for the baby, when he gets here. I thought I could use it in a quilt. Wouldn't that be nice?"

"The baby?" He frowned, trying to remember if she'd mentioned anyone they knew expecting a baby. "Whose baby, Ma?"

Shaking her head and laughing, she swatted at Jason's knee. "Why, our baby, silly! Seriously, Jimmy, you're getting more forgetful every day!"

Jason's heart sank. Jimmy. That was his father's name. His father who had passed away nearly seven years ago from an aggressive pancreatic cancer. By the time they caught it the summer after high school, it was already too late. James Archer hung on until late the following spring then passed away in his sleep, peaceful on the painkillers that had become the only thing keeping him together at that point.

Looking her over she seemed perfectly content, at least. There were no signs of distress or fear, so he could count that as a good thing. She was somehow lost in a memory from before he was born and she was happy. Jason saw no reason to mess with that.

"Well, Libby." He patted her hand and called her by the pet name his dad had always used. "I think that is a fine little pretty for the baby. Just fine. Look at those colors! Why don't you tell me what else you've been up to today."

———

Jason pulled into the circular drive at T&M Ranch, put the truck in park, and just sat quietly for a moment. All day he'd been on edge, what with worrying about his mother and thinking about Charlotte. While he'd missed her fiery temper, what he'd really missed was her laugh. That was the goal for tonight: to make her laugh and earn that sweet smile. When he didn't see anyone wandering around in the yard or peering out the windows his heart sank. Had he assumed too much? It would be just like Charlotte to refuse to come out with him just to piss him off. She was never one for being told what to do. He smiled. That was one of the things that was so exciting about her.

After several minutes of sitting with the truck running, he decided he'd better bite the bullet and just go knock on the door. She was probably lying in wait to punch him in the mouth and then chase him off the property.

Stopping in front of the porch steps, he gazed up at the house. There was a time when he wasn't expected to knock. He was considered part of the family and was welcomed with open arms. He and Bran had been tight even then, and Jason had never missed one of his band's performances. Things had gotten a little hostile after he broke things off with Charlotte and she left town. Even now, he didn't think he'd been forgiven for breaking his sister's heart. But Zearing was a small town, and they couldn't avoid each other forever, so they started hanging out again. They just never talked about Charlotte. Ever.

There was no sound coming from inside the house, and Jason wasn't sure if they were all hiding or if they'd just left rather than see him again. Only one way to find out. He took the steps slowly, like a man climbing to the guillotine. When he reached the front door without setting off a booby trap, he breathed a sigh of relief and knocked. That's when he heard the muffled, angry voices inside.

"I think this is a bad idea, Char, that's all. Are you sure you want to go on a date with him?"

"First off, it's none of your damn business who I do or do not go on a date with. Second, why is it okay for you to hang out with him but not for me? And last, it is not a date. We're going into Zearing for a couple of drinks and some food. As friends. So butt out."

Before he could hear Brandon's response, the front door flew open, and Charlotte nearly knocked him on his ass. Jason jumped back just in time. It seemed that she didn't see him, because once she was through the door, she stomped down the steps and toward his truck.

"Well, come on." Her voice carried to him even though she didn't even turn her head. "Unless you'd rather just stand there on the porch like a dope and wait for Brandon to come out and bury you in the pasture, I suggest you get in your truck and start driving."

"I heard that, Charlotte Rose!"

At the sound of her brother's indignation, Charlotte snorted out a laugh and glanced over her shoulder. Every time. Every damned time she smiled at him he just wanted to dissolve into a puddle at her feet. Tonight needed to come off perfectly, if he were to have a chance with her.

That plan was already going off the rails: she was almost to the truck without him. He jogged to get in front of her and barely reached the door before she did. "Here, let me get that." She rolled her eyes and gave him a withering glance, but she climbed into the cab anyway.

When he looked back over his shoulder, Jason could see Brandon's silhouette in the doorframe, arms crossed. "Bring her home in one piece, Archer. Or I *will* bury you in the pasture."

An awkward silence hung over them until they had pulled onto the highway that led into town. Charlotte shook out her hands and took a cleansing breath.

"Sorry about that. He's being a little overbearing. And don't open the door for me. I'm fully capable."

Jason chuckled. "Well, good evening to you, too, Charlotte. You look beautiful. Oh, I look quite dashing, if you say so yourself? You're too kind."

She didn't say anything, but he caught the corner of her mouth twitching and decided that was good enough.

"And it's okay. Brandon's a good guy and good friend, but you're his little sister. I don't blame him for being protective. Especially after I—well, I get it, that's all."

She stared at her hands, folded in her lap, and didn't say anything. He kept peering at her profile from the corner of his eye, waiting for her to demand he take her home, but the miles passed by without her calling it off.

When the lights of their small hometown appeared on the horizon, Charlotte perked up. "What am I in for tonight, Jay? The town looks bigger. Is it bigger? It's changed so much while I was gone, I guess I just don't know what to expect." She sat straighter in the seat and peered out the windshield.

Glancing at her, Jason's breath caught. She looked exactly the same as he remembered from the last time they'd taken his old pickup into town. Her golden eyes were bright and wide, a small smile curving her lips. It was hard for him to tear his eyes away, but he'd miss the turn if he didn't.

He parked on the street and tried to get around to open her door, but Charlotte was already waiting for him on the curb. How was it possible that he'd have the same butterfly reaction to this woman that he'd had when he was a teenager? She was wearing a floral-print dress that flowed around her knees and a denim jacket with the sleeves rolled up a couple of turns. Of course, she had on a pair of cowboy boots. There was enough of a breeze that her hair waved around her, making her hold her bangs out of her eyes, just the way she used to when they were young. The ache in his chest let him know that he'd missed her more than he'd realized.

"Everything okay?" She was squinting up at him, one corner of her mouth lifted. "Was there something else you wanted to do tonight or just...this?"

With a start, he realized he'd been daydreaming, staring at her with one elbow resting on the bed of the truck. "Right. Of course there's more." Jason stepped up on the curb next to Charlotte and offered her his arm and a bright smile. "Shall we?"

THIRTEEN
CHARLOTTE

Charlotte rolled her eyes at Jason's chivalry but looped her arm with his anyway. He was being kind of adorable, and she was determined to have fun tonight, despite the way her heart was racing. It wasn't as though this was a date, or anything. This was only spending time with someone she grew up with. So why were her palms sweating?

"All right Archer." She lifted an eyebrow and smiled up at him. "Show me what you've got. And it better be good."

"Oh, it's like that, is it? You're throwing down the gauntlet right out of the gate?"

Bumping him with her hip, she laughed. "How long have you known me? I'd be shocked if you expected anything else."

The corner of his mouth twitched. "I would never." When he straightened his arm and waited, she let her hand slide down until it fit into his. "Besides, I want to see the look on your face after you've had the best date of your life."

Stopping abruptly, she pulled him around to face her. "First, no one said this was a date. What kind of crazy person would go on a date with their ex after the kind of history we have? Second, I wasn't throwing down any kind of gauntlet.

But now that you've mentioned it, I kinda like the idea of a friendly wager."

Her knees wobbled a little at the look he was giving her: lowered eyelids, mouth curved wickedly, the tip of his tongue touching his top lip. *Not a date. This is NOT a date.* Maybe if she told herself enough times, she'd believe it.

"A wager, you say? I can get behind that. What are the stakes?"

Shit. What *were* the stakes? "You've promised me an amazing time, and I expect one. If I don't feel you've delivered by the end of the night, you have to spend a Saturday mucking the stables with me."

"Seriously?" He narrowed his eyes and stepped closer. God, he smelled good. It took all of her concentration not to retreat or bury her nose in the crook of his neck. "And if, at the end of the night, you have been ruined for all other dates in the future—"

"Not a date."

Rolling his eyes, he huffed. "Fine. If you find you've been ruined for all future non-dates," his eyes twinkled down at her, catching her breath, "I get to make you dinner."

"You…what?" She blinked several times. "How is that a reward for *you*?"

He tugged her hand and tried to head down the sidewalk again, but she held her ground. "Don't worry about it. It's what I want when I win."

Tilting her head, she looked into his eyes. God, those deep blue eyes sucked her in every time. What game was he playing? How could cooking for her benefit him in any way?

"Ha! You won't win. I have very discerning tastes, and it will take a lot to 'ruin' me." It actually probably wouldn't. She hadn't been on a proper date in years outside of throwing dinner parties for friends or hanging out at a bar in a group. But there was no way she'd tell Jason that. "Fine. You're on."

As they continued walking, she knew she should take her

hand back. This wasn't a date, after all. But the warmth of his fingers around hers was nostalgic and comforting, bringing back a slew of memories. She was here to help her dad and her brother, to take care of them and try to save the ranch, but it all weighed on her. And she hadn't told anyone but Bran about the face in the window, about the phone call from the barn. Truth be told, it had her on edge, not wanting to be outside after dark, closing all the curtains at night, jumping at every little sound. And she hated it. Being with Jason right now somehow made her feel strong. Protected. Cared about. It was nice.

At the corner, he pulled her to a stop. She could hear voices and there was a smell wafting through the air that made her stomach growl.

"Are you ready?"

"I don't know, Jay. Depends on what I'm in for. If we turn this corner and you're handing me off to a tribe of cannibals, then no. I'm not."

When his head dropped back and he laughed, a wave of warm gooeyness rolled from her head to her toes. How had she been away from that–from him–all these years? Being near him was soothing and exciting and made her feel things she hadn't felt since…She shook her head.

She hadn't felt this way around anyone since she left Zearing. Since he *made* her leave without him. That was a memory she didn't want to poke at tonight, but it brought her back down to Earth. It would be so easy to let herself drift back into the way she felt about him all those years ago - shit, those feelings were far closer to the surface than she'd realized - but she wouldn't let him crush her heart like that. Not again.

Slipping her hand free, she folded her arms and tried to ignore the hurt that flashed across Jason's features. It didn't matter; he'd get over it. This was *not* a date, after all.

"No cannibals this time, but it's not completely off the table." Walking backwards, he led her around the corner with a sweep of his arm. "Welcome back to the Zearing Annual Chili Cookoff."

Charlotte stared with a hand over her mouth, a giggle bubbling up in her chest. "No way." The street in front of them was lined with tables on either side and filled with people laughing and talking and eating from small bowls as they walked around. "How did I not remember this was going on this weekend? My family and I didn't miss a year when I was growing up. I remember the year you entered the contest and made it into the top five. Please tell me you still use that recipe."

He laid his warm palm against the bare skin at the base of her neck as they started to walk. She debated squirming out of his reach, but decided she didn't hate the way it felt. Besides, there were a lot of people in this small space and her scalp prickled thinking that one of them could have been at her home, watching her. Jason's touch anchored her to him as they made their way through the crowd, giving her a sense of safety in the sea of unfamiliar faces.

"I do use that recipe, to an extent. I've made some improvements on the original." He ducked his head and cleared his throat. "Actually, I have the first-place trophy from last year in a corner of my kitchen."

"Jay, that's terrific! But I never doubted that you'd take them all by storm one day." If she knew one thing about Jason Archer, it was that he had a gift when it came to food. Somehow, he knew the best combinations of spices and flavors and was a genius at mixing up new tastes that you'd never think of as going together. The fact that he walked away from culinary school hurt almost as much as his walking away from her.

She cleared her throat and pushed the past back into the past. "Well maestro, this is your show. What's first?"

Jason led her around the square, feeding her a bite of cornbread at one stand, a spoon of chicken chili at another, and many bites of Texas chili at varying degrees of heat. Charlotte's mouth was on fire after the first two, but Jason seemed unaffected. She was not going to let him beat her at anything. She was going to keep up with him if it killed her, and at this rate, she thought it just might.

As they walked, Jason kept a hand on the small of her back. If they were stopped at a booth talking to the cook, his hand rested between her shoulder blades. No matter what, he seemed to be touching her every moment. That was something Charlotte generally disliked, but with Jason... Somehow with him, every touch sent the butterflies in her stomach into a frenzy. She loved it.

But she hated it, too.

Why would she think this whole 'date' was anything more than a chance for him to rope her into falling for him again? This was very low-risk for him; she'd been the one sent away, the one whose heart had been stomped on, and the one who stood the chance of going through every painful minute of that all over again. Jason, on the other hand, probably got a great boost to his ego every time she smiled at him, or he made her laugh. As far as he knew, she was only here for a little while, giving him the opportunity to woo her and then send her away. Again.

"Hey."

Jason's voice broke into her thoughts. Had he been talking? She realized she didn't have any idea what he'd just said. "Hm? Sorry, I think I missed that."

Steering her out of the flow of foot traffic around them, he stopped and turned her to face him. "What's going on? What are you worrying about?"

"Who, me? Worry?" She tried to laugh it off but couldn't meet his eyes. "Nothing is going on. I'm fine."

"Oh yeah?" He tipped her chin up until she couldn't avoid him. With one finger, he smoothed the skin between her eyes. "Do you know that you get this little crease, right here, when you're thinking really hard on something, trying to fix it?"

She pushed his hand away, her cheeks burning. "I do not."

"You do." He didn't say anything more, just stood there while he scanned her face. The intensity behind those deep blue eyes made her heart race and she couldn't stand still. It was like he was reading her mind - or trying to, at least. Just when she was going to blurt out every single thought in her head, he shrugged and wound his fingers through hers.

"Okay. Ready to move on to the next phase of our non-date?"

FOURTEEN
JASON

T hings were going well.

At least he thought they were. Charlotte was smiling and laughing and didn't pull away when he touched her—which he couldn't seem to stop himself doing.

But more than once, he'd also seen her frown, looking like her mind was far away, trying to work out a puzzle. He knew she'd never tell him what was bothering her. It was going to take more time to earn back her trust.

And he was determined to do just that.

"There's a second phase?" She raised her eyebrows and smiled.

"Oh darlin', there is so much more in store for you tonight." Tucking her hand in the crook of his arm, he had to work to keep his pace even as he led her to the next stop. It had been Mitch's idea, something he mentioned in the midst of brainstorming, but as soon as the words were out of his mouth Jason knew it had to be part of the big night.

When they stopped, Charlotte pressed her lips together and watched him from the corner of her eye. That only made his smile grow twice as big. She was in for a surprise, and he couldn't wait to see the look on her face.

"Are you lost, Jay? Picking something up here?" She waved a hand at the sign on top of the building, as though he didn't know exactly where they were. "You do know what goes on inside the Jackalope, don't you?"

Nodding, he led the way through the door and into the noisy bar. Lively country music filled the room, and the dance floor was crowded with couples two-stepping around their circuit.

"Come on, let me get you a drink." He nodded to the bartender and held up two fingers. Before they even sidled up to the bar, there were two cold bottles of a local beer waiting. After he handed one to Charlotte, he tapped the neck of his bottle to hers. "Cheers."

She kept her narrowed eyes on his while she drank and the power move sent a wave of excitement through him. Charlotte Trevino was not a woman to be pushed around or lied to, and that was one of the things he most admired about her. She was no shrinking violet or submissive partner; she was a woman who spoke her mind, told you what she wanted, and didn't take anyone's shit.

It was sexy as hell.

"When was the last time you were here?" He leaned against the bar and watched her face as she started to mouth the words to the song blaring through the speakers. "When we were still in school?"

"No." She ducked her head and took a swig. "I came here the second summer after I left for San Francisco."

He frowned. "You did? I didn't even know you were in town then. I thought you only came back at Christmas. Were you here the whole summer?"

Nodding slowly, she folded her arms against the bartop. "I was here for three months. Mostly at the ranch, but I came here to dance a lot because I knew it was the one place I was sure I wouldn't run into you."

That admission was an arrow in his chest. Three months

that she was right here in Zearing, actively avoiding him. And he didn't blame her. "How did I not know any of this? It's a small town and folks around here love to gossip."

"They wouldn't dare." The corner of her mouth lifted, and she looked up at him through her lashes. "Because I threatened bodily harm to anyone who went running to you."

Only Charlotte could manage to look contrite, proud, and challenging at the same time. Jason laughed and shook his head. "Well, that sure as shit would keep me from telling a soul. It would have been all 'Charlotte who?'"

They laughed together for a minute but then her smile faded, and she picked at the label on her bottle. She had her bottom lip trapped between her teeth and she shrugged before turning to him. "Brandon dragged me out here, to be honest."

"Really? I didn't know Bran was so into the two-step that he'd bring his sister as a date." He also didn't know that someone he considered a close friend had kept something like that from him for all these years.

Head tipped to the side she searched his face for a moment. "That had nothing to do with it." Then she turned back to shredding the label, keeping her eyes down when she spoke again. "He didn't want to be here either, but he had to do something. I was...not okay."

His heart squeezed at her words, and he held perfectly still until it started beating again. The way she'd said those words sent fear coursing through him. There were a million questions he wanted to ask but he bit his tongue.

"San Francisco was great, but I was horribly homesick. I wasn't sleeping much, I hardly ate, my grades were suffering. My roommate Katie was worried enough that she called my dad, and they made arrangements—behind my back, mind you–to make me take a break." She shook her head, but the ghost of a smile curved her lips. "Assholes."

"I'm sorry Char. I wish I'd known."

Her golden eyes flashed as she turned to him. "And what

difference would that have made? Would you have come running to my rescue? Because you are the only possible reason that I was feeling bad, right?"

"How bad was it, Char?" He kept his voice low, refusing to be baited. Watching her from the corner of his eye, he knew she was trying to deflect but he wasn't going to let her. It was hard to think about this full-of-life woman being so low that her friends and family had to run what was essentially an intervention.

One shoulder lifted. "I don't know, if I'm honest. It's so hard to remember what it felt like, what was going on in my head, ya know? Like, I think I know but then again, what I remember can't possibly be right. If I hadn't written some of it down, I wouldn't believe it myself. I was so far away, missing my mom, and everything was just so *hard:* my classes, working to make spending money, even just trying to make friends. Everyone around here, I'd known since we were in kindergarten together. It was quite a rude awakening trying to learn how to connect with people. And there were students from all over the world, people well-traveled and interesting and I just felt..." She sighed. "I just felt so ordinary, you know?"

"Ordinary?" That was never a word he would have associated with her. Gently, he turned her toward him and cupped her face in his hands. Her skin was so soft, and her golden eyes shined in the lights flashing all around them. "I'm so sorry you felt like that. Just know that you, Charlotte Rose, are anything but ordinary."

She started to argue with him, but he didn't want to hear it. With his hands on her shoulders, he walked behind her and propelled her across the room. He leaned in until his lips were almost pressed to her ear. "I bet none of those 'interesting' people pushed Steve Hankins nearly a mile in a wheelbarrow after he broke his arm falling out of the tree at the edge of your property, all the way back to the stables. And did any of *them* sweep the horse competition at the state fair, winning four blue ribbons in one year?"

They'd reached the dance floor and if Charlotte knew what was coming, she gave no indication. Jason spun her around and pulled her against his chest. He draped her arm up over his shoulder, positioning them as he spoke. "And I know for a fact that not one of those snooty bitches beat the shit out of Greg McManus when he called her 'shrimp', pulled her hair, and pushed her into a locker."

That one got her to smile. Her whole face lit up like the Fourth of July as she laughed. "That suspension was one thousand percent worth it."

Now that she was paying attention, it seemed she realized where they'd stopped a split second before a Keith Urban song filled the air. Her head snapped up to gape at Jason, soft lips slightly parted, eyes wide, and his stomach flipped. *Right there. That was exactly what he was waiting for.*

"Ready?"

Her mouth opened and closed, and she shook her head. "You don't dance, Jason Archer."

Pressing his cheek to hers, he pulled her flush against him to whisper in her ear. "I've learned a few things while you were gone, Charlotte Rose." Then he locked his gaze on her amber eyes and led her onto the floor in a smooth two-step.

Her mouth hung open for the first trip around the floor then she let her head drop back and laughed. "You are just full of surprises, aren't you?"

"You ain't seen nothing yet, darlin'."

It took almost no time at all for her to relax in his arms, letting him lead her through the steps. Her laughter floated around him whenever he spun her without missing a step. And when he switched their positions to the sweetheart two-step, she leaned back against him, and they moved together like they'd been doing this their whole lives.

Laying their joined hands against her stomach, he wanted

to stay in this moment. For the first time since she'd arrived back in town, she was letting her guard down and trusting him. Sure, it was only while they were dancing, but it was something. She was warm in his arms and she smelled so good. It was hard not to press his face into her hair or bend down slightly to drift his lips down the creamy skin of her neck.

Before he let his mind wander too far into that territory, he spun her out and back in so they were face to face. "Mind sufficiently blown, Trevino?"

She gazed up at him with dreamy eyes and flushed cheeks and her lips were curved. "To say the least. Not sure what I expected tonight, but I can tell you that it was NOT this."

Just then, the music changed, and the strains of a classic Garth Brooks ballad filled the air. He felt her stiffen under his hands and she stepped back.

Shit.

This had been their song, the song playing during their first kiss, the first time they'd stumbled past just kissing, and when she first said she loved him. But in this moment, when she tried to slip free from his embrace, he stopped her.

"Char." Her eyes were guarded when she looked up at him, searching his face. "One more dance? Please? Then we'll go."

She hesitated, chewing the corner of her mouth with her eyebrows drawn together. God, he was about to lose her. The night had been amazing so far, and this one song dredged up so many memories—good and bad—that she was ready to walk away.

When she dipped her head in a quick nod, the relief he felt lightened the weight that had settled on his chest. He didn't say anything, just spread his fingers on the small of her back and waited until her head was on his shoulder and her hands clasped around his waist.

The few other couples were still stepping around the floor,

cheeks pressed together as they passed, but Jason and Charlotte were barely moving. The words washed over them, their
meaning pulling on his heart and twisting his stomach.

I know you haven't made your mind up yet
But I would never do you wrong
I've known it from the moment that we met
There's no doubt in my mind where you belong

Suddenly the tension released from her shoulders and her
hands slid up his back until she was gripping his shirt. Her
body melted against him and all he could think was that he
wanted her closer. He needed her even closer. Brushing her
hair out of the way, he cradled the back of her neck in one
hand. They drifted through the song, feet barely moving, and
her head nestled into his chest like he'd never let her leave in
the first place.

Like he'd never pushed her away.

The song ended but they stayed wrapped around each
other for a few seconds longer. His lips brushed over her
temple, and she tightened her grip for a second. Then she
heaved a sigh and moved back, breaking the spell. Her smile
was soft and a little sad and she tucked her hands into the
pockets of her dress before dropping her eyes to the floor.

Shit. Jason kept his hands to himself even though all he
wanted to do was wrap her up and hold her tight. "You all
right? We can grab another beer if you want."

She shook her head. "No, thanks. Can we go? I just kind of
want to go."

Following her to the door, he waited until they were out on
the sidewalk, and he fell into step next to her, still fighting the
urge to touch her. Instead, he dragged his hand through his
hair and tried to figure out if he could salvage the night.

"Are you up for the final phase of the night?"

"Final phase?" Her skeptical glance was promising. "Do

we have to fight the big boss or something? Not sure I'm wearing the right shoes." Then she looked up at him and the twinkle was back in her eye.

Thank the gods.

"No fighting necessary. I promise. Just a quick stop for some dessert."

FIFTEEN
CHARLOTTE

The song was unexpected. Hell, the whole night had been unexpected. Jason had been notorious for having two left feet when it came to dancing and he was never really interested in learning. He was fine with a swaying slow dance, but the two-step?

Tonight, he seemed like he'd been dancing his whole life, smooth and coordinated and really, really good.

But then god damn Garth Brooks had to pop up in the middle of it all and nearly rip her heart out of her chest.

How many notes had they passed back and forth with the lyrics standing in for the feelings they were too young to express? How many nights had they laid in each other's arms and listened to the song on repeat? In college, her roommate Katie had tried to soothe her homesickness by playing any country song she could think of, but Garth Brooks was expressly forbidden. Childish? Sure. But it was the only way she knew to protect herself.

As soon as the first notes played, she wanted to bolt, to slip out of Jason's embrace and run for the door. Maybe even run all the way back to the ranch. But hell, she was already out with him, already pressed up against him, already feeling those old feelings.

So…she leaned into it. She held onto him like a lifeline, burying her face against his shirt where she could inhale his scent and just be there with him. The way he cradled her head with one hand while the other pressed into the small of her back gave her a sense of safety, a sense of home she hadn't felt since landing in San Antonio.

Everything had been so rushed. She flew in not knowing what had happened to her dad, then she found out about the loan being late and the other problems with the ranch. One thing after another had bombarded her: Chancellor, the face in the window, feeling followed, getting the phone call. She felt like she'd been on high alert forever, waiting for the other shoe to drop.

With Jason, she felt like she could finally relax. That everything was going to be all right and she didn't have to keep her guard up every minute of every day.

She hadn't felt that in a very long time. So she just gave in to his soothing touch, let the music and the memories envelope her. Until the song ended and reality came back into the picture.

"Dessert, huh?" She linked her arm with his again as they strolled along the sidewalk. "What's even open at this time of night?"

The corner of his mouth curled. "Nowhere, really. This is an exclusive event for just the two of us."

What in the world could he be talking about? "Ooookay. Aren't you a bit bougie."

That made him laugh, a deep rumble in his chest that she felt in *her* chest. And other places. Glancing up she was glad to see that he was not looking at her and couldn't see the flush of her cheeks.

"You won't think so once we get there."

They walked quietly for a few moments, and then Charlotte cleared her throat. "Are you going to tell me about the dancing, Archer? I cannot accept that you were just holding out on me all that time when under it all you were so fleet of foot."

He took in a breath and turned to her but then seemed to change his mind about whatever he was going to say. When he did start talking, his voice was low and heavy.

"It was my mom. After my dad was gone, she started to fade. They were high school sweethearts, too, and I don't think she knew how to exist without him." He paused, pressing his lips into a thin line. "Actually, it was my Uncle Jed's idea. My folks had loved dancing when they were younger, so he set me up with some lessons and I'd take my mom two-stepping through the whole house until she was smiling and laughing again."

There was something blocking Charlotte's throat as she listened to him. A thousand things to say popped into her mind: *I'm sure she appreciated that. I'm glad you got to share that with her. What a sweet gesture from your uncle.*

"I can't imagine how hard that was, Jay."

He shrugged. "Doesn't really matter now. It's a good skill to have on occasion, but I don't think she remembers it at all."

Charlotte pulled him to a stop and turned him toward her. "I don't believe that for one second. I think that it's a memory that she cherishes, that she plays deep in the parts where her mind is still *hers*. She'd never forget something like that. Not really."

She waited for him to laugh or to tell her she was silly or idealistic. Instead, he blinked a few times and then bent down to wrap his arms around her waist and press his face in the crook of her neck. They stood that way for a few moments, and she was unsure whether or not she should move. Because she didn't want to.

"Thank you."

His whisper tickled her skin, sending goosebumps rushing

over every inch of her. Stroking the back of his head, she kissed his cheek. "You're welcome."

"Will you two break it up and get down here, please?"

Startled enough to jump back from Jason, Charlotte looked around to see Mitch standing just outside his shop. His hands were on his hips, and he was shaking his head as they approached.

"You guys are too much. I've been waiting."

"What, exactly, are you wearing, Mitch?" Charlotte eyed his long-sleeved t-shirt made to look like a tuxedo.

He smoothed his hands down the front, smiling wide. "Jay told me to look nice, and I thought, what looks nicer than a tuxedo?" Leaning forward, his eyes opened wide, and he lowered his voice. "Do you know how much one of those costs?"

After locking the door behind him, he scuttled around the store to get in front of them. He stopped next to a little card table set up with two chairs. When Charlotte took the opportunity to look around the room, her mouth dropped open.

Mitch had strung fairy lights from the ceiling, making it look like a blanket of stars above them. Every flat surface was covered with candles, and she swore she heard some sexy R&B playing in the background somewhere.

"Mitchell, this is beautiful! I can't believe you did this for us."

"Dont worry about it." He winked, then cleared his throat and dropped a towel over his arm. "Mesdames et monsiers, I welcome you to be the first to try something I've been working on. It's called 'Adult Ice Cream' because I can't come up with anything else that is less shitty than that name."

Slipping behind the freezer, Mitch started dishing up some scoops. "As far as we can tell, there's no one else doing this yet. Shakes and malts–yes. But not this."

Jason held out Charlotte's chair, settling into his once she was seated. "You're going to love this. Mitch and I have been working on this for a few months."

Looking across the table, she almost laughed at the blatant excitement on Jason's face. He was nearly bouncing in his seat, rubbing his hands together. Had she ever seen him look so eager? It squeezed her heart with old memories of that bright smile from when they were kids and he had always smiled at her like that.

"Voila!" With a flourish, Mitchell set down two bowls holding a frozen dessert that was the most unusual color of blue. "I present to you the very first perfected adult-flavored ice cream. This one's called The Icy Underwire."

"It looks amazing." She turned the bowl around on the table. "What's in it?"

Now Jason leaned forward, his blue eyes shining from more than just the lights on the ceiling. "Blue curacao. We found a way to keep the bright color and the alcohol while sweetening up the citrus flavor. Try it."

Both of them were watching her expectantly, leaning in with wide eyes and almost manic smiles. "You're making me nervous."

"What?" They glanced at each other. "How?"

"You look like crazed ten-year-olds waiting for a practical joke to hit an unsuspecting target." She narrowed her eyes. "Is this going to turn my mouth blue for a week or does it taste like ass or something? I'm not sure I should trust you. Either of you."

Just then Mitch's phone dinged from the counter and his face split into a wide grin when he read the screen. "That's a wrap for me, kids. My special lady friend is waiting for me up the block."

"Is this Kelcie from last week? What is this, your third date?"

"Fourth, m'man. Fourth." Mitch waggled his eyebrows and slapped Jason on the shoulder before leaning in and pecking a kiss to Charlotte's cheek. But he paused and lowered his voice so only she could hear. "Be nice to him. He's trying really hard to impress you. Tonight is a tremendously big deal for him."

The heat filled her face as she kissed Mitch's cheek in return. She'd been watching Jason's face while Mitch whispered in her ear and the way his eyes jumped from her to his friend and back showed just how nervous he was. It was kind of endearing and yet confusing. Sure, she knew he wanted to show her a good time, but she figured it was more about showing off. It never occurred to her that he genuinely wanted to impress her.

So far, the night had caught her off guard at nearly every step. Correction: *Jason* had caught her off guard. He'd been funny and considerate, charming and sweet. Was she surprised because she'd spent the last several years vilifying him and he was proving her wrong over and over?

Or was she surprised by how thrilled she was to be wrong?

It was no secret she was still attracted to him. Her body reacted to his touch in ways that she both loved and hated. The rush she felt when he held her hand, the way heat and longing bloomed low in her gut when she was in his arms: it was all so exciting and infuriating. She hated feeling out of control, that sensation of butterflies in your stomach when you're perched at the very top of a high hill on a roller coaster. And that's how she felt around him all the time.

Once Mitchell was gone and they were alone, she looked up to see Jason watching her. "What?"

The corner of his mouth curled, and he lifted one shoulder. "I don't know. Nothing, really. It's just...the way these lights hit your eyes they really look like warm honey. And they sparkle." He cocked his head to the side. "Did I already tell you that you look amazing tonight?"

Even though she rolled her eyes, she felt the blush rise in her cheeks. "In fact, you did. When you picked me up and I was kind of being a brat."

He nudged her foot under the table. "Kind of?"

"Shut up. Do we eat this, or what?"

"Right! Yes. Please."

She took a small spoon of the dessert, unsure what to expect. But the flavor exploded in her mouth, that little hint of alcohol underlying the sunshiny orange. She rolled it around in her mouth, eyes wide, then swallowed it with a small moan.

"Are you kidding me? You two yahoos made this?"

The grin on Jason's face was both relieved and proud. "Mitch perfected this batch but yeah, we made it." She felt his eyes on her when she took another, bigger taste and made an even louder noise that she was powerless to stop. "So I'm guessing your moans mean you like it?"

"Oh, yes. Absolutely. If you hear me make that noise again, you can bet it's from pure pleasure."

Jason was watching her closely, his bottom lip between his teeth. Then he leaned forward, one eyebrow raised, and started drawing lazy circles on the side of her bare knee. "Is that so? Because I would very much like to make you moan like that again, and again."

Charlotte knew she should move away, but she was thoroughly enjoying his teasing touch. Goosebumps broke out over her thighs, and she had to press her lips together so she didn't make that noise again. They were so close to each other that it would take almost no effort to escalate things to the next level and satisfy the drowning need she felt to know what his mouth tasted like.

She was completely lost in his eyes and the way her heart was racing when reality dawned on her. The delicious warmth spreading through her chest, the ache to guide his hand under the hem of her skirt, was from more than simply being near Jason; she looked down to see that her ice cream was almost gone. She blinked and gave her head a little shake before setting her bowl on the table. "Hoo, it's a little strong though, isn't it?"

Sitting back, Jason ate a big bite of his own ice cream and chuckled. "Yeah, we noticed that. Not sure yet if we're going to tame it or keep The Icey Underwire this boozy. There are a lot of problems that could come from it being so potent."

Yeah, no shit. She'd noticed. "How'd you come up with the name?"

Now it was his turn to look a little abashed and he rubbed at the back of his neck. "Well, let me preface the explanation by saying that we'd already been through a couple tastings when we landed on that name."

"Ah." She nodded and ate the last of her serving, unable to resist the refreshing flavor. "I will keep that in mind."

"Um, well, it was supposed to hint that it would get a girl's nipples hard." He scrubbed a hand over his face and shook his head. "God, we sound like degenerates."

"That's because you are."

They locked eyes for a moment then he laughed.

"Where'd you find him? I know he's not from around here."

"I think Doc Angus told you some of it already. Mr. Scutter was getting ready to retire, and he was looking for a buyer. He'd just gotten too old to keep those hours, but he couldn't afford to hire more than the couple of kids who'd come in evenings and weekends. He'd reached out to a real estate agency looking for suggestions on how to find a buyer and they helped him create an online ad. One day, he gets a phone call from a young man saying he's looking for a fresh start and he'd like to buy the shop, sight unseen. Scutter didn't believe him. At least, not until he rolled into town carrying a check for the whole amount and then some."

Charlotte frowned. "Didn't that seem suspicious? Wasn't anyone looking out for Mr. Scutter?"

"Oh, I was. His financial advisor works at my uncle's firm with me and had been talking with different folks in the area who were thinking about buying the place. But they were all trying to set their own price. Wasn't happening. So Scutter asks us to come down to the shop to meet with him and this new buyer, just to make sure things were on the up-and-up. I was early and Scutter and I were making small talk, when the front door flew open and in walked this tall, burly, red-curly-haired guy who couldn't be more than twenty-five or so, wearing the biggest, toothiest grin I'd ever seen."

"I'll bet a red-haired stranger in the middle of Zearing caused quite a stir. Not something you see very often."

He nodded. "Exactly. And the way he walked in—it wasn't a stroll, but more of a swagger. Like he'd been watching too many John Wayne films, and his boots were too loose. He came right up to us and stuck out his hand to Scutter first. 'Thanks for meeting with me again, m'man. Really decent of you.' Then he looks me over and grabs my hand, pumping it up and down like he thought he'd get water out of it."

Charlotte threw her head back and laughed. "Oh god, that's quite the visual!"

"You're telling me." Shaking his head, Jason laughed along with her. "Long story short, he was legit. He came out from Florida, trust fund baby or something like that, just looking for a quieter life. When he saw the shop in person, he fell in love with it and the sale was done the next day. Scutter retired to South Padre Island and Mitch has been a source of entertainment ever since. He's a good man."

Watching him tell the story, Charlotte was struck by how comfortable this all was. Sitting under these lights with Jason, talking and laughing the way they were, made her feel eighteen again. She had to admit she liked it.

"He sounds like just what this town needed. I hope he doesn't get you into trouble."

"Mitch? Nah. That was always Brandon. A fight here and there, a couple of speeding tickets, and the occasional rescue from crazed groupies. Those were some of the wildest times of my life. I don't think either of us could survive them now. Mitchell is a little out there, but he's always got my back."

Charlotte's heart hurt for a moment, thinking about how she and Jason used to be like that, too. They would have done anything for each other once upon a time.

"So, tell me about San Francisco. Is it really as expensive and crowded as it seems?"

"Shoot, you have no idea," she mumbled around the bowl of her spoon. "My roommates and I were lucky to get and keep this townhouse near the college. The rooms were small and I'm not sure they all qualified as legitimate bedrooms, but we got along and shared the cost of food, and I'm really sad to have to move out."

"Why do you have to?"

Glancing up at him from under her lashes, she tried not to make solid eye contact. No matter how sweet he'd been all night, she wasn't sure how he'd react to her news. "Well, because I'm not going to be living there anymore. I'm, uh—I'm moving back to the ranch. To Zearing"

She felt him stiffen next to her where they leaned against the counter and the little store was completely silent for a moment. Then he pushed away and started straightening the chairs around the little table Mitch had set up for them, keeping his head down.

"That's uh, that's great." Jason stopped suddenly and frowned at her, hands in his back pockets. "When was this decided? Were you even going to tell me?"

Charlotte cocked her head. "Why would I tell you? It's got nothing to do with you."

"Oh, really?"

"Yes, really, you cocky jerk. I decided that my dad needed a little more help than he was letting on and it just made sense for me to pick up the slack. At least until he - and the ranch - are back on their feet."

What the hell was his problem? She followed him as he

strolled around the store, chewing on his lip and straightening the items on the shelves as he passed. It almost seemed like he was mad that she was moving home. Not really the reaction she expected.

"How long will you stay, Charlotte?" He cleared his throat and paused near the door. "Don't you think you'll get restless and need to leave again? You never really wanted to be here in the first place."

Her jaw clenched. "I didn't go to San Francisco because I didn't want to be *here*, Jason. I wanted to see what was *out there*. We wanted to." Swallowing the lump in her throat, she pushed back the hurt she still felt, after all this time. "After you backed out, I went because I didn't feel like I belonged here anymore."

Pressing his lips tight, his gaze roamed over her face before he spoke. "I'm sorry you felt that way–that I made you feel that way. It wasn't true."

"Yeah, well." She shook her hair back off her shoulders and smoothed her dress over her legs. How did he think she'd react to that? Did he think the last eight years would just be swept away with a simple apology?

He was watching her from the corner of his eye as he led her out of the store and turned to lock the door behind them. "What's your plan? You'll just save the ranch and live happily ever after?"

Their eyes locked and her heart fluttered. He looked so sad and hopeful at the same time, like he wanted her to come back but was afraid of what would happen if she did. It was such a big gamble, and she didn't have a solid plan. Yet.

"Does that exist, Jay?" It was subtle, but she saw him wince at her words. Damn it. She didn't want to be cruel, she didn't mean to. But sometimes the hurt that still bubbled under her skin escaped. She waved a hand. "It'll be fine. I'll be close to my family for holidays and whatever else they need. And I'm sure I can get certified to teach around here without much trouble. I appreciate your concern, but we Trevinos are a hardy bunch."

The corner of his mouth lifted, and he focused his dark blue eyes on hers. "Don't I know it."

———

"I have one more stop planned, if you're up for it."

The beer and the high from dancing and the boozy ice cream all had Charlotte feeling more relaxed than she'd been in a long time. And despite the fact that this was NOT a date, Jason was charming and funny and still god damned gorgeous. And she wasn't ready to go home just yet.

Leaning back against his truck, Charlotte was acutely aware of how close together they were standing. He watched her from under his lashes, one hand braced against the door behind her, and she was finding it hard to breathe. "Aren't you full of surprises, tonight?"

Twisting a strand of her hair lightly around his finger, he leaned close to whisper in her ear. "You have no idea."

The sudden ghost of his warm breath against her neck made her shiver and her body arched into him on instinct. When his lips began a slow exploration of her neck, she forgot everything except the delicious rasp of his scruff on her skin. The rest of the world melted away, leaving nothing but his body pressed against her. He had worked his way along her jaw and when he finally reached her mouth, a moan rumbled up from deep in her throat. The kiss was sweet and tentative, letting her know that she could stop this at any time, that the next move was hers. But she didn't want to stop—not quite yet. Kissing Jason had always been intoxicating, and she was glad to know that hadn't changed. She wrapped her arms around his waist and pulled him closer, lightheaded and tingling.

The sudden blare of a car horn startled them, and they

jumped apart. Stepping up on the curb, they found they'd been blocking one of the parking spots and had just given quite a show to the people who'd been waiting for them to move.

Jason was laughing, his fingers linked with hers, but Charlotte had been jolted back to reality. What the hell was she doing? She let herself get swept up in nostalgia and maybe a little loneliness. This couldn't happen. Her heart wouldn't survive another rejection from him, and she couldn't help thinking she had a pretty good idea how this would end.

But holy hell, she liked being around him and making him smile and kissing him—especially kissing him. Seemed she'd found her kryptonite, and his name was Jason Archer. She took a couple steps back, slipping her hand free, wrapping her arms around herself.

"You know, I'm pretty tired. It's always an early start on the ranch, and the booze in the ice cream is playing with my head. Maybe we should call it a night."

He didn't move for a second, just stared at her with his head tipped to the side. But she heard his quick inhale, like he wanted to argue with her and convince her to stay out with him. She half wanted him to try. Instead, he sighed and opened the truck door, eyebrows drawn down. "Right. Of course."

Charlotte kept her hands folded tight in her lap and stared out the windshield while she waited for Jason to climb behind the wheel. This whole night had been a mistake, she could see that now. What the hell was wrong with her? A couple of weeks back home and she was falling into old patterns. She and Jason had barely spoken in years; he practically packed her bags and pushed her onto the airplane when she left for college. And now, after one night of fun and good conversation, she was ready to fall into his arms without a second thought.

When Jason finally joined her in the truck, she was so irritated with herself and her behavior that she could hardly think straight. Keeping her jaw clenched tight so she wouldn't say anything, she didn't even glance at him again until they were on the highway heading back to the ranch. He didn't say anything, either, which somehow incensed her further.

Several minutes of tension-charged silence passed and then Jason sighed. "What did I do wrong this time?"

"I don't know what you mean."

"Ha! You're obviously pissed at me; you're doing that teeth-grinding thing you always do. Did I say something? Come on, just let me have it. I'm a big boy."

She took a few deep breaths through her nose and crossed her arms. "No, Jay, you didn't say something wrong. And what do you mean, 'that teeth-grinding thing'? What the hell do you know about what I always do? You hardly bothered to talk to me in the last eight years!"

"Is that what this is? You're feeling slighted?" He laughed without humor and gripped the steering wheel, his knuckles turning white. "When was the last time you reached out to me? The phone works both ways, sweetheart. And what does that have to do with anything tonight, anyway? I don't know about you, but I had a good time. With you. Until now, that is."

"Don't turn this on me," she snarled. "It was your idea to go out tonight, your idea to get beers and then what? What was this other stop you wanted to make? Let me guess—you were going to take me out to some dark field outside the city where you can see every star and wait for me to tear my clothes off and ravish you. Am I close?"

"Jesus, Charlotte, you're impossible! I didn't kidnap you. If you remember correctly, you came along willingly, and you were having fun." He cleared his throat and shifted in his seat. "I didn't hear any complaints when you were kissing me."

"When *I* was kissing *you*? You're delusional." She threw her hands in the air and turned to face him. "So, because I let you kiss me, you're entitled to something more? Is that what your misogynistic brain is telling you? Because that is not going to happen. Not now, not ever."

"Misogynistic?"

"Yeah," she jeered. "Do you need me to spell it for you?"

Jason clenched his teeth, the muscle along his jaw twitching, and stared out the windshield. When he spoke again, his voice was quiet and full of hurt rage. "No. I know what it means. And I never once expected anything more from you than reconnecting. God, when did you become so jaded?"

"Obviously sometime in the last eight years." They exchanged matching sneers as Jason turned the truck into the circular drive of the ranch. "And I don't need you to swoop in and romance me, like some white-hat cowboy. I've been doing just fine without you around, thank you very much."

Without responding, he threw his door open and jumped out. It took Charlotte a second to realize what he was doing, and she scrabbled at her seat belt.

"Don't you dare open that door for me!"

His muffled voice accompanied his quickening footsteps. "God damn it, Char, will you just let me? What's the big deal?"

Finally freeing herself from the belt, she shoved the door open with all the force she could muster. Unfortunately, she realized too late that Jason had reached the door at the exact same moment and managed to stop its motion with his head. Charlotte heard the 'thunk' and caught a glimpse of him stumbling back before he fell hard on his ass in the dirt.

"Oh my god!" Her hands flew to her mouth, and she sat immobile for a moment. Pushing the door open again inch by inch because she wasn't sure where Jason was just then, she called out, "Are you okay? Please don't be dead." When she heard his low groan, she jumped into action.

Jason was sitting up with his head cradled in both hands, moaning. Kneeling next to him, she tried to coax him into letting her take a look at the damage, pulling on his wrists. "I'm so sorry. Come on, let me see. Are you bleeding?"

He dropped his hands into his lap and Charlotte gasped. There was an ugly purple knot forming on his forehead, just above his left eyebrow. "Oh, Jay, honey. I'm so sorry. Come on, let's get some ice on that."

Hauling him to his feet, she threw his arm around her shoulders and wrapped hers around his waist. She steered him toward the house, all the anger of a moment ago dissipated.

Once they reached the kitchen, she sat him at the table and gathered a clean dish towel, wrapping it around a handful of ice cubes. Then she pulled another chair up in front of him, gingerly pressing the cold compress to his head. "How are you feeling? Are you nauseous or dizzy? Look at me."

"I'm fine, Charlotte. And give me that." He tried to take the towel from her, but she slapped his hand away.

"Hold still." She leaned in closer to look in his eyes and their faces were only a few inches apart. There was that scent of him again, warm and male and enticing. Her gaze kept drifting to his lips, and she chanted in her head, *Don't lean in, don't lean in.*

To her complete humiliation, Jason noticed, and his soft mouth curved into a grin. "My eyes are up here, Trevino."

"I know. Get over yourself." She took a deep breath and bit the corner of her lips to keep from inhaling him.

Jason laughed deep in his throat and ran the backs of his fingers lightly over her cheek. "Not that I'd complain, mind you."

God, could he hear the way her heart was hammering against her ribs? Hell yes, she was thinking about the kiss earlier. And hell yes, she wanted more. But in the back of her mind, she knew that was only a disaster in the making.

"I need to look at your pupils, you dope, to see if you have a concussion. If they're different sizes, I'll need to take you up to the hospital and get you checked out. Probably not a bad idea, anyway."

He rolled his eyes. "Oh, please. This is nothing."

"I'm really sorry, Jay." She frowned and shifted in her seat. "I swear it was an accident, but I shouldn't have gotten so mad."

He grinned. "I guess I just bring out that passionate side of you. It was always so easy to push your buttons, even if it wasn't on purpose. Mostly."

Sitting back, she cocked her head and studied this man. Jason should be a stranger to her after all this time, but somehow, he still felt so familiar. He was leaning back with his eyes closed, holding the ice on his head, giving her the chance to take in every feature: the long eyelashes laying against his cheek, the way his hair curled around his ears, the scar on his chin from jumping out of the loft after a particularly fun make-out session. Then her gaze fell on his mouth. She knew that mouth so well. Knew it smiling or crying, yelling or laughing, and definitely knew what it was like pressed against hers. His full lips were slightly parted as he relaxed. She found herself drawn closer, the urge to taste his lips again almost a burning sensation in her chest.

"What the hell's all this?" Brandon was standing in the doorway, eyebrows arched as he looked from Charlotte to Jason and back again.

"Go back to bed, Bran. It's nothing you need to worry about."

He took a step into the kitchen, arms crossed over his chest. "Sure it is. It's a little late for a social call, isn't it Archer? Did she kick your ass?"

"For fuck's sake, Bran. I'm almost thirty years old. Mind your business."

Jason handed the towel back to Charlotte with a chuckle and stood. "It's okay, I'll go."

"The hell you will. Sit down." Whipping around, she

planted her feet and glared at her brother. "I invited him here, Brandon. He's welcome as long as I say he's welcome, at whatever time I want him here. So go back to bed."

Shaking his head, Brandon leaned down and whispered to Charlotte. "I hope you know what you're doing."

Did she? Was she letting their past override her common sense? She had to remember what he'd done, how he'd treated her, and the fact that he'd crushed her heart. Was she willing to risk that again?

"It's fine, Bran." She smiled and shrugged. "I've got it under control."

"If you say so." His eyes swept between the two of them before he shook his head at Jason, then climbed the stairs to his bedroom, leaving them alone again.

"You didn't have to do that." When she sat down again, Jason was fidgeting with the tassels on the end of the towel of ice. "He and I are friends, but I can understand why he doesn't want me here."

"Does it matter that *I* want you here?"

He didn't lift his head, but she saw the flash of his dark eyes from under his lashes. "You do?"

"Don't make me regret saying it, Archer. Come here." She leaned toward him, checking to see if the knot on his head had gone down and looking into his eyes again. They were so close that their knees were slotted together, her bare skin heating up where they touched, and Charlotte was surprised by the tingling waves of pleasure that contact sent through her body. *Knees? Really?* That had never seemed like an erogenous zone. But with Jason, it was. She was tempted to scoot a little closer and climb onto his lap. Instead, she sighed. "Okay. How are you feeling?"

He brushed her bangs from her eyes, letting his fingertips linger as he traced the shape of her face. Making the mistake of looking in his eyes at the gentle touch, her breath caught in her throat. The way he was looking at her, with a longing that made her ache to touch him, to lose herself in his kisses, set off an inferno low in her belly. When he answered, his voice was thick and low. "I feel...really fucking good, Charlotte."

Lowering her gaze, her cheeks blazed with heat and so did other, even more sensitive parts of her body. With a quick shake of her head, she cleared her throat. This is exactly the situation she was trying to avoid tonight. Being alone with Jason, feeling all those old emotions, getting drawn into his deep, night-sky eyes. Brandon was right: he shouldn't be here. They were dipping into dangerous territory, warning bells telling her he had to leave before there was no turning back.

But damn if she didn't want him to stay.

Suddenly he slapped his hands on his thighs and stood up. "But I don't want to overstay my welcome. I'll just head on home and get out of your hair. Thanks for a great night, Charlotte."

"What are you talking about?" She didn't realize her heart had stopped until it thudded back to life. Throwing her hands in the air as she followed, she stopped him at the door. "I ended the night with a temper tantrum and gave you a head injury. What, exactly, are you thanking me for?"

With the corner of his mouth lifted, Jason locked Charlotte in his gaze. He slipped his hand into her hair, lightly cupping the back of her head, and drew her in. She knew she needed to stop this, that kissing Jason again was going to ruin her and she'd end up letting him break her heart once more. But she was powerless against her own body's reaction. Her eyes fluttered closed as his warm lips first brushed over hers then fitted to her mouth so perfectly that she wondered how she could have existed so long without kissing him. His other hand spread out on the small of her back, bringing her body flush against his, and that hand was basically all that was keeping her on her feet. Melting into him, her hands twisted in the fabric at the front of his shirt, and every part of her was thrumming.

There was no urgency to the way his mouth moved with hers, his tongue slipping along her upper lip slowly as though he was savoring the taste of her. Oh god, had she ever been kissed like this, been kissed so deeply and thoroughly that coherent thought was no longer possible? In this moment, there was only Jason, his soft lips gentle and demanding, and she would willingly drown in the sensations coursing through her.

She nearly fell forward when he pulled away and gazed down at her with fiery eyes, his voice rough. "Thank you for reminding me what I've missed by letting you go."

She fell back against the door frame, her whole body trembling and almost too weak to stand and watched him walk back to his truck. Had anyone ever worn blue jeans like that? The ache to touch him, to let her hands roam over that impossibly perfect ass, to have his hands on her body and his mouth wherever he damn well pleased, was quick and intense. This was no teenaged boy, sneaking into her barn for late-night makeout sessions and fumbling caresses. No, he was all man and seemed to have learned a whole slew of new tricks. Imagining this grown-up version of Jason in her bed had her skin flushing and desire blazing between her thighs. As his taillights disappeared in the dark, she pressed her lips together, the feeling of his mouth still lingering.

She was in some serious trouble.

SIXTEEN
JASON

While things hadn't gone quite as expected with Charlotte the other night, Jason was still thrilled with how it had ended. He touched the tender spot on his forehead where the bruise had faded considerably and smiled. Head injury aside, he couldn't stop thinking about the kisses they'd shared.

Charlotte Trevino was exciting and passionate and holding her could sometimes be like trying to hold onto a lit rocket. Was it going to be an exhilarating, wild ride? Or would it blow up on take off? Every time he'd touched her on their date–and it *was* a date, no matter what she said–his stomach flipped, and his heart raced, and he had to hold himself back from just crushing her against him.

Dragging his hands through his hair, he sucked in a deep breath. What was wrong with him? Why the hell did Charlotte have such an effect on him? Sure, it was probably the memories of first love and all their shared history. He'd been with other women, had dated here and there over the years. But this feeling that sat low in his gut, this constant sense of arousal that spiked when he was near her was something new. And he was sure it was going to kill him.

He grabbed his coffee mug and headed to the kitchen for a refill. If he wasn't able to concentrate on finishing up this proposal right now, he was going to end up putting in some really long hours and he'd need the extra fuel.

On the way back to his office, he nearly ran headlong into his uncle, walking with a man who looked more like a cartoon character than a real person. Dressed impeccably in a light gray suit, steel-tipped cowboy boots, and an enormous Stetson, he stroked his snowy white mustache with one hand, holding an ornate white cane in the other.

"Jason." Jed's eyes were wide, and he glanced at the man next to him before clearing his throat. "What're you doing?"

Lifting his mug, he raised his eyebrows. "Coffee."

When his uncle didn't make any move to introduce him to this colorful character, Jason stepped forward and offered a hand. "Jason Archer. Nice to meet you."

The stranger barely acknowledged him, laying both hands on the silver head of the cane. Jason frowned and cocked his head. Who did this fucking clown think he was? Whatever. Jason didn't have time for this.

He was about to turn away when Jed stepped forward and clapped a hand on his shoulder. "Jason, this is—"

"Gerard Chancellor, of Chancellor Enterprises."

"Mr. Chancellor, this is Jason, my nephew and top analyst. Mr. Chancellor is one of my new clients." At a sideways glance from the haughty stranger, Jed paled. "Uh, one of my most important clients."

What the hell was going on here? Jason watched his uncle stammer and wipe his sweaty hands on his pants. When was Jed ever nervous?

"Good to meet you, boy. I've heard you're quite the shooting star around here."

Jason prickled at the condescending tone and fought to keep his expression neutral. He really, really wanted to let this pompous prick know where he could stick his cane, but one look at Jed gave him pause. His uncle was watching the visitor with wide eyes, chewing on a fingernail. He looked like he was waiting for the next words from Chancellor like they were table scraps for a stray dog. What the hell?

Chancellor kept both hands wrapped around the head of his cane and widened his stance. "Keep up the good work and you just may rescue this sinking ship, yet."

He frowned. "Sinking ship? I think you've been misinformed. Under Jed's leadership we've become the top investment firm in central Texas."

"Is that so?" Chancellor slowly turned toward Jed with a greasy smile that made Jason feel like he needed a shower. "That's fantastic news. I'm counting on your reputation, Mr. Archer, to help me get what I want. Don't disappoint me."

Jed coughed into his fist and avoided Jason's direct gaze. "Let me walk you to the elevator, Mr. Chancellor. I'm sure you've got a busy day ahead of you."

Jason watched them disappear around the corner and shook his head. If he'd ever had a more disturbing encounter with someone, he sure as hell couldn't remember it.

"Good, you're still here." His uncle bustled back into the hallway, dragging both hands down his face.

"What the hell was that, Jed?"

His uncle didn't answer right away. He stopped and stared at the floor with his hands in his pockets, gnawing on his bottom lip. Then he glanced over both shoulders. "Come on down to my office. We'll talk there."

Then he was gone.

Jason frowned and took a deep breath. Something was definitely wrong.

When he got to his uncle's office, he found Jed pacing in front of his big window, fingers pulling on his bottom lip. He didn't notice Jason at first, giving him a chance to really look at his uncle.

He hadn't seen him like this for...well, for a very long time.

Even from across the room it was easy to see the dark circles under his eyes. His tie was loosened and askew, his suit coat crumpled into a ball on the red leather sofa.

"Did that pompous ass seriously just call me 'boy' or did I imagine that?" He shook his head and paced from the door to the desk. "That was not a real person. Couldn't be. He's got too much of a villain vibe to be human."

But when he turned to look at Jed, he stopped in his tracks. Jed slouched against his desk as though all the air had been sucked out of him. "Oh no, he's real, all right."

The defeat in Jed's voice made Jason's blood run cold. Suddenly, this man who had been larger than life, who had stepped in and been there for him and his mother after Jimmy died, was small and tired looking. It made his throat dry and his palms sweaty. "Who is he, Jed? What have you gotten wrapped up in?"

"It wasn't supposed to be like this, Jay. I just needed a little help, and this seemed like an easy way to fix things." He turned pleading eyes on his nephew. "No one else was supposed to get tangled up in it, swear to god."

Cold seeped into Jason's chest and he narrowed his eyes. "Tangled up in what, exactly?"

He watched Jed palm away the sheen of sweat from his forehead before lowering onto his desk chair. Had he ever seen his uncle look so...frightened? It set a finger of fear crawling up his own spine. Jason shoved his hands in his pockets and tried to stay calm. He waited for Jed to start talking, but the longer the silence dragged out, the more uneasy he became.

Finally, Jed heaved a sigh. "I've been investing for decades. I am not new to this, and I have made a lot of people a lot of money. Myself, included." He glanced at Jason, but he seemed unable to hold eye contact, and he stared at his hands on the mahogany desktop. "An investment opportunity came across my desk—one that I researched and vetted–and it looked like a no-brainer. It was going to double the company's capital and allow me to retire *very* comfortably a lot sooner than I'd planned."

Realization creeped over Jason, and he groaned, his shoulders slumping. "Oh no. It tanked?" Jed barely nodded, his cheeks flaming and beads of sweat popping up on his hairline. "How much, Jed? How much did you lose?"

"A lot. Enough to put the company in jeopardy." He groaned and covered his face. "Everyone could lose their jobs and we'd all be ruined."

"Shit." Jason's hands dug into his hair, and he couldn't keep still any longer. He started pacing. "Shit. Shit."

When Jed looked up, his eyes were wild and pleading. "It wasn't supposed to happen this way! On paper it was flawless, it was a sure thing. And then it just…wasn't."

"And Chancellor?"

The sigh that came out sounded like it was escaping from the depths of Jed's soul. "Chancellor came along at just the right–or wrong–moment with his offer to keep the doors open in return for me doing some local market research. And for keeping it quiet. It seemed harmless at first, but every time he showed up or called, he pushed my boundaries a little farther. Before I knew it, he was asking me to do things that aren't exactly above-board and now I'm in so deep, I can't see the surface anymore."

His mind spinning, Jason didn't need it spelled out for him: Chancellor had his uncle by the throat and was squeezing. If they told Chancellor to stick his money up his ass, they would likely lose the company, their clients, their reputations. And if they continued with what they were doing, well…there was a good chance Jed would lose his soul along the way.

"Okay. Let me do some research and find out what exactly we are facing and how we can get out of it with the least amount of damage."

Jed sat up straight, shaking his head, the color flooding back into his cheeks. "No. Absolutely no way. I don't want you involved in any of this. I will take the fall if things go south, you can still salvage the company and everyone's jobs. I don't want you involved."

"It's a little late for that." The words snapped out of his mouth before his anger even registered. Jed winced and turned to stare out the window again. "Look, I won't let you swing out there alone. If you let me see the files, tell me all the details, I can help figure a way out of this."

"No."

"What do you mean, 'no'?"

Laying his head back on the chair, Jed sighed. "I mean no. I won't drag you down with me. Just go back to your office. I'll figure something out."

Jason raked his hands through his hair. "You are a stubborn old man." When he was halfway out the door, Jed called him back.

"Jay?" He faced the man who'd been his rock for almost a decade. "I'm sorry."

SEVENTEEN
CHARLOTTE

Pacing in front of the stables, Charlotte was about to slide into a panic. Brandon was here, helping her with the lessons, but Hank hadn't shown up all day. Now they were getting ready to take the girl scout troop—their biggest group yet— out for their ride of the trails and there was no way to do that safely with just the two of them. Arthur was gone for the day with Dr. Angus who had kindly offered to drive him an hour away to his physical therapy, and he hadn't been cleared for riding yet anyway. She was quickly getting to the point of drawing blood on the fingernail she'd been worrying for the last twenty minutes, and it was time to make a decision.

Brandon loped over from the edge of the paddock, tucking his phone into a pocket, eyebrows raised. "Well? Did you get a hold of him?"

"No." She scowled at her brother. "He won't pick up his phone. Milo is still in classes, and he'd never be able to get here on time, anyway. When I get my hands on Hank..."

"Calm down, Char." Brandon laid a hand on her shoulder and looked over the crowd of girls starting to get bored chasing each other around. "It's not over yet."

She rolled her eyes. "Don't patronize me. I hate to say it, but I think we're going to have to either rain check this group or refund them entirely. In the future, we'll have to limit our groups to no more than six at a time."

Hands on her hips, Charlotte stared at the ground, trying to work up the apology she'd be offering the troop leader in just a minute. Refunding their money would be a blow. Why hadn't she come up with a contingency plan? "Crap. Best to get it over with, I guess."

But before she could take more than a couple of steps, a familiar black pick up drove into the yard.

Jason hopped down from the cab of the truck and waved a hand at the mass of little girls in the paddock. "Hey Charlotte, Bran. I heard you guys might need a hand today."

Brandon clapped Jason on the back and shook his hand. "Thanks for coming on such short notice."

"Hold on, what the hell is this?" She scowled, almost as irritated at their smug looks as she was by the butterflies that kicked up in her stomach at Jason's dimpled smile.

He cocked his head at the quickly devolving group as Brandon ran off to corral them. "I'm here to help."

Charlotte barked out a laugh before she could stop. "Sorry. You? I don't remember you being an expert horseman."

He leaned in so his lips were only inches from hers and she felt her knees wobble a bit. "There's a lot you don't know about me, Charlotte Rose." Straightening, he waved a hand at the soon-to-be-chaos. "I'm not sure you have any other options. You need another set of eyes and hands, I'm here, so put me to work."

She bit her lip. "I can't ask you to do that."

"Technically, you're not asking–Brandon did. Besides, I'm offering."

She needed the help, there was no denying that. The tours and the lessons were starting to make a dent in what they owed to the bank, but if she had to refund this group something was going to fall through the cracks. Jason leaned against the paddock fence wearing a crooked grin, chuckling as the little girls giggled and chased each other, and it melted her heart.

Why did he have to be so damned adorable? She'd spent eight years casting him as the villain, and now he was showing up to save the day just when she needed him. Taking her out on a date, kissing her in a way that curled her toes and made her blush thinking about it–it was all so confusing. It would be so easy to let him in again and see where things might go, but could she trust him?

Only one way to find out.

"Fine. But you do what I tell you when I tell you and if you fall off we're leaving you. Oh, and if you hurt my horses, I'll break your legs." She grabbed him by the elbow and dragged him toward a grinning Brandon.

"All right. Get him on a horse." When Brandon opened his mouth–most likely to point out how he'd saved the day–she punched his arm and shoved past him, calling over her shoulder. "Don't say anything. Just get them all ready. We're doing this ride."

Once everyone was saddled up and given their final instructions, the group took to the trail. Brandon rode up front, pointing out different rock formations, giving them a heads-up about where the trail would turn ahead, naming the different flowers and trees along the way.

Charlotte rode up and down the ranks, making sure the horses—and the girls—were behaving properly, while Jason took up the rear to make sure there were no stragglers. Seeing him in the saddle was something of a shock for her. She'd tried to teach him to ride when they were kids, but he was more of a farmer, working with his hands. His nerves made the horses uneasy and everybody suffered for it. But today was different.

Every time she had an opportunity, she turned to watch him. There was an easy smile on his face, and he would periodically take in a deep breath through his nose or gaze dreamily up at the puffy clouds. She'd never seen him like this. The reins were loose in one hand as it rested on the pommel and his other hand was splayed out, relaxed, on his thigh. You'd think the man was born on a horse. She shook her head, making a mental note to get more information out of him later.

And then he was so easy with the kids, teasing and encouraging and teaching. Who was this man? By day, he was a suave, suited financial analyst, every hair in place, exuding an air of professionalism and trustworthiness.

But this Jason? Butterflies woke in her stomach as she watched him. *This* Jason was relaxed, smiling wide with an easy laugh, his hair flopping in his eyes every time he turned to catch her eye and wave. All of her worries about the ride dissipated as he charmed the whole troop with his terrible dad jokes, somehow remembering every name.

"You're drooling, Charlotte." Brandon rode up next to her as Jason took the lead, a teasing note in his voice.

"Am not," she mumbled. "I'm just confused. Who *is* that guy? That's not the Jason I remember."

Her brother was silent for a minute. "A lot of things changed while you were gone, Char. Archer included." Then he rode ahead, leaving her to wonder about what some of those other changes might be.

The rest of the ride was leisurely and took a little longer than expected, but the troop leader wouldn't accept any apologies. She was thrilled with the whole afternoon and named off at least three badges the girls had earned just that afternoon. And, judging by the pink cheeks and bright smiles all around, Charlotte felt that the day had been a tremendous success.

She had to admit that having Jason along had been a bonus. Not just because of the flutter in her chest every time he caught her watching him or she looked up to find him watching her. It was more about seeing him in a different light, about realizing that maybe there was more to him than she thought.

And she wanted to spend some time finding out what that was.

EIGHTEEN
JASON

"That was amazing," Jason gushed. "Did you hear Lulu when we really got going? She was encouraging her horse the whole time. 'You're doing great, Ace. You're such a big boy for not being scared.'" Rinsing the soap off his hands he chuckled. "I could spend every day out here, sitting on a horse, taking kids out for their first ride, just meandering through that tall grass. Today was the happiest I've felt in a long time."

All the horses had been returned to their stalls, the tack cleaned and put away, and Charlotte was watching Jason with narrowed eyes while they finished washing up.

"All right, spill it, Jay." Reaching her hands over her head, Charlotte gave her back a good stretch. Jason's eyes traced the shape of her curves where the movement pulled her clothes tight against her. Dear lord, he wanted to touch her. "You were the worst thing I'd ever seen on a horse when we were kids. What changed?"

He chuckled and followed her out of the stable toward the old barn. "Nothing really changed, I guess. Brandon and I started hanging out, he taught me some stuff, and I just stopped being scared of the horses. And you weren't around to make me feel like such a lost cause, so..." He shoved his hands in his pockets and shrugged.

"What do you mean by that? I never called you a lost cause."

"No, but you didn't have to." They walked in silence for a while, but he knew right away that he'd screwed up. The words had come out sounding a lot harsher than he'd intended, and the way she was picking at her fingernails told him she was already analyzing the shit out of them. Charlotte could take honest criticism but had a hard time letting go of what she saw as a personal slight, and he immediately regretted saying it. She'd worry about it for the rest of the night, poking and prodding it until she'd convinced herself it meant she was a terrible person. He was such an ass.

When they finally reached the barn, he led her to the far side and an old bench positioned just right for watching the sky change colors every morning and evening. Jason placed a light hand on the small of Charlotte's back, guiding her to sit before he did. Draping an arm along the back, he relaxed into his seat. But she sat straight, hands on her knees, chewing the corner of her mouth, and he just watched her.

On the surface, Charlotte was hot-headed and assertive, and she didn't suffer fools lightly. Inside, though, he knew her heart was as big as Texas—and so was her self-doubt. There was no one more critical of Charlotte Rose Trevino than she was.

"Hey." He laid his palm between her shoulder blades, his fingers stroking the back of her neck. The tension drained out of her shoulders almost immediately, making him smile. "I didn't say that you tried to make me feel bad. I did that all on my own."

She grunted, but relaxed onto the bench, not moving away from him. And he was glad. God, he wanted to bury his face in the crook of her neck and breathe her in. "I'm not saying you made me feel bad, but you were always so natural with them. It was one of the things that I couldn't share with you, and I was a little salty about it."

She frowned as she picked at her fingernails. "I'm sorry. I never meant to make you feel like that. If I'd known, I could have taught you the stuff Bran did. I wish you would have told me how you felt."

"No, Char, why would I do that?" He slipped his hand from the back of the bench to the back of her neck, fingertips tracing tiny circles on her skin. "It was amazing to watch you in your element, and I was always so proud to be there with you."

With a sigh of contentment, she tipped her head forward, leaning into his feather-light touch. Her eyes drifted closed. "I was always proud of you, too. I hope you know that."

He snorted. "For what? I didn't do anything even remotely interesting. You were the star."

Charlotte's head snapped up and she turned toward him, frowning. "No, I wasn't. What does that even mean?"

"Oh, come on. Salutatorian, class president, National Honor Society: all of that while also being one of the best young horse trainers in the county and holding your family together after your mom passed. I was in awe of you every single minute."

She looked up at him just then, brows drawn down and lips pressed together. Lifting his hand, he drew his fingertip over the crease between her eyes until it disappeared. She was gazing at him with those gorgeous amber eyes looking like she wanted to believe him but wasn't quite there yet. He didn't blame her.

With a quick shake of her head, she jumped up and started to walk out into the field. "It's too nice out here and I'm so happy about today I can't sit still. Come on."

Jason trailed behind her, wondering what was on her mind. Her palms drifted over the top of the tall grass, her pace leisurely in the fading light. When she turned to smile at him over her shoulder, his lungs forgot how to push air in and out. The light behind her turned her hair to gold, a light breeze ruffling her bangs. And her smile... Ah, that just about ended him.

"What're you doing back there, slowpoke?"

There was no hesitation about her, no distrust or anger anywhere in her tone. He jogged a few steps to catch up to her and was a little surprised when she looped her arm through his and dropped her head to his shoulder. The afternoon heat was still radiating from her body, and there was some intoxicating scent surrounding her, like sunshine and wildflowers. His chest tightened and he had to fight the urge to pull her into his arms and kiss her.

"Thank you so much for today, Jay. I don't know what we would have done without you."

"No big deal, I was happy to help." He brushed his lips over the top of her head. "Brandon's been a pretty good friend over the years. And the added bonus of getting to show off for you was an irresistible pull."

"Is that what you were doing?" She laughed and shook her head. "Well, I was impressed so I guess I'll allow it. But seriously, didn't you have something else going on or family to hang out with today? It is Saturday."

He tried not to wince at the word family, and he was lucky that she wasn't looking up. "Nope. I'm all on my lonesome."

"Really? What about your mom? Doesn't she put you to work on the weekend, like she used to?"

Shit. Did she not know?

They reached a spot where they had a perfect view of the fields around them, the clear blue sky stretched out endlessly. "I will never get tired of this view." Standing side-by-side, their shoulders almost touching, he felt Charlotte's deep cleansing breath before she nudged him. "I imagine your mother still gives you a list of chores to do."

"Uh, no." He squinted at her, head to the side. "You haven't heard about my mom? Brandon never told you?"

Alarm passed behind her eyes. "Oh no, Jay, don't tell me–"

"No, no, she's still alive. She's just not living at home anymore." Why was it so hard for him to talk about? Libby Archer had been living at the care facility for several years, but he was having trouble telling Charlotte. "Not too long after my dad passed, she started showing signs of early onset dementia. She has her good days and her not-so-good days, but she's been living out at Serenity Center for at least five years now."

She didn't respond at first and he knew she was trying to process that. His mom had been like a surrogate mother to Charlotte. Twining his fingers with hers, he watched her and waited. Her shoulders sagged and her head dropped forward, and he saw a single tear slide down her cheek.

"I'm sorry, I should have told you a long time ago."

"What?" Her head whipped toward him. "Don't you apologize to me Jason Archer, I'm the one who's sorry. I am so very sorry that I never asked how she was doing. I knew that your dad passed away and I never checked in with her." Pressing her lips together, she frowned and tucked her hands in her pockets. "I never checked in with you."

Jason didn't know what to say. She was apologizing to him after he'd broken her heart, had convinced her that he didn't love her anymore? It tightened his throat, and he had trouble swallowing. God, she hadn't changed. Still the biggest heart in Texas. He felt like such an asshole.

"Charlotte." Cupping her chin, he tipped her face up so he could look into her amber eyes. "Don't do that to yourself. I gave you every reason to never talk to me again, no matter how you felt about my parents. They knew you loved them. And you were the daughter they never had. I am the one who wrecked all of that. I am the one who hurt everyone with my stubborn bullshit."

Damn. The way the light of dusk played over her face, made her eyes shine and turned the streaks of red and gold in her hair into fire, mesmerized him. In front of him stood the same woman he'd loved as a girl, grown and strong and thrilling, but still able to make his heart turn cartwheels. He leaned in and touched his lips to hers then smiled.

"She still talks about you."

That seemed to surprise her, and she blinked up at him. "Seriously? Even with dementia?"

He slipped an arm around her shoulders and turned them to look out over the gleaming fields as they quickly succumbed to the setting sun. "She thinks one of the nurses is you and keeps trying to get her to marry me."

Charlotte laughed and wrapped her arm around his waist. "I'm sure that nurse appreciates her match-making. Have you taken her out?"

"Don't be ridiculous. She's not you."

The words were out before he realized what he was saying. Under his arm, Charlotte stilled but didn't respond. It seemed that they were both a little stunned by his admission. *Huh*, he thought. *Mitch would love to have heard that.* Deep inside, he'd already known that was why he didn't date much, why he hadn't been with anyone for more than a couple of months.

None of them could hold a candle to Charlotte.

Clearing her throat, she leaned into him. "I'd like to go see her."

"You would?"

He felt her nod before she pulled away and looked up at him. "I really would. When are you going next? I could just tag along."

Warmth bloomed in his chest, and he swept her hair off her forehead with a smile. "That sounds great. Tomorrow afternoon?"

The corner of her sweet mouth lifted. "It's a date."

NINETEEN
JASON

Veronica led them to Libby's room after Jason introduced her to Charlotte. "Ah so you're Charlotte! I understand why she would remember you."

They paused at the door, and Veronica laid a hand on Jason's arm. "She's been in and out today, so don't be surprised if she doesn't seem to know you. She does, even if she calls you Jimmy."

He looked down at Charlotte after Veronica left, raising his eyebrows. "Are you sure you want to do this? It's not too late to back out if it's going to be too much." She wasn't looking at him but was watching his mom where she was rocking in her chair and knitting. The way her brows were drawn together, he was sure she'd change her mind. He never should have invited her here; this wasn't hers to deal with.

To his surprise, though, she slipped her hand in his, winding their fingers together and smiled at him. "I'm not going anywhere."

In that moment, he wanted to wrap her in his arms and weep. She had no obligation to be here, no real ties to him, but she wanted to be here. His uncle had been a great help, but there really hadn't been anyone he could lean on and talk to about his fears and what he was going through. Charlotte was the last person he thought would support him and comfort him, and yet...

"Thank you." He leaned in and brushed his lips over hers. "This really means a lot to me."

Laying a hand on his cheek, she kissed him a little more firmly. "It means a lot to me, too."

They walked into the room together, hands still joined. "Hey, Ma. Look who came to visit." He watched his mother's face very closely as Charlotte stepped forward.

"Hey there, Mrs. Archer, how are you?" She paused and waited, and Jason held his breath.

He'd seen his mom on her good days, bad days, and really bad days. He'd seen her lash out at whoever was standing near her when she got too overwhelmed and she knew she was losing herself. In that moment, however, she simply looked from Charlotte to him and back again, blinking and pursing her lips, before she cocked her head and stared at the young woman kneeling in front of her.

Jason's heart lurched as he watched clarity wash over his mother's face. Shoulders straightening, eyes clearing, the corners of her mouth curling, Elizabeth Archer was suddenly the woman she'd been before her husband got sick.

"Why, Charlotte Trevino, where the hell have you been?" She framed Charlotte's face with both hands and leaned forward to kiss her forehead. "I haven't seen you in far too long. How's San Francisco and school and, oh just tell me everything. You know my son doesn't like to talk a whole lot so he doesn't fill me in."

When she turned an accusatory look at him—at *him* and not Jimmy—Jason almost broke down. He had to swallow several times before dislodging the lump enough to squeeze words past it. "When you're right, you're right. I'll try to do better, Ma." Moments like this had been few and very far between, and he was terrified of doing or saying something that might

145

flip the light switch off again. He caught Charlotte's eye just as she wiped a tear from her cheek and her smile was warm and genuine and full of affection.

"Shame on you for keeping her all to yourself, Jay." She turned back to Charlotte. "How's your daddy doing? I don't see Arthur around nearly as often now that you all are grown."

"He's good, Mrs. Archer."

"Stop that. You know you can call me Libby. In fact, I insist on it. Mrs. Archer was my mother-in-law, bless her soul, and I do not want to be confused with her." She rolled her eyes and patted Charlotte's knee.

"You got it, Libby. My dad had a fall a little while ago but he's on the mend and trying to raise hell." She leaned forward conspiratorially. "Like always."

Jason wanted to drop to the floor and wrap his arms around her legs when his mom threw her head back and laughed. It had been too many years since he'd heard that sound and he wanted more, needed more. Pulling a couple chairs over and holding one for Charlotte before he lowered himself into the other, he cocked an eyebrow. "Come on now, you did your fair share of hell-raising. Don't deny it."

"Who, me?" She batted her lashes, laying a palm on her chest. "Never. That was all Jimmy."

A cloud passed behind her eyes just for a split second, and Jason's heart jumped into his throat. But it was gone again just as quickly. Glancing at Charlotte he could tell by the tightness around her mouth that she'd seen it, too.

"I hear tell that you're a kindergarten teacher, is that right?"

"Yes ma'am. It seemed like a logical progression after so many years with your son." She winked at Libby. "I already had lots of practice."

"Hey, now!" Jason tried to be offended, but it didn't quite land through the face-splitting grin he wore. Besides, he was far too grateful for what was happening here to really care. "I wasn't that bad."

His mom's eyes were sparkling with mischief, and she pretended to whisper behind her hand to Charlotte. "He really was. You should have seen the tantrums he threw when I picked up the wrong ingredients for one of his famous gourmet meals."

"Where are my manners?" Libby's hand covered her cheek. "Can I get you some iced tea or lemonade? Then you can tell us all about San Francisco, sweetheart."

Needing a moment to himself, Jason popped up and started for the door. "Don't you worry yourself, Ma. I'll get us something to drink and see if I can scrounge up some cookies." Smoothing her hair from her face, he pressed his lips to the top of her head. "You two go ahead and I'll be right back."

Once Jason was out in the hallway, emotion crashed over him all at once: relief, fear, love, joy. He fell back against the wall, eyes closed and just breathed. It was temporary, he knew that. There wasn't any reversing her condition, there would only be continued deterioration ahead of them. But for the moment, he had his mom.

Veronica found him there and seemed startled when she saw that his cheeks were wet. "Oh my god Jason, what happened? Is Libby okay?"

"Everything's good." He placed a hand on her arm to keep her from flying into the room but pointed through the open doorway at the two women laughing together. "I'm on the hunt for some tea and cookies so she can entertain her guest."

"I can hardly believe it. Look at how aware she is–I don't think I've seen that light in her eyes as long as I've known her."

Nodding, he didn't trust himself to speak. He scrubbed a hand down his damp face, unable to tear his eyes away. His mom, who barely shuffled around her room most days, was getting up out of her chair, looking determined and moving as though her old joints were twenty years younger. Charlotte jumped up and followed her, watching closely with hands at the ready while Libby rummaged through her dresser drawers.

"That girl is something special, Jason." Veronica narrowed her eyes as she looked at him and smiled. "But you already know that don't you? You get back in there and I'll go get your refreshments."

"Thanks Veronica. But I think I'll just wait for you here." The two women were sat on Libby's bed like a couple of schoolgirls, leafing through a yearbook. They were laughing and talking, and he was afraid of breaking whatever spell Charlotte had weaved. "But yeah, she is special."

TWENTY
CHARLOTTE

Crossing the threshold of the Archer family home, Charlotte was nearly giddy.

"Jason, that was the best afternoon I've had in a long time. Your mom is still so sweet and funny." She turned to face him as he shut his front door behind them. "Three hours went by so fast, but I could have stayed forever."

She looked around at the familiar house where she'd spent most of her teen years. Not much had changed. There were more photographs of Jason with his folks, photos showing the good years, the laughter, the love that had permeated every inch of the home. It made her heart hurt for everything Jason had lost.

"If you want, we could make that a regular thing." Perching on the arm of the couch, she watched him and waited. "I'd be happy to go see her with you every weekend. I missed her."

And you, she wanted to add. *I missed* you.

He was leaning against the door and staring at his feet. What was he doing? There was no tension in his shoulders to indicate that his silence on the drive had been anger, but there was nothing about his posture that showed sadness, either. Maybe he was trying to figure out how to tell her kindly that he didn't want her tagging along again.

Oh god, had she monopolized Libby's time? He'd taken her to see HIS mom and she'd butted in there like a rhino, never giving him a minute with her. Why hadn't she thought of that? Her stomach twisted with guilt.

"Or not." She smoothed the fringe of the little hole in the couch's fabric, trying to keep her voice even. "I didn't mean to get in the middle of everything, Jay. I should have backed off and let you have time with her. Libby is YOUR mom, after all, and it seemed like she was having a good day so I should have let you have that with her."

A shift in the air startled her and she looked up to see that Jason had moved to stand directly in front of her. Without a word, he took her hand and eased her to her feet, his gaze locked on hers. His expression was placid and searching, his deep blue eyes pulling her closer.

Cupping her neck, fingers tangling in her hair, he brought her toward him with a hand on the small of her back. When their lips met, the kiss was unexpected, slow and deep and strong, and she felt it all the way to her core. Her hands slid up his back, palms flat to feel the heat of his skin through the t-shirt, and she melted into his embrace.

There was no lust in this kiss, no need for satisfaction and no stripping clothes off in the heat of the moment. And yet, it was the most passionate and intimate kiss Charlotte had ever experienced. It was as though all the intense emotions of the last eight years were wrapped in that kiss, flowing between them and around them and through them and the strength of it made her want to weep.

When it ended, Jason stayed very still, his cheek against her hair. "I don't know that I have any words, Char. Thank you a thousand times for today."

She didn't have any words, either, but she buried her face against the front of his shirt. Breathing him in, she wanted to carry this scent of fresh wood and green grass with her always. This was what home and comfort smelled like to her.

She was afraid to break the spell of what was between them, but she needed to know more. "Do you want to talk about all of this? About your mom and her illness and what happened today?"

He seemed reluctant to let go of her at first, then he drew in a deep breath and slipped out of her arms. "Yeah. Yeah, I suppose we should." Looking dazed for a minute, he shook his head and raked his hands through his hair before turning to her with a smile. "Can I cook for you? I believe I owe you a home-cooked meal after that mind-blowing non-date the other night."

"Oh, you think you won that bet, do you?" Of course, he had. She would never go on another date that would top that night, head injury and all.

"I know I did." The smile he shot over his shoulder made her heart race.

"Fine. But just because I'm hungry." Charlotte followed him into the kitchen and sat on a stool at the counter while he rummaged in his refrigerator. "What's on the menu?"

"Let's see–how about a simple carbonara? I still have some guanciale in here somewhere, eggs, pasta. Should be easy enough."

Here was her Texas boy, clean-cut financial analyst, horse and Girl Scout wrangler, moving around the kitchen with ease as he cooked dinner for her. A dark curl of hair flopped over Jason's midnight-blue eyes, and her insides melted. Then, when he flashed a grin over his shoulder, the most delicious rush of electricity ran through her veins.

Damn. She didn't want to admit it, hated the truth of it, but after all this time, her heart was still his.

"You know, a lot of people think there's cream and a ton of onions and other stuff in a carbonara, but the traditional Roman dish only has four ingredients: black pepper, guanciale, pecorino cheese, and eggs."

"Isn't there bacon in it, too?"

Raising an eyebrow he grinned. "Yes and no. You can use bacon in a pinch, but guanciale is honestly so much better."

"And what is that?"

The grin broadened. "Pig's cheek. It's cured for three months in salt and chili powder and black pepper, and the flavor is like super-bacon. Trust me, you'll never eat Americanized carbonara again."

She could tell that he was waiting for her to balk at the revelation, but he seemed to forget that she'd lived in San Francisco for close to a decade. While they may not find many adventurous food offerings in their small town, she had a little more experience. "What can I do to help?"

"Well, there's not a lot to do, but if you want to start the water boiling, that would be good."

Without being told, she went straight to the cupboard with the beat-up pots and pans and was instantly back in her senior year of high school, cooking for Jason's parents and her dad and brother every Sunday. Thinking of Libby, she cleared her throat.

"Wanna tell me about your mom?"

He didn't answer, but she heard his heavy sigh. Waiting patiently, she filled the pot and set it on the lit burner.

"It was little stuff at first. She'd misplace her glasses or forget what she went to the store for. I assumed it was more about missing dad and didn't think much about it." His movements slowed a little before he continued. "Then she'd call me Jimmy and when I corrected her, she'd look at me like I'd grown three heads. But after about a minute, she'd laugh and swat my arm and say, 'I know you're Jason. It was just a slip of the tongue' or something like that. When she went missing, though, Jed and I knew this was serious."

"Oh my god. She went missing?"

"She'd gotten in the car one morning to go to the store and missed her turn. Nothing looked familiar, I guess, so she just kept driving. We didn't realize she wasn't where she was supposed to be until after work that night. She'd been gone for seven or eight hours and wasn't answering her cell phone." Pausing, he let his eyes drift closed. "Then we got a call from the owner of an ice cream parlor in Oklahoma City. She'd wandered in there, looking lost, and after a while he asked if she had her phone and she handed it to him."

Thinking back to that phone call after her father had just broken a couple bones, her heart squeezed. She laid a hand on his back. "That sounds terrifying."

"It was." The smile he gave her was warm and grateful, and he leaned down to kiss her forehead. "But I had Jed to help and we took her to the best doctors in San Antonio. They ran a ton of tests, MRIs, a thousand scans and determined that she most likely had a form of early-onset Alzheimer's disease. Once we knew–once she knew–it was like she gave in to it. Things went downhill fast and the windows of her still being *her* got smaller and smaller."

Jason paused his stirring and sighed. "Today was like nothing I've seen in at least five years. I hope you understand the magic you brought to me—to us—in that room."

"I don't know why you keep saying that. I didn't actually DO anything." She waved her hand at him. "Whatever happened in there was just really good timing."

He shook his head. "Huh uh. It's more than that. Did I tell you that she thinks most of the nurses are you? That she's looking for your face in every woman that she sees?"

She stared at her hands and shrugged "You mentioned it."

"Charlotte, you are a shining spot in her mind, one that is

tied to her memories, and seeing you cleared all the haze and brought her back to herself. I've never seen anything like it."

What the hell was she supposed to say to that? "If my being there somehow helped, I'm glad." But she had a sinking feeling in the pit of her stomach. She hoped that Jason wouldn't be angry when it didn't happen again.

TWENTY-ONE
JASON

When was the last time his mom had been so…alive? So much like herself? Two days later, Jason was still marveling at the transformation. He didn't think the facility had changed her medications at all. There was simply no explanation other than Charlotte.

He knew better than to think that there honestly was something magical about his old flame that brought Libby back to the surface. Did he want to believe it? Oh yeah, he did. At this point, he'd do his own ceremonial dance nude in the town square if he thought that might help her.

No matter what, he was glad his mom was coherent when Charlotte was there. Hell, if he hadn't been there himself, he'd never have believed it. Jed would have been thrilled.

Shit. He hadn't even told his uncle about it yet. Until this moment the idea of recording the day hadn't occurred to him, but even with that kind of evidence it'd be a tough sell.

Jason knocked on the edge of the door frame. "Hey Jed, can I come in?"

When his uncle looked up, Jason's stomach dropped. The dark circles under his eyes were even more pronounced and his pale skin had taken on a waxy sheen that made him look a little inhuman.

"Sure, kid." He dragged a hand down his face and offered a weary smile.

Pulling the door closed behind him, Jason sat in the chair across the desk. "You look like shit." Jed chuckled, but Jason didn't join in. "Are you sleeping? When was the last time you ate?"

"Quit crawling up my ass, kid. I'm fine. Just a little out of sorts today." After taking a long drink from his mug, he leaned back in his chair and smiled more naturally. "But you look good. Been spending your time with that pretty Trevino girl? Getting any…exercise?"

He immediately felt his cheeks heating up. While nothing had happened between him and Charlotte beyond a few kisses —remarkably hot kisses—Jason had certainly done his fair share of thinking about 'exercising' with her. More than his fair share. "First off: rude. Secondly: I do feel good. I went to see Ma the other day, and I took Char with me."

"Oh?" Jed sat up straight in his chair, his grin widening. "Did you, now? Rekindling something with your old flame?"

"Don't be a dick. But yes, I am. At least I'm trying to. Remember I told you that Ma thinks one of the nurses is Charlotte?" When Jed nodded, Jason continued. "Well, Char came with me to the facility, and it was like a miracle. A god damned miracle, Jed."

"What are you talking about?"

Jason relayed the story, tears pricking the backs of his eyes just like every time he thought about it. It warmed his heart to see the color bloom in Jed's cheeks, his eyes lighting up as he listened. When Jason finished, Jed stared at him, open-mouthed and still as a statue for a minute.

"Son of a bitch. That's fantastic, kid! Let me know next time you're going, and I'll tag along."

Even though he looked better, Jason was still worried about his uncle. "What's the latest with Chancellor?"

Jed dragged his hands down his face and leaned back in his chair. "Nothing new, really. He's got me sniffing around a couple pieces of land that are behind in their loan payments to see if we can finagle a deal with them. It all just makes me want to take a shower." From the corner of his eye, Jed looked Jason up and down. "Things are going to hell in a handbasket around here. You should get the Trevinos to sell. Almost all their neighbors have moved on already."

Stomach turning, Jason shook his head. "What the hell does he need all this land for, anyway? Some kind of golf course or some shit?" He reached for the folder on the desk, but Jed jumped up and slapped his hand over it, sliding it out of his reach.

"The less you know, the better, kid." Without making eye contact, he dropped it into one of the desk drawers, locking it with a key he tucked away in his pocket. "I can't tell you anything more so stop asking about it."

Fuck. Whatever Jed was tangled up in was bad. Really bad. "How much trouble are you in?"

Narrowing his eyes, Jed stood tall and faced Jason. "This is my mess, I'll deal with it." His phone broke the thick silence that followed, and he waved toward the door. "I have to take this. Get back to work."

He opened his mouth to protest, but the glare he got from his uncle told Jason the discussion was over.

TWENTY-TWO
JASON

As he pulled into the yard, he spotted Charlotte perched on the paddock fence, leaning forward on her knees. She didn't even look up at the sound of his truck, so he killed the engine and watched her for a moment. The sun was rising out in front of her, gilding her silhouette in pinks and golds. Her hair almost looked like it was on fire, especially with the way the light morning breeze lifted the tendrils and waved them around her face. She was magical.

When he shut his door, she turned her head to the side just enough to see him, so he waved.

"Morning, Char!"

She raised her coffee mug in response, and he frowned. Why wasn't she demanding to know what he was doing there? Was she already done with the morning routine? It was too early for her to have exercised all the horses. He leaned his elbows on the top rail next to her.

"What're you up to?"

Her thumbs tapped a staccato rhythm out on the sides of her mug as she stared at the ground. "Hank quit."

"What? Why?"

Blowing her bangs out of her eyes, she shrugged. "He

heard about the trouble with the bank, that we turned down a purchase offer, and he's got a wife and a baby on the way. Can't take the chance of ending up unemployed."

Jason laid a hand on her back. "I'm sorry to hear that."

Charlotte squirmed away from his touch and jumped off the fence. "Yeah, well, thanks. But that isn't going to help us with the rest of the groups I have scheduled." Pacing inside the paddock, she sipped from her coffee. "I mean, I get it. If I were in his shoes, I'd do the same. But it still sucks."

"What about Milo? Can he help?"

"No, Jay. I told you—he's still in school. And before you ask, Bran is against calling Calvin back. If we could even find him." She stopped pacing and set her mug on the fence post. "It's not just that, though. These groups are great and everything, but they won't last. And we haven't gotten one request for private lessons. This isn't a long-term solution."

This was his chance, a perfect opening to broach the subject. He cleared his throat. "What about selling?"

She glared at him from the corner of her eye. "That offer was insulting and the goal here is to try to keep the ranch in the Trevino family. Or did you forget that part?"

Ouch. Jason stood back from the paddock and shoved his hands in his pockets. "It was just a suggestion."

"I know. Sorry." Charlotte sighed and let her head fall back to stare at the light spring sky. He probably wasn't supposed to notice, but the light caught a tear that slipped out. "I don't know what else to do. My brain is fried and I'm just sick about all of it."

He hated seeing her like this. There was such hopelessness etched into her features, and it made his chest ache. Charlotte was not the type of woman to give up, ever, and yet she seemed so depleted and worn down. Well, today wasn't going to be the day she threw in the towel—not on his watch.

Reaching over the top of the fence he held out his hand. "Come on."

"What?" She narrowed her eyes and took a step back. "Where?"

"I'm not sneaking you away to murder you, if that's what you're worried about." When the corner of her mouth twitched, his heart skipped. "Let's just take a walk."

After a long moment of staring at his hand, she grabbed it and climbed out of the paddock. "Fine. I've got a little bit of time before things have to be done."

As they walked, Jason started asking questions. "Okay. Brainstorm. Besides horse training and riding lessons, what else could you do out here to make some money?"

"Shit, I don't know. Bran and Dad already sold off a couple of acres and that didn't buy us much time."

He ran a hand through his hair and nodded. "Right, that's not gonna fix anything. Let's think of steady income. Renting out the stable? Boarding horses?"

"We already do that. And if we take on any more at a time, we'll have to hire more help, which negates the whole point of taking on more boarders." She stopped abruptly and turned a frown at Jason. "This is pointless. Jay, I don't know if I can fix this."

"But why is it all on you?" Laying his hands on her shoulders, he bent his head to look into her eyes. Holy hell, those eyes. "I know you don't want to hear it but maybe it's just time to let the ranch go. You could look into selling and get out before it drags you all down."

Her eyes popped open wide, and she jabbed a finger in his chest. "No. This is what I do. I fix things. I refuse to accept failure here. This place is my home, where my grandparents met, where my mom met my dad, where they raised us, where she passed. And all the family that came before are counting on me to keep that legacy alive. I can't let them down."

She took off at a faster clip and Jason had to rush to catch up with her. Amazing to him, since she was so small. His legs were way longer than hers so how the hell did she cover so much ground so quickly? Lost in his own head, he didn't see that she had stopped again and nearly ran her over. "Whoa! What gives?"

Following her line of vision, he spied the old Dutch-style barn that had housed the ranch's horses before the new, modern one was built closer to the house. It wasn't in bad shape, but the Trevinos had the opportunity to erect a state-of-the-art building with facilities for Dr. Angus and more storage all in one place. And they never tore down the old one.

It was once a bright red barn with pristine white trim, the kind of barn you see on postcards and in children's books. The exact image you'd conjure anytime someone said the word 'barn'. But now, it was obvious it hadn't been updated in years. The paint was chipped and peeling, the roof had numerous shingles missing, and the surrounding ground was overrun with weeds.

"What do you think?"

He glanced at Charlotte. "What do I think about what?"

"The barn, of course!"

Tilting his head, he looked it over again, trying to imagine what she wanted to hear from him. What did he think about tearing it down? About the general state of it? "I don't know, Char, what do you mean? It needs some work, but it's good-sized and the structure is sturdy. You could rent it out as RV storage, maybe."

She grabbed his arm and dragged him behind her until they were right in front of the big front doors. "You're not thinking big enough. When I was in San Francisco, there was no end to the cathedrals and fancy hotels and mansions where you could hold amazing weddings. But almost every couple I've known since I started college has opted for a rustic, farm-style wedding, away from the city."

"Oh." As she worked her idea out, he could see the barn and all its possibilities through her eyes. "Oh!"

Walking around the structure, still keeping Jason in tow,

her eyes got brighter, and she became more animated. "Think of it! We're less than an hour from about six smallish towns. It wouldn't be any big thing for folks to drive out here for the ceremony at the gazebo and then a kick-ass reception in the barn. Twinkle lights all around the beams, soft candlelight on each table, plenty of room for Texas-style dancing. And people pay a ton of money for weddings."

He had to admit, it was brilliant and fairly simple and would pay for itself with the first couple of bookings. Texas weather was conducive to outdoor parties and the space could be reserved all year round. And it would save the ranch, there was no doubt in his mind about that.

"I think it's a great idea, to be honest. Who's going to do the work, though? Won't that get expensive?"

She put her hands on her hips and cocked her head. "I'll do it."

Before he could stop himself, Jason laughed. The sound died in his throat, however, at the murderous glare Charlotte turned his way. "Sorry, that was uncalled for. I know you have the stubborn drive to do it all yourself, but...what do you know about repairing a roof or refinishing a floor? How are you going to have time to do all this work and take care of the horses now that Hank is gone? And you're going to need money for supplies–money you don't have. Let's just stop and think about this for a minute."

He trailed behind her as she walked the perimeter of the building. It was easy to see the wheels spinning in her head, making plans, estimating what she could and couldn't do herself, costs, and potential income. Jason was doing the same thing, his heart thudding as he watched her. This was a bad idea, really bad. But god, he wanted to be the reason she smiled for once.

"You're right. I'll need help. Between Brandon and me—"

"I'll help." The words popped out of his mouth before he'd

really thought them through, but her enthusiasm was catching.

"You want to help?" It seemed Charlotte had the same thought because she pivoted slowly, brows drawn together. "To rebuild the barn to save the ranch?"

"Yeah, why not? I know Jed'll let me take the time, and you definitely could use the help around here."

He knew Charlotte. What she lacked in stature she more than made up in determination, with a stubborn streak a mile wide. If anyone could turn things around it was her. But, if she somehow couldn't make this work out, the Trevinos would have no other choice but to sell and that would destroy her.

"That's an awful lot of work, Jay. And what do I know about throwing a wedding?"

"You don't need to know—that's what wedding planners are for." He watched as the possibilities spun around in her head.

"Come on, Char. What have you got to lose?" Turning her toward the barn, he leaned in, his mouth brushing the shell of her ear as he whispered. "Can't you just picture it? A cool spring evening, soft light spilling out of the windows, laughter and music filling every inch of the building as friends and families celebrate the beginnings of a new life, creating unforgettable memories all thanks to you and the romance of T & M Ranch. Weddings, birthdays, graduation parties, bar mitzvahs...all of it allowing you to keep the ranch safe and in the Trevino family."

"I don't know." She scrunched up her nose and tucked her hands in her back pockets. "Like you said, I'll need money for supplies. I can't get a loan, not with our current one such a mess."

"How about an investor?" Her eyebrows shot up and the hope in that golden gaze broke down any doubts he might have been holding onto. "Me. I'd like to invest. In you. I'll pay for the supplies and anything else I can't barter for, and in return you pay me back five percent of profits after the bank is paid up."

Her mouth dropped open, and she shook her head. "You're insane. That's a terrible arrangement."

"Hey now, I'm the financial advisor here." As he spoke and painted her the picture he was seeing in his own mind, he felt the tension slipping out of her shoulders. "We'll repaint the outside a bright, fresh coat of red, and I'll replace any of the broken boards on the doors and shutters. Plus, I've got a few clients who owe me favors I could cash in. Hell, I may even be able to bribe Mitch to give us a hand on the weekends."

"But why?" Narrowed eyes and hands on her hips, she shook her head. "Why would you want to do something like this?"

Because I want you to stay. Because I need to make amends for all the years I missed with you. Because I gave you my heart nearly a decade ago and I don't want it back.

There was no way he could say all of that to her. Not yet. "Look, it's a sound idea. You know that people from San Antonio will love the rustic charm and won't mind driving an hour for something this unique. And anything that draws people to Zearing is good for the whole town."

Grabbing her hands, he pulled her behind him to the big front doors and pushed them open. She walked into the dusty gloom, and he trailed behind her as she turned in a slow circle. He could see the wheels already turning, working out all the details, and he smiled.

"We'll have to tear out some of the stalls to make it a more open floor plan, and we'll need lots of cleaning." She tapped a finger against her chin and tilted her head. "Once the outside is done, we can decide if we want to stain or paint the beams inside. The wiring will need to be updated, too, and a railing installed on the loft—ooh! Couples could hold the ceremony in the loft, overlooking the guests down below! And then the cake-cutting and bouquet-toss, and everything that needs to be visible can be up there, too."

And that was it. That was all it took, and he was sunk. Fuck Chancellor and his smarmy villain bullshit. Jason would find another way to keep his uncle safe. He'd have to. Because looking into those golden-brown eyes gazing up at him with the tiniest spark of hope, he knew there was nothing he wouldn't do for this woman.

Charlotte leaped forward and threw her arms around Jason's neck, squealing in excitement. It was spontaneous and genuine and made his heart beat out of rhythm. He lifted her from the ground and spun her in a circle, both of them laughing. When he set her on her feet again, her fingers playing with the hair at the nape of his neck, the air around them shifted, and he couldn't breathe.

Damn, she was beautiful. She inched closer to him until his skin burned at every place her body met his; from their thighs up through their hips, across his fluttering stomach to where her full breasts pressed against his chest. When her eyes dropped to his mouth and her tongue slid along her own bottom lip, that burn burst into flames, and he couldn't hold back anymore.

Cupping the back of her head, he captured her mouth, and she let him. Her lips parted for him, and he couldn't stop the moan the invitation pulled from his throat. The sound seemed to spur her desire on, and she gasped, sucking his tongue further into her mouth and gripping his hair with both hands.

God, what was she doing to him? Every inch of him was on fire and he couldn't get her close enough to ease the ache building in his gut. She dragged her teeth along his chin before burying her mouth in the hollow of his throat, her tongue darting out as she kissed her way across his skin.

"Jesus, Charlotte," he growled and slid his hands over the curve of her hips, gripping the backs of her thighs and lifting her off her feet. She wrapped her legs around his waist, her head dropping back and giving him access to the creamy skin just below her jaw. He nipped and licked, her soft whimpers shooting straight to where his arousal already strained against his zipper. Walking them backwards until her back was pressed against the stall, he was hyper-aware of the way she was moving against him, the friction driving him wild.

"I want you out of these clothes, Jason Archer." When she scraped her teeth along his earlobe, he shuddered. "I need to touch you, to see you. All of you."

He groaned into her mouth, stretching his fingers to stroke the seam of her jeans between her legs. "Do you have any idea how hot that is? Tell me what you want, Charlotte." He nipped her chin, soothing the spot with his tongue immediately after. "I want you to tell me, in detail, where to put my hands, where to touch you."

"Everywhere," she panted.

But before he could put his mouth on her skin again, the sound of an engine caught his attention.

"Charlotte? Are you out here?"

"Shit!" At Brandon's voice, Jason lowered Charlotte back to her feet and they both scrambled to straighten their clothes. Through the window, he could see Brandon driving the Gator around to the front of the barn.

He maneuvered to the other side of the half wall, untucking his shirt and praying the tails were long enough to hide what Charlotte did to him. She winked at him and ran her hands through her disheveled hair seconds before Brandon loped through the doors.

"There you are." As he drew closer, his eyes found Jason and he stopped suddenly. "Hey, Archer. What's going on?"

Shit. Could he sense what they'd just been doing? He felt like it was written all over his face that he'd just been about to take Charlotte hard and fast up against the damned wall.

Bran's gaze traveled from his sister back to Jason, and his eyes narrowed.

Tucking her hands into her back pockets, Char stepped toward her brother and smiled. "We were just talking out some ideas for this old barn. Did you need something?"

"Yeah. Uh..." He gave them both one more disapproving glare before shaking his head. "Our feed shipment didn't come, again, so I'm gonna drive over to the Hansons' place to borrow some."

Jason saw Charlotte's brow furrow and she moved closer to Bran. "Seriously? Again?"

"This has happened before?" Walking out to join them, Jason was surprised by what he was hearing. "Is there another option, another place to order from?"

"This *is* the other place we've ordered from." Charlotte didn't look away from her brother as she answered.

"Actually, it's the second other place." Bran ran his hand down his face and sighed. "Our regular supplier lost the order a few months ago, then the next one said we canceled our order when we absolutely hadn't, and now this one is dealing with quote-unquote shipping delays."

"Each time, we've had to make other arrangements, and it's cost us twice as much." Turning back to Jason, she shrugged, defeat shining out of those golden eyes. "So yeah, any progress we've made by doing group rides and lessons has been eaten up by things like this."

"That's bullshit." Jason grumbled the words under his breath. "There's no way all three of these suppliers are just making errors."

"No shit, Sherlock." Brandon rolled his eyes.

"We don't have any proof, but we're pretty sure someone's trying to sabotage us, make it impossible for us to catch up on the loan so we'll have to sell." Charlotte shook her head. "I'll give you three guesses who, and the first two don't count."

Jason frowned. *Chancellor.* "They can't do that."

"Yeah, well, they are." Brandon hitched a thumb toward the Gator. "Come on, I'll drive you back up to your truck and Charlotte and I can go get what we need. We'll sort out the rest later."

TWENTY-THREE
CHARLOTTE

True to his word, Jason called in every favor he had that would help get the barn fixed up. Over the years, he'd given such great investment advice to several businesses that included painters, roofers, flooring installers, and others that they were all willing to volunteer their time to get the barn into top shape. Charlotte couldn't believe how much progress had been made in just a few short weeks.

And she had Jason to thank for it.

"The door-hanging project is done and put to bed, m'lady." Mitch skidded to a stop next to Charlotte, red curls flopping, and his signature grin covering his face. "Gimme something else so I don't get in trouble."

Laughing, she pulled up the to-do list on her tablet and checked a box before scrolling through what was left. "You're the best, Mitchell Drew. What do you want to do now?"

"No idea. Everything. Anything." He bounced up and down on the balls of his feet. "Use me as you will."

She sighed. Most of the things still on the list were waiting on other, professional-level projects to be done, first. There was still so much to be done before the grand opening she'd already started planning and yet permits and supplies and just time were not on her side. "I don't know, Mitch. I just don't know what to do next. The bathroom stalls need to be put in but the plumbing for the toilets isn't done yet. Before we can finish the storage in the kitchen, we need all the appliances on site. I just–" She dragged a hand through her hair and looked around at all the busy work being done and everything that was still waiting. She pushed her hand against her stomach as though that might keep it from twisting in on itself.

"It's all good, Char, no biggie." Laying a hand on her shoulder, Mitch steered her toward the door. "I'll see if there's anything I can help with on the grounds. I'm not so bad at landscaping and whatnot. In the meantime, why don't you get some fresh air and get something to drink."

She nodded, tucking the tablet under her arm and taking a water bottle with a grateful smile. "Thank you."

Closing her eyes she took a long drink and just let the breeze brush over her. The sun was beating down on her bare shoulders and even though it was hot as hell out here, it had a great relaxing effect on her.

When she felt a little more settled, she decided to take a walk around outside to hand out water and see who needed a break. It was also a great opportunity to take stock of everything that was already done, instead of what wasn't.

She paused and said hello to the familiar faces who had been showing up, day after day, to help out of the goodness of their hearts. It was wonderful and heartbreaking all at once. Several of the neighbors who'd lived in the area her whole life but had lost their properties to Chancellor, volunteered to keep things moving forward. Some gave their time, some brought materials. Others were more than happy to supply drinks and meals for every single person toiling in the heat. For her family.

It was amazing.

Rounding the corner, she slowed her steps and smiled. Jason was there helping to shim up a window, his shirt nowhere to be seen and the sight was…mesmerizing. His skin glistened with sweat over the muscles of his back and biceps as he stretched before turning her direction. Every line of his chest was like it had been sculpted from marble and it stole her breath. How was he real? She caressed each curve of his chest with her gaze, drifting over the flat plane of his stomach, along the low-hanging waist of his jeans. God, she wanted to put her mouth right *there*.

"Everybody, take a break!"

The sound of his voice calling out over the rest of the noise snapped her attention back to his face. Of course, there was a crooked smile lifting the corner of his mouth as he walked toward her. "So, how does it look?"

She blinked at him, the heat in her cheeks having nothing to do with the Texas sun. "Do you mean the barn, or…"

Jason had reached her, and she felt the rumble of his laugh through to her core when he leaned in and brushed his lips over her cheek. "Both."

Waving a hand at the nearly finished outside, she proclaimed, "Amazing!" Then she turned back to him, losing herself in the blue of his eyes, lowering her voice for just him to hear. "Absolutely amazing."

The brilliant smile he gave her in response quickened her pulse. "You'll have to tell me all about it in more detail. Later."

Dr Angus and a few of the spouses came around then, passing out water and sandwiches and little towels where needed. The small crowd gathered around to rest in the shade fell into a low buzz of conversation while they ate. But the way Jason was looking at her made all the rest fall away.

"You need to eat something." She ran her fingers through the shock of dark hair on his forehead. One of his eyebrows lifted with a wicked smile.

"Something?"

Damn. What was it about this man that just that one word, that half smirk, had her pressing her thighs together and

SHARON L. CLARK

trying to calm her stuttered breathing. "It's a little crowded here, don't you think?"

"Well, let's take a little walk, then." He twined his fingers with hers and they set off toward the other side of the barn.

All the workers were gathered where the food and drinks were, so there wasn't anyone in sight when they slipped through the door on the far end of the building. Spinning quickly, Jason bent and lifted Charlotte by gripping the backs of her thighs. She wrapped her legs around his waist with a giggle and a flurry of kisses down the side of his face. Moving them along the wall, he set her on top of a workbench before turning his face toward her.

"Hi."

She thought her heart was going to thud through her ribs at the heat in his eyes. "Hi."

Tunneling one hand into the thick hair at the base of her neck, he used the other to skim under the back of her shirt, pressing her body closer. He nipped at her bottom lip, and she gasped before she fitted her mouth to his. No matter how many times she kissed him, she could never get enough.

Cupping the back of his neck, she angled into the kiss, their tongues colliding and slipping together. He dug his fingertips into her hips and tugged her closer until he was pressing his arousal hard between her legs. Her head fell back with a moan, and she rocked her hips into him, his lips burning a trail across her throat.

Trying to remember how to breathe, she moved against him. "You've been out in the sun all morning–how are you not just exhausted?"

Jason's mouth drew kisses, hot and needy, over the line of her chin before answering. "I *was* exhausted, until I caught you looking at me with those 'come fuck me' eyes and I got my second wind."

"I do not have 'come fuck me' eyes." She scooted to the edge of the table, angling her hips for a little more contact, a little more friction. "I was merely admiring the scenery. And thinking about all the ways I could pleasure it."

Groaning against her collarbone, he passed both hands over her bare, heated skin, wrapping his fingers around her ribs on either side. "You are going to be the death of me Charlotte Rose." When she ran her palms over the chiseled curves of his chest, circling her thumbs over his nipples, his breath caught. "And every single thing you do pleases me."

He pulled back and locked on her eyes while he stroked his fingertips up and down her inner thighs. Bracing herself with her hands, she leaned back and let the sensations of his touch wash over her. His thumbs wriggled under the legs of her shorts, moving closer to exactly where she wanted his hands.

"Someone could walk in any minute," she managed to say on an exhale.

"Let 'em. That kinda makes it that much hotter." Lightly biting at her breast through her shirt, he growled and moved his thumbs farther up her legs until he was stroking her through the dampness of her panties. "Your skin tastes like sunshine and oranges, and every little noise you make drives me crazy."

Bypassing the last barrier, he slid his finger inside her and they both gasped. Then his mouth was on hers again, hot and insistent, his tongue moving in rhythm with his hand and she started to unravel. Her body trembled from the pleasure coiling low, tighter and tighter, as she whimpered and panted over his lips.

"God yes, Charlotte. I want to watch you come, feel you around my fingers and know that it was for me, it was all mine."

Tipping her head forward, she gripped his shoulders to keep herself anchored in the moment. "Open your eyes. Look at me, Charlotte."

She did as he commanded and locked onto his gaze. His other hand had dropped below the edge of the table, his bicep flexing rhythmically, and knowing that he was stroking himself and her at the same time made it hard for her to hold on much longer. "Jason…" His name came out as a gasp, all of her breath being consumed by the electric tension coiling in her stomach. Her legs started to tremble, and everything around them faded into darkness. When he groaned and leaned in to kiss her hard and deep, she was undone.

The pressure inside her exploded, and there was nothing but pleasure shooting through her. Pressing the back of her hand to her mouth to stifle her cry, she watched his gaze unfocus before his head fell back and every muscle tightened under her touch. Then his forehead was on her shoulder, both of them fighting for air while he twitched and sighed.

Then he pressed a kiss to her jaw, pulling back so they could see each other, and grinned. "Hi."

Releasing a shaky laugh, she smiled back and stroked his hair off his forehead. "Hi." When he kissed her this time, it was soft and slow, warm and languid, and she wanted to drown in it. His arms wrapped around her, and she wondered if she'd ever felt so safe, so precious.

When conversation and laughter drifted to them in the silence, they realized they'd better join the rest of the crew before they were missed. Charlotte felt like her skin was glowing and that it would be obvious to everyone what they'd been up to. Grabbing a sandwich and handing one to Jason, she settled on the ground and listened to the chatter around them. One of her neighbors, Cooper, was shaking his head as he spoke.

"All I'm saying is that it's sketchy as hell."

Her eyebrows lifted. "What is?"

"Go on Milo, tell them what you saw."

Everybody turned their attention to teenaged Milo and his face immediately flushed. "I don't know if it means anything, but it just seems odd."

"What do you mean?" Jason leaned his shoulder against the barn.

Milo drew in a deep breath. "So, it's probably nothing but I've been past some of the properties that have been bought lately and nothing has changed."

"That's a good thing," a voice called from behind Charlotte. "So what?"

"Well, it's not quite true to say that *nothing* has changed. Everything's overgrown, all the lights are off, there's no tracks going in or out." When people started shifting and murmuring, Milo raised his voice to be heard. "It just looks like it's been abandoned. I thought he was taking over operations at all of these places. But he's not even tearing anything down."

Cooper shrugged. "It's none of our business what Gerard Chancellor decides to do with *his* land. If he wants it to all go to seed and let the earth take it all back, let him."

Charlotte didn't share her former neighbor's lackadaisical viewpoint. "No matter what he's doing, that sleaze is up to no good. He came around here again last week with another ridiculous offer. He keeps harassing us, I know he bullied a lot of the rest of you, and local law enforcement won't do anything about it. But Gerard Chancellor will get his hands on this ranch over my dead body."

Conversation rose and fell like a wave around the little group, and Charlotte looked for Jason to hear his thoughts on the matter. But he was gone.

TWENTY-FOUR
JASON

"Shit! Shit! Shit!"

Fisting his hands in his hair, Jason paced in front of the little house, well away from everyone working at the barn. *Chancellor* was the shithead coming after Charlotte's family? He'd just thought it was a representative from the bank, coming around and reminding them they were behind on their payments, telling them to find a buyer before they foreclosed.

He should have known that shitstain was behind all of this. Jed never said which properties were being purchased, never said that Charlotte's was one he was researching. He should run right back down there and tell Charlotte everything, tell her that his uncle was helping Chancellor with his land grab. Then he should call his uncle and bitch him out for being such a dumbass.

Freezing in the midst of his path, he paused. What would happen if Jed walked away and told that smug bastard to shove it? Would he expect Jed to pay him back whatever money he'd invested in the firm? Would he take it over, force Jed out and liquidate all the assets, putting all their employees out to swing in the wind?

He frowned. There was a very real possibility that Chancellor would ruin his uncle. He'd destroy his reputation, end his career, and leave Jed with nothing. He couldn't let that happen.

But the Trevinos were his found family. They were working their asses off - hell, half the county was working to help them save their land. He'd encouraged her, he'd given her money and called in favors to make this dream a reality–for *her*. Nearly every day he'd been there, putting his own sweat into the project. How was he supposed to convince them to just walk away from it all when they were so close to making it work?

And Charlotte. What about Charlotte? He pulled his hands down his face. Jesus, he could still smell her on his hands, feel her mouth under his. He knew without a doubt that he didn't deserve her. She just hadn't realized it yet. Eight years ago, he'd made the biggest mistake of his life and convinced her that he didn't love her. That he didn't want her. Now she'd come back into his life and turned it upside down in the best way. Just hearing her voice put a smile on his face. Every day, she showed him something new. No job was too hard for her and she would never ask anyone else to do something she wouldn't do herself. At every turn, Charlotte Rose proved herself to be one hell of a woman.

There had to be a way for him to fix this. He had to get his uncle out from under Chancellor's thumb. And somehow keep from betraying the only woman who had ever held his heart.

TWENTY-FIVE
CHARLOTTE

"I'm telling you, it was amazing. This wedding planner is going to be a big client for us." Charlotte was tapping her thumbs on the steering wheel, excited energy flowing through her. "She already named three of her local brides who are looking for exactly what we've got! And she said they wouldn't think anything of making the hour-long journey from San Antonio or even from Austin. Sure, it's a little harder once you're off the interstate and have to navigate these desolate rural roads to get there, but we'll find a way to make it easy on the city folk."

Jason's voice rolled out of the speakers, warm and affectionate. "I am so proud of you, Char. This is all you! Your ideas, your plans, your tenacity. It's going to be an enormous success. You are saving the ranch single-handedly."

God she was grateful to have Jason in her life. Being around him made her feel like a giddy teenager all over again. When they weren't working on the barn, Jason helped her work with the horses, and he was getting to the point where he could train them by himself. They talked about the future, about the past, about their dreams and fears. And anytime they had a break, they'd find a secluded spot in the stables to steal a few hot kisses.

When he had to be in the office, he texted her throughout the day. He'd ask her how things were going without him, type out funny stories that had her in stitches, and then tell her he couldn't stop thinking about her and how she'd felt under his hands. It made her stomach flutter and her skin flush with the heat of her own wicked thoughts.

Arthur and Brandon continued to chip away at the bank loan, keeping them one step ahead of foreclosure. There were no more strangers peering through the window, no more phantom phone calls, and even their luck seemed to even out with no breakdowns or major issues slowing them down.

And Charlotte was happy. Truly happy for the first time in...well, she didn't know how long.

"Oh, no. Everyone has chipped in and played a huge part in this little adventure. And you..." Her chest filled with gooey warmth. "You called in favors, you invested, you put together test menus. And you encouraged me along the way. I don't know how I can ever thank you enough."

"I'm sure I can think of something." His low, raspy voice filled the car. "Want to come over?"

The giddy thrill that fluttered in her stomach made her breath catch. They hadn't been alone–really alone—together since the day they had their hands all over each other in the barn. "I'll be there in thirty minutes."

"Can't wait."

After disconnecting the call, Charlotte settled into the seat, a smile stretching her lips. Things were good. They were so good! Her dad was almost completely healed, the doctor allowed him to take the sling off as long as he promised to take it easy. And Dr Angus was making sure he did.

Brandon's band was getting more work, and they were more than willing to offer up their services for weddings and parties in the barn. They had a small following in San Antonio, and Brandon even had his own personal groupie. Dale had stuck around after one of the shows, bought the whole band drinks, and he and Brandon just hit it off. They weren't quite dating, yet, but they were definitely dancing around the idea. And she'd never seen her brother so happy.

In fact, she felt like they were all the happiest they'd been in a while, herself included. Sure, Jason was part of it. A big part of it. He was sweet and kind and funny and sexy as hell. It was easy being around him. Not only did Jason make her feel adored and important, he made her feel safe. But it was so much more than being with him that made her happy.

Fixing up the barn, coming up with a business plan—all of that gave her a sense of purpose. She felt like she was really doing something and making a tangible difference. Sure, she made a difference as a kindergarten teacher, but this was different. It was looking like she really was going to be able to save the family ranch.

Out of nowhere, bright headlights filled her rearview mirror. "What the hell?" She flipped it to the nighttime setting, trying to reduce the glare, but it didn't do much good. The truck was gaining on her and the lights were only getting brighter as they got closer.

"That's it...go around me." She watched its progress, waiting for it to overtake her and pass her on the two-lane highway. Then she'd be able to see again. She still had another twenty minutes before she got home, and she didn't need to be stressing out about some asshole with a lead foot.

But instead of swerving around her, the truck pulled close behind her and turned on its high beams. What game was this douchebag playing? She rolled down her window and stuck out her arm, waving them around her, but they didn't move.

"You're joking, right?" Closing the window again, she frowned and tried to shade her eyes. A kernel of fear popped up in her stomach; this was a long, desolate stretch of road and besides this truck, she hadn't seen another driver for a while. Hadn't she grown up being told to be aware of her surroundings at all times and to NEVER pull over in the middle of nowhere? There was no way to know if this was something or if she was overreacting, but she hated being unsure and afraid. It just pissed her off.

Charlotte hit the button on the steering wheel to connect to her cell phone, but it just beeped and disconnected. Glancing down quickly, she saw that there was no connection.

"Shit. Shit, shit shit." She was so used to being fully connected in San Francisco that she forgot there were still no-service areas in parts of Texas. That definitely amped up the threat posed by whoever was behind her.

Okay, she thought, *Keep it together. It's probably nothing.* She pressed the gas pedal down a little more, trying to put some distance between them, hoping that this driver was just an asshole with poor depth perception. But deep in her gut she didn't really believe that. The truck was slowing down then speeding up until it was almost touching her bumper, then backing off again.

"Damn it!" She didn't like being scared, but this was really getting under her skin and that just made her angry. It was very tempting to screw with them, too, slowing down until they were creeping behind her, but that would only make her more vulnerable. She could speed up and try to outrun them, but she wasn't familiar enough with this road to go too fast. If she crashed, she'd be at their mercy. With no cell service, her GPS wasn't working either, so she had no idea if there was any kind of turnoff coming up ahead, or if she was just all alone for the time being.

Glancing at the rearview again, the truck was backing off considerably more than it had before, and Charlotte let out a breath of relief. Thank god, they were done messing with her.

And then the headlights disappeared.

"What the hell?" She hadn't seen them turn or go off the road or anything. The lights were just gone. The hair on the back of her neck stood up.

They'd turned the headlights off.

Hitting the phone button over and over again, every beep that indicated no signal made her breathing hitch. She was alone. How much time had passed since she hung up with Jason? Ten minutes? Only three? Her heart was hammering against her ribs, and she checked the mirror again, turning her head to look in her blind spots, then doing it all over again. Did she hear an engine revving behind her or was that her own car?

There were no streetlights or city lights ahead of her as she followed the curving, tree-lined road. "It's okay, you're okay, they just turned. You're almost home. It's okay. You're okay. It's okay."

She was looking in the mirror and trying to catch her breath, but something was wrong. It was so pitch black out here it was hard to see much of anything, but she could swear there was something behind her, some odd sort of movement on the road. Or maybe her eyes were just playing tricks on her

From out of nowhere, the truck lights blinded her again and the same huge vehicle was bearing down on her much faster than before. She pressed her foot down, adrenaline mixing with her terror, and her need to get away as fast as possible took over. She had the pedal almost flat, the speedometer needle inching higher and higher, but the truck was still gaining on her.

A sob forced its way out of her throat, her pulse loud and fast in her ears. What was she supposed to do? What could she do? There were no turn-offs, no other cars, nothing to do but to keep flying down the road toward her home and safety. The speedometer needle was creeping toward ninety and they were still almost on top of her.

"What do you want?" Her scream ricocheted around her,

only making her fear creep closer to hysteria. She couldn't keep this up, couldn't keep speeding along these curving roads like this. Something was going to give, and it would likely end up with her dead; whether with her car wrapped around a tree or whatever the driver chasing her down had planned for her, she didn't want to know.

Her hands were aching from their white-knuckle grip on the wheel and her lungs were struggling to capture enough air. Easing her foot up a tiny bit at a time, she slowed enough to feel a bit more in control, her eyes flitting from the threat in the rearview to the tree line speeding past to the road stretching out ahead. The demon truck kept pace with her, maintaining the distance between them for several more miles, not drawing closer or slipping back.

What was the game here? Why were they doing this? When it first started, she thought maybe it was a group of asshole kids out too late with nothing to do, but this was far beyond bullshit joyriding. This was an honest-to-god threat chasing her on these dark, desolate roads.

And she was one hundred percent at their mercy.

Coming around the next curve, her heart soared: the lights of Zearing were finally a visible glow on the horizon. She'd never been so happy to see her little hometown in her entire life. Relief surged through her, bursting out as a wet, choking laugh. Safety. People. Home. It was all right there.

An engine roar sounded behind her, and she whipped her head up, casting over her shoulder in time to see the truck barreling toward her with determination. The impact to her back bumper sent a jolt up her spine and the steering wheel jumped under her hands.

Her eyes wide, she watched the monster on her tail fall back slightly and then accelerate impossibly fast, zeroing in on her once again.

This was it.

The shock of contact nearly ripped her hands loose, her

head snapping back on the headrest before her forehead made contact with the steering wheel. She could feel the back end of the car fishtail as she smashed her foot onto the brake and fought for control, but knew she wouldn't win. The side of the road raced toward her as her tires tried and failed to find purchase on the pavement.

With a thump and a final bounce, her car crunched into a post and came to a shuddering stop.

Dazed, Charlotte was barely aware of the hulking mass of metal slowing down to pass her only feet away on the road. Then, before she could let the terror of her vulnerability sink its claws into her, she heard squealing tires, and the truck peeled away.

Her breath was ragged, scraping in and out of her raw throat. Tremors overtook her body, a chill tearing through her veins and replacing her blood with what felt like ice water. Afraid to move, she tried to focus on the sounds around her but could only hear her own heartbeat filling her ears.

Looking over at the road cautiously, she watched a pale light drawing closer from in front of her. Her throat closed off, fear clawing its way through her chest. They were back. They came back to what? Finish her off? Kidnap her? What other plans could they have for her?

A white dually pick-up slowed to a stop next to her, and when the window slid down, it revealed a familiar face staring at her with wide eyes.

"Why, Miss Trevino! Are you quite all right? What in the world happened here?"

Charlotte blinked at the raised bushy white eyebrows of Gerard Chancellor as he watched her, and she tried to make sense of what she was seeing.

His eyes narrowed and he glanced up and down the empty road, the corners of his mouth curving. "You know, it's not safe for a young thing like you to be out here all alone at night." Pausing, he locked his gaze on her, baring his teeth.

"Any number of accidents could occur, and you could be very badly hurt."

Her mouth fell open, but no words came out. The back of her neck prickled as every hair stood on end. There was no mistaking his meaning; this had been no accident. This was a warning.

He could get to her, could hurt her, and no one would ever know it was anything more than a tragedy.

Chancellor sneered and slapped his palm on the door, putting the truck in drive. "I suggest you think very carefully about your safety in the future, little rattlesnake. Give your father and brother my best regards." Without another word, he drove away until his taillights faded in the distance.

The sudden ringing of her cell phone made her jump and clap a hand over her mouth. With trembling hands, she pressed the button to answer the call. "Hello?"

"Hey Char, could you stop and grab some wine on the way here? It's the one thing I forgot to pick up for tonight." Jason's voice spilled out of the speakers, cheery and warm, and Charlotte came undone.

"Jason…" Her voice broke on his name.

When he spoke again, she could hear the tight edge to his voice. "Where are you?"

Swallowing the lump in her throat, she pressed her shaking fingertips to her lips. "On the highway just north of town."

"Don't move, lock your car, turn off your lights. I'm coming to get you."

TWENTY-SIX
JASON

"Are you all right?" Jason threaded his fingers with Charlotte's as they sat in her kitchen.

She nodded and squeezed his hand. "Just a little shaken up. No harm done."

But her pale skin and her wide eyes told a different story. God, why did she have to be so tough all the time? She'd been scared, there was no doubt. Trembling in his arms when he finally reached her, she'd broken down and he just held her. He didn't know what had happened out there in the dark. Charlotte wanted to drive her car home, but Jason convinced her it, and she, was in no condition. Now they were gathered in her kitchen, Arthur pacing while they waited for Brandon to get home.

"I wish I'd been with you." His throat closed, remembering the panic in her voice. "I should have been with you."

But she shook her head, her brow pinched. "You couldn't have done anything, Jay."

"I could have protected you."

"No. You couldn't." She pursed her lips and pulled her hand free. "I don't know what you think you could have done that I didn't already do but having you in the car would have changed nothing. And I'm not as breakable or helpless as you think I am."

He shook his head. "What? I never said that."

With a loud bang, Brandon barreled into the house and made a beeline straight for his sister, forcing Jason to jump out of the way. "Jesus Char, are you all right? Are you hurt?"

"I'm fine." Pulling her from her seat, Brandon crushed her against his chest, Arthur wrapping an arm around them both. Over her brother's shoulder, she rolled her eyes at Jason, and he had to cover his mouth to hide his smile. "I said I'm fine, but now you're going to smother me to death."

Keeping out of the way, his shoulder propped in the kitchen doorway, Jason watched the little family huddle around the table, and he felt a sudden ache in his chest at how close they were. He missed having that with his own parents, and turned his head, swallowing the sudden lump in his throat.

"Tell me what happened." Brandon leaned toward his sister, eyes filled with worry and rage as she launched into the story.

Jason's own rage simmered low in his chest as he listened, horrified at how close she'd come to being seriously hurt, or worse.

"The black truck drove off just before he pulled up with his smug face and his ridiculous mustache, asking if I was okay. As though he hadn't been behind the whole thing."

Brandon reared back in his chair. "You've got to be fucking kidding me."

Watching the flush race up Arthur's neck and Brandon's hands balling into fists, Jason pushed himself away from the door jamb. "Chancellor? He was there? He talked to you?"

"He just smiled down at me, acting like he hadn't orchestrated the whole thing."

All the blood drained from Jason's face and his hands turned to ice. He was going to throw up. What in the holy hell was Jed tied up in? This was so much more than just a land grab. "So, because you're working to make the ranch liquid again, he tried to hurt you."

"Or at least scare her, and us, into giving up and selling to him." Arthur's mustache twitched in anger. "That man is nothing but bad news with bad intentions and an inability to lose."

And his uncle was in his pocket, tied to him through desperate circumstances, helping him. Pushing out the people who are struggling the most. And did Jed know what that sack of shit was up to when he told him to get Charlotte to sell?

"What the hell is he after? Did Charlotte tell you what Milo saw?"

The three Trevinos shared a look before Brandon looked him in the eye and nodded. "We've noticed all that, too. Why would he push to purchase all that property just to let it sit vacant? Doesn't make any sense."

None of this made any sense. Jed obviously wasn't telling him everything. The whole thing was sketchy as hell, and Jason was going to find out what it was.

Anger still simmered just below the surface when Jason got up the next morning. How much his uncle knew was a question he'd grappled with all night. On one hand, there was no way he could believe that Jed would put Charlotte in danger. Put anyone in danger. But then again, he was stuck between a rock and hard place where Chancellor was concerned. Did he know the lengths that asshole would go to get his way? Was that why he was pushing so hard to get Jason to talk to Charlotte?

Driving to work on a Saturday morning, he was half pissed that his uncle wouldn't be there. Jason wanted nothing more than to shake the shit out of Jed the first time he saw him after Charlotte's little 'accident'. Whether he had an active hand in it or not, he knew what Chancellor was and he still helped him. It was useless trying to pry information from his uncle without raising suspicion and making him even more secretive. He was evasive and short-tempered these days, rushing off to meetings or changing the subject at every turn, so that didn't get him anywhere. Any time he walked into Jed's office, he slid a file folder into the top left drawer, locking it and pocketing the key. Whatever Chancellor was up to was in that folder and Jason was determined to learn what it was.

When he got to the floor with their offices, he walked through the shadowy halls to his own office. Jed took his drawer key with him when he left, but there might be another way to get in without leaving any signs that it had been tampered with. The desk in his office was identical to his uncle's. Jason was hoping that meant the locks were also identical. He pocketed his key and made his way down to Jed's office.

One thing he was thankful for was that even though the office doors were closed, none of them were ever locked. There had never been a need, because no one who had access to the building would ever steal a coworker's files.

Until now.

Inside Jed's office, Jason sat in the desk chair and sent up a silent prayer that his assumption would prove true. He slipped the key into the lock, turned it, and huffed out a breath of relief when he heard the click. The file he was looking for was right on top and he eagerly laid it out on the desk.

"Let's see what you're up to, old man."

The top page wasn't anything he didn't expect: it was a spreadsheet of the properties in the area that were in financial trouble, showing the acreage, full amount of the loan, and how far in arrears they were. There were four properties with lines through them, and Jason surmised that meant they had been acquired. T&M ranch was about halfway down the list, highlighted in yellow.

Behind that was a map showing the locations of each of the properties. The ones marked were pretty evenly spread out in a sort of meandering line. The Trevino ranch was central to the other parcels and was positioned in such a way that it would connect all the other properties. What the hell was he doing?

There were confirmation letters showing the transfer of water bills and power bills, insurance documents, an accounting of every building on each property. He found other maps measuring distance and the time to travel from one property to the next.

"What the hell are you up to? And what does it have to do with Charlotte?"

The sound of ice clinking in a glass made Jason jump up from the chair.

"It doesn't have anything to do with Charlotte, Jason. I told you to leave it alone."

Jed was standing in the doorway, a nearly empty glass of amber liquid hanging loose from his hand. With his heart leaping into his throat, Jason stood tall and watched his uncle shuffle into the room. Jesus, was Jed drunk? It broke his heart to see him like this. Everything Chancellor touched went to shit, everyone who got near him was screwed.

As much as he was saddened by his uncle's behavior, he was still pissed and he wanted—no, needed answers. Keeping his hands fisted at his sides, his jaw tight with rage, and he said nothing. Jed dropped heavily onto the arm of his couch and took a drink.

God, he looked so tired. Jason knew he was in over his head, but it seemed he didn't have any clue just how far below the surface he was. It took all he had to squeeze the words from his throat, not wanting to hear the answer, but needing it. "Did you know he was going to go after Charlotte? That he'd try to hurt her?"

Staring down into the glass as he swirled the ice around and around, his shoulders drooped. "It wasn't supposed to be like this, you know." Jed looked up and sighed. "When this started, I didn't know what I was getting into. All I saw was a way to save the business."

"That's not an answer."

"No." He looked up then, eyes bloodshot and red-rimmed. "No one was supposed to get hurt. I told myself that if I didn't know about it, there was no way it was my fault. Ya know?"

Coming out from behind the desk, Jason watched the older man's movements with some concern. He was sluggish and unsteady, as though he'd had more than a couple glasses of whatever he was drinking.

"Tell me what this is, Jed." He fanned the papers out on the desk. "What am I looking at here?"

"That, kid, is a whole lot of shit you don't want to get mixed up in. I wished to Christ that I wasn't." He rubbed his hands down his face. "Stay the fuck out of it, Jay. I mean it."

Pushing the sheets around, he tried to put it all together, but none of it made any sense. "What's he doing out there, Jed? Why does he need the Trevino land?"

"I have no idea, kid." Jed's laugh was without any trace of humor, and he waved a hand in the air. "He didn't say, and I didn't ask."

Dropping into the chair behind his desk, Jed let his head fall back and he stared at the ceiling. "Look, what I do know, though, is that this situation is unstable." He turned his bleary eyes toward Jason and the raw fear there made his blood run cold. "These people are unstable."

"Are you in danger?"

"Don't worry about me, kid—worry about yourself. If he knows you're poking around where you don't belong, he'll come after you with both barrels."

"Fuck him."

Closing his eyes, Jed pinched the bridge of his nose. "Stop and think for a second, dumbass. If they come after *you*, don't you think they'll come after what means the most to you? Charlotte? Your mother?"

His blood ran cold. He hadn't thought about that, figured they'd come after him and just him. What the hell was he supposed to do? Chancellor needed to be stopped, needed to be called out for the trash human he was. But at the expense of his mother's safety? They'd already come at Charlotte without him being involved, and she'd been lucky. Wrapping a hand over his mouth, the possibilities of how much worse things could get washed over him.

"You know I'm right. If you get in the way of what they want, they *will* hurt her: and Brandon, Mitch, anyone close to you." He turned with a steely glare. "Get that family to sell. That's the only way to keep her safe."

Jason groaned. "I can't do that. I invested a lot of time and money in this barn idea. The grand opening is a month away! This will be a boon for Zearing, there's a lot of interest, and it can *save* the ranch. I can't tell her to walk away now."

"Don't you get it, kid? Chancellor isn't going to *let* them succeed. He wants that land, and he will get it, by any means. Tell them to sell and get the hell out of here."

His stomach tied in a knot; Jason shook his head. "I can help you. Let me help get you out of this. There has to be something we can get on Chancellor."

Jed groaned and shook his head. "I don't want you involved, Jay. Go home."

"No. No way. Let me dig up something to make him walk away, something to get him to leave you and Charlotte's family alone." He started pacing, running his hands through his hair as fear and desperation clawed at him. "I know there's something in that file we can use; some leverage. If I could—"

"No!" Jed slammed his glass on the desktop so hard, the tumbler cracked. "Damnit kid. The less you know, the better. You probably already know too much. I won't drag you any further into this. Convince them to sell. Chancellor will make it worth your while then you and Libby can get out of here and never look back."

Backing away, his throat closed so he nearly choked on his words. "I don't want his money."

Jed sighed and sat back, turning his head toward the window. "Suit yourself. But you're going to get everyone hurt. Now go home."

Jason slowly made his way to the door, nauseated and his heart full of dread. What was he going to do? Chancellor was obviously doing some seriously shady shit, threatening Jed, trying to hurt Charlotte, and he'd get away with it all if Jason kept his mouth shut. But if he fought back, if he tried to force Chancellor to back down, he could end up making the people he cared the most about suffer. He was trapped between a rock and a hard place, and he couldn't see a way out. Not yet.

Before he crossed the threshold into the hallway, he heard Jed call out to him.

"And kid?" Jason paused without turning around, his chest heavy at the edge in his uncle's voice. "Don't you ever go through my desk again."

TWENTY-SEVEN
CHARLOTTE

Charlotte ended the call and tucked her cell away, disbelief making her smile. Had that just happened? Her dad was going to lose his mind when she told him the news. Unable to hold in her own excitement, she spun in a circle, whooping into the sky.

"Good news, Char?"

Whipping her head toward the voice, her heart swelled. Jason was carrying two cups of coffee as he approached, the corner of his sweet mouth lifted in a grin.

"Thanks." Taking the offered cup, she ran her gaze over him in his light gray suit, the tie loosened and a curl of dark hair flopping over his forehead. She smoothed the hair back into place and let her hand drift down his cheek, where he turned his face in and kissed her palm. Would she always feel these butterflies when she was with him?

God, she hoped so. "Hell yes, it was great news."

He lifted his eyebrows and threaded his fingers through hers. "Do tell."

"I just got off the phone with that wedding planner I visited last week, and she's already got a handful of brides interested in our place, and one of them is putting down a deposit today. A *big* deposit." She thought her face was going to crack from smiling, but she didn't care.

Pulling her into his arms, he lifted her from her feet, then buried his face in her neck and spun her in a circle. "That's terrific! How big are we talking?"

"Just this one deposit is a third of what we need to catch up on the loan." She tugged his hand to make him stop walking and look at her. "A third, Jay. In a year, if things go as well as I think they will, we could pay off the whole damn thing. This is going to work!"

With one hand on the small of her back, he pulled her in for a kiss, his mouth warm and tasting of coffee. "Never doubted you for a second." He slung his arm across her shoulders and propelled them down the sidewalk. "Okay boss, what else do you need to get while we're here? Just point me in the right direction."

"All we need are the tables and chairs, but those will be delivered sometime in the next week. Then you can start planning the menus and Kelcie and I will work on decorating the suites for the bride and groom and that should be it." She steered them off the sidewalk so they were out of the way, and she looked up at him.

"None of this would have been possible without you, Jay." Shit, she didn't want to cry, but the relief was overwhelming. Blinking quickly, she swallowed the tears. "I think you're my lucky charm."

He tucked her hair behind her ear before cupping her cheek. "This was all you, Charlotte Rose. Your idea, your determination, your refusal to give up are what will save this place." Tracing the curve of her bottom lip with his thumb, he smiled. "You are nothing short of remarkable."

There it was again, that warmth that spread from head to toe when he looked at her like that. And when he complimented her, it was an eruption of butterflies in her stomach. How was he hers? If Katie or anyone had told her a year ago, hell, six months ago, that she'd be in Jason's arms, she would have had them committed.

Somewhere, the Fates were having one hell of a laugh.

Wrapping a hand around the lapel of his suit coat, she pulled him close and whispered against his lips, "I could well say the same about you, Jason Archer."

When had she become a woman who essentially made out with her boyfriend—*boyfriend?*—in the middle of the street? Melting against his chest, she already knew the answer. When that boyfriend kissed the way Jason did, deep and slow, and the rest of the world disappeared until only the two of them existed.

"Jesus, you guys are disgusting."

Reluctantly, she pulled back and shot a dangerous look over Jason's shoulder to Mitch. He was hanging out of the General Store's front door, nose wrinkled.

"Oh please. You and Kelcie are just as bad these days."

As though saying her name had summoned her, Kelcie's smiling face popped out from behind Mitch. "And I make no apologies. Hi, Charlotte!"

Mitchell shook his head but the grin splitting his face said it all. "Fine. But it's gross when you two do it."

"Wanna go down and get some ice cream?" Charlotte cocked her head and lifted an eyebrow, already imagining how it would feel to kiss Jason with his mouth cold and sweet. "We could even get some to take home."

The corner of his mouth lifted, but then he tipped his head toward the building next to them. "You go on down. I need to slip into the utilities office real quick. Need some estimates for a project I'm working on."

"I don't mind. I need to check emails, anyway." He kissed her forehead before disappearing through the door.

Off to the side, she leaned back against the bricks and lost herself in work for a few minutes. This was never a direction she thought her life would take, and yet she was loving every single aspect of getting this business up and running. The hard work everyone had put in to repair and refurbish the barn, the word of mouth referrals from local retailers, making lists and thinking of every single thing that could go wrong so they could head them off before they were problems.

She chuckled. At last, her Type-A personality traits were getting an opportunity to shine.

"Well, if it isn't the little rattlesnake."

That voice. In the time it took for her to lift her eyes from her phone, white-hot rage had filled her gut. She pushed away from the wall and stared him down, her chin lifted. "Just keep on walking. I don't want to hear anything you have to say."

"Are you sure about that?" He placed the tip of his cane on the sidewalk in front of him, clasping the grip with both hands. "What if I simply wanted to congratulate you on your coming success? I hear you've got a brand-new venture that will solve all your little troubles."

She narrowed her eyes. "Yes, it will." What was he up to? There is no way he would be happy for them. In no universe would Gerard Chancellor wish them well.

"I hope you're right, Ms. Trevino." The greasy smile that spread slowly over his face sent a chill down Charlotte's spine. "Because it only takes one little mistake, one little accident, one person getting hurt to shut a venue down for good."

Her stomach dropped. There was no way that wasn't a threat. But was it against her? Or the venue and the people who came to celebrate? The blood drained from her face; this man really would stop at nothing to get what he wanted. He wasn't bothered by any kind of moral compass and had never known regret a day in his life.

How could she fight someone like that?

"Okay Char, I'm ready." Jason walked out of the utilities office but then froze mid-stride when his eyes fell on Chancellor.

Keeping her eyes on the sleazy cartoon of a man in front of

her, she couldn't see Jason's face. But she definitely saw the way Chancellor stood taller, his smile widening and curling maliciously at the ends when he saw Jason. And it made the hair on the back of her neck stand up.

"Please don't let me keep you, Ms Trevino. It seems you are in the middle of something here. Do say hello to your father for me." Then he turned that chilling grin back to her. "And please tell your uncle I said hello. It's a pleasure to see you again, Mr Archer, and I look forward to our continued partnership."

He walked away, but Charlotte barely noticed, as the ground fell away beneath her.

TWENTY-EIGHT
JASON

Jason couldn't move, couldn't speak. Fuck, he could barely suck in a breath through the fear clutching his throat. The way she was looking at him was so much worse than he expected. It wasn't rage or sadness or confusion.

It was pure, unadulterated betrayal.

"Charlotte, please let me explain." He held up a hand and took a step closer. But she took a step back at the same time and his stomach turned.

"What was that, Jason?" Her voice sounded too thin, too far away. "How did he know who you were? Have you been– have you been *helping* him?"

"It's not like that. Charlotte..." He tried to reach for her again, needing to touch her, but she jerked back and slapped his hand away.

"Don't." Pressing her lips into a thin line, she stared at him. "What is it like, then, Jason? Does he know you, or not?"

"Yes. He knows who I am. But I'm not working with him, I'm hot helping him, I swear it." He took a deep breath and held up the papers he'd picked up inside. "Actually, I've been trying to find a way to stop him. You see, Jed–"

"Your uncle?" She shook her head. "Your uncle is the one

helping to push people off their land? And you knew about it?"

Shit. This was going from bad to worse. He didn't have a plan, he didn't have anything solid on Chancellor, and he wasn't about to drag her into this. She was already on Chancellor's shit list and didn't need an even bigger target on her back.

Tucking the papers into the inside pocket of his suit coat, he scrambled for something to say. "It's not that simple, Charlotte."

"Well, that seems like a pretty simple question to me, Jason." He flinched at the venom in her tone. "Did you know your uncle was helping him?"

His shoulders fell as he nodded. "Yes."

"When?"

With a sigh, he looked up and then immediately regretted it. There was no fire in her eyes, no emotion at all, even though he knew she was livid and burning up on the inside. "When, what?"

"When did you know?" Her voice was low and the flat calm of it sent a chill down his spine. "Did you know Jed was working with him before you took me to see Libby?"

He tried to swallow the boulder in his throat. "Yes, but–"

"Did you know when you kissed me in the barn?"

"Charlotte." Passing a hand over his face, he clenched his teeth. "It wasn't like that."

"Did you know that night when he ran me off the road? That night when you picked me up and comforted me?"

He nodded. "Please, Char. I..." He what? What could he possibly say to her to make anything okay?

"I see." Her fists clenched at her sides, but she didn't raise her voice, didn't yell. And that honestly made it feel so much worse. "Don't say another word. I will pay you back every cent that you put into the barn."

He groaned. "Please don't do this."

When he looked at her again, looked into those molten gold eyes, his heart fell into his gut. She was looking at him like she'd never seen him before, like he was a complete stranger. And it was like a knife in his chest.

"It's already done. And that's on you."

He rubbed his knuckles across his chin. "Right. Right, I expected as much." He started to turn away, a hand on the back of his neck, but he couldn't leave things like that. "Before you walk away from me–from *us*–I need you to know how proud I am of you. How enormously impressive you are, Charlotte Trevino, and that I do care about you." He looked into her eyes and swallowed once, then twice, before speaking again. "No matter what, you need to know that."

"And you need to know that you've hurt me for the last time. You need to know that you have destroyed any affection I may have had. Now I truly hate you." She closed her eyes then, as though she couldn't look at him for another second. "Go home, Archer. I'll find my own way back." Without looking back, she walked across the street and was gone.

A couple miles down the road, Jason pulled onto the shoulder and gripped the steering wheel until his knuckles were white. Fucking hell. He wanted to puke. He wanted to scream, he wanted to punch something until his hands were bloody and broken.

Jesus, her face. He laid his head back and groaned. It hadn't been ten minutes since he left her, and he already knew he would see that pain–the pain *he* caused–every time he closed his eyes. Just like the last time.

He should have told her about Chancellor. He should have told her as soon as he knew that Jed was tangled up with that piece of shit. Together, he had no doubt they would have found the answer. They would have figured out a way to bring Chancellor to his knees. But what would that have done to his uncle? To the rest of the employees at the firm? If Chancellor was willing to chase a woman off the road because she was trying to save her family ranch, what would he do to a grown man who got in the way of him making money?

Grabbing his hair with both fists, he tried to think. What else could he have done? He never wanted to hurt Charlotte. Shit, he never thought he'd see her again, much less get close to her. She was kind, smart and beautiful. Nothing was more important to her than family. For fuck's sake, she gave up her old life to try to fix things for her dad and her brother. There were no bad ideas to her, no job was too big or too small for her to jump in and lend a hand. Charlotte Rose Trevino was like no one he'd ever met before.

And dammit if he wasn't in love with her. Had never *stopped* loving her.

No matter what she said, no matter how many insults she threw his way, she cared about him too. At least she was starting to until he'd lied to her. She'd let him in again, and he couldn't be honest with her. Couldn't put her first like she deserved.

But he owed his uncle *everything*. Without him, there was no telling where he and his mother would have ended up. Jed gave him an education, a career, a life. He stepped in and let Jason lean on him when everything felt hopeless.

Jason pressed the heels of his hands against his eyes. There had to be a way to fix this. Pulling out the utility estimates he'd picked up less than an hour ago, he stared at them without really seeing them. There was something he was missing. He knew he could put it all together if he could just find all the pieces. Chancellor was a thug and a criminal. But he was also a billionaire who probably had a roster full of crooked law enforcement and politicians who would keep him out of jail, no matter what.

Thinking back on the papers he'd snuck out of Jed's office, there was something off. Why would a billionaire go pick off a bunch of barely-functioning farms and ranches? Wasn't every fiber of his being geared toward *making* money? These were all failing family businesses. So why?

He felt like there was an answer skimming just below the surface, barely out of reach. But what? He'd already stared at everything for hours to the point he could see them in his sleep. That was a problem for another day. Right now, he just wanted to drown himself in work until all thoughts of Charlotte were out of his head.

Why he thought he could accomplish in one afternoon something he hadn't been able to do for eight years, he'd never know.

TWENTY-NINE
CHARLOTTE

After parking her car, Charlotte checked her makeup in the mirror and took a deep breath. This would be fine, she could do this. She was here to support her brother and have a good time with her friends and family. So what if Jason had lied to her, had worked against her, then disappeared, leaving her with a sour stomach and a headache from not being able to sleep.

Screw. Him.

She felt like such a fool. A colossal fool. She had reservations from the start, but he'd smoothed over every excuse she brought up. And then his kisses, his hands, the way he looked at her like she was the answer he'd been looking for, all distracted her from what she already knew: Jason didn't care about her. Not really. But he seemed more than willing to let her think otherwise, as long as he got paid by that piece of garbage.

Jason had waited two days before he started calling her. When she refused to pick up, he resorted to texting. But those were easy to deal with; she simply deleted each and every one of them without opening any. He sent gifts, he sent flowers, he sent letters and cards. And when he showed up at the ranch one morning to ambush her in the stable, Brandon had been more than happy to tell him to get lost and chase him away.

She had to give it to him, he was good. And she'd made it easy for him. He played on her weaknesses, dredging up memories that slipped her into old feelings and making her think they were new ones. When she expressed guilt that she hadn't asked about his mother, he let her believe it meant something to him. It had all been so carefully orchestrated, and she fell for every single lie.

Tears pricked behind her eyelids, and she slammed her hands on the steering wheel. Damn it, no! She'd cried over him for far too long. He didn't deserve one more tear from her.

Arthur and Dr. Angus were waiting for her outside the Jackalope, loud, raucous music and voices spilling out every time the door opened. Jan stepped forward and pulled her into a warm embrace.

"Don't you look gorgeous! That dress is perfect on you."

Smoothing her hands down the ruffled skirt of the cap-sleeved white dress, Charlotte blushed. "Thanks."

Her dad grasped her hand and pressed a kiss to her cheek. "Brandon will be so thrilled to see you out there in the crowd, cheering for him. Thanks for coming, darlin'."

"I wouldn't miss it for the world." She meant every word and the surge of pride it gave her spread the first genuine smile in days across her face. "Come on, what are we doing out here? The dancing's inside!"

The place was packed, and everyone seemed to be having a great time. It hadn't been an exaggeration that the whole town was there. It took her twenty minutes to get through the crowd to the bar, stopping every few feet to say hello to familiar faces and get hugs from old friends she hadn't spent nearly enough time with. Then it took another ten minutes to weave her way close to the stage where she could wave and whistle at her rockstar brother.

Couples whirled around the tiny dance floor and Charlotte

found herself pulled into the rotation by neighbors, old school friends, and even a stranger or two. But she didn't care. This was exciting and fun, and it kept her from wallowing.

There was no way Jason Archer was going to drag her down. Not again, and not tonight.

Her old math teacher, who was older than her dad but knew his way around the floor like a man half his age, spun her out and back before shaking his head. "All right missy, that's about all these old bones have in them tonight. I need a beer and chair before I need an ambulance."

She kissed his cheek and turned to find her dad but was stopped by a familiar face standing in her way with a hand outstretched.

"Miss Charlotte, you are a vision of loveliness tonight." Mitchell Drew bowed low over her hand, pressing a kiss to her knuckles. "Can I talk you into a dance?"

"Mitch! I can't believe you came." She wrapped her arms around his waist and gave him a squeeze. "All you have to do is ask, and I'm all yours. Where's Kelcie?"

Taking her hand and placing it firmly in the crook of his arm, he led her back onto the floor and into the fray. "My darling girl will be here a little later. Hope you don't mind keeping me company."

She smiled and followed him out onto the dance floor. The conversation was light and easy and, thank god, he never once brought up Jason, asking what happened between them. Maybe Jay hadn't said anything to him, or he was keeping out of it, but either way she was grateful to just relax and have fun for the first time in weeks. In no time, he had her laughing as he enthusiastically sang along and led her like a pro, pretending not to know the steps and then surprising her with a spin. When the song ended, she followed him to the bar where he offered to buy her a beer.

"Thank you so much for coming out tonight! It means the world to me, and I know that Bran is incredibly grateful."

"No thanks necessary. I'm having a blast." He squeezed her hand as they snaked through the crowd, then he turned to her with an apologetic grin.

"Before we get to the bar, just believe that I adore you and truly value your friendship."

She laughed. "I value you, too, Mitch. And I will always consider you a friend."

"Yeah, well, I'm gonna hold you to that. No takebacks." Then he stepped aside, revealing a contrite Jason. As soon as their eyes met, he pushed off the bar and gave a hopeful smile.

She glared at Mitchell. "You rat."

"Please don't hate me." He kissed her cheek and tried to be heard over the noise. "He's my best friend and he's hurting."

"*He's* hurting? Tough shit." She tried to walk away, fuming, but Mitch stepped in front of her with his hands up.

"Please, just hear him out." He glanced over her shoulder then offered a crooked grin. "If you don't like what he has to say, you have my full permission to kick his ass. God knows he'd deserve it."

Narrowing her eyes, she glared at Jason, but her heart wasn't fully into the rage she wanted to feel. His hair was hanging over his forehead, the dark blue of his fitted t-shirt nearly matching the color of his eyes. With his hands jammed into his pockets, he looked so unsure and nervous that her traitorous heart skittered in her chest. *Oh no, not you, too.* "I don't have anything to say to him, Mitch."

Jason took a tentative step forward and swallowed. "I just need a couple minutes, then I promise I'll leave and won't bother you again."

She was insane for even considering this, right? She should tell him to eat shit and then walk away without another glance. Shouldn't she? But the glimmer of hope in his eyes cracked her resolve and she couldn't say no.

"Fine. I'll give him one song to say what he needs to say. But that's it, do you hear me?" Her throat tightened with a fresh wave of hurt when she looked over Mitch's shoulder at the one person who could cause her this much pain. Then his mouth lifted in one of his crooked smiles and she was overwhelmed by the swell of affection it invoked. *Damn it.* "One song, then I'm out of here."

Mitch wrapped his arms around her and lifted her from her feet, planting a loud smack of a kiss on her head. "Atta girl!" He set her down and pushed the two of them closer, before smacking Jason on the back of the head.

"Ow! What the hell?"

"Don't mess this up." He offered Charlotte a wicked grin. "Now you crazy kids get out there and hash this shit out. Go on - git!"

With one more gentle push, he shooed them to the floor.

Charlotte led the way, sliding between patrons with her jaw clenched and without looking back to see if Jason was following her. This was a bad idea. She didn't owe him anything and this little exercise was bound to do nothing more than shatter her heart further. If that was even possible.

When she reached the floor, she expected to see Jay well behind her, still fighting his way through the press of bodies. But he was less than a foot away, the hint of a smile curving his mouth. "Thanks for this, Char."

She put her hand on his waist while he positioned his on her shoulder and then shook her head. "I'm not doing this for you, asshole. Mitch is a good guy with a heart of gold, and I care about him. I'm doing this for *him*. That's it."

"Fair enough."

While Jason led her through the steps and around the floor, she refused to look at his face. At this point, her heart was duct taped together with anger and pain. And those god damned midnight eyes would chip away at her resolve, so she was not going to give him a way in. But in her refusal to meet his gaze and by locking her eyes straight ahead, she found herself staring straight at his mouth. Her stomach lurched then flipped when his tongue wet his bottom lip before settling between his teeth.

Son of a bitch.

She dropped her eyes to the hollow of his throat where she could still see the beat of his pulse, but at least it kept her from thinking about how his lips tasted.

"You wanted to talk; so talk. This song won't last forever."

His Adam's apple bobbed before he cleared his throat. "You're absolutely right, I am an asshole."

"Thank you! I'm glad you admit it. Goodbye." She tried to pull out of his embrace, but he held fast and steered them to the side of the dance floor, out of the way of the other couples.

"Charlotte, please."

Against her better judgment, she looked up into his eyes and regretted it instantly. She pressed her lips together and kept her hands hanging loose at her sides, even though he kept his on her shoulders. "Say what you need to say so we can go our separate ways."

He winced but nodded. "I should have told you about Chancellor, I know that, and I was going to. I just needed a little more time."

"Time for what? To get me to trust you implicitly so I would do anything you asked?" Hurt started to overpower her fury, and she felt tears thickening her throat. "Been there, done that. Eight years ago. And you treated my feelings exactly the same—as though they didn't matter. As though I didn't matter."

"I never wanted to hurt you, Charlotte. Not when we were kids and not now. But I was trying to fix this whole stupid mess before I came to you. Jed is tangled up in something bad with Chancellor and I didn't want to put him or you in any more danger. I just want to explain."

Lifting one eyebrow, she crossed her arms and lifted her chin. "This should be good."

His sigh was heavy, and he flexed his hands on her shoulders. When she looked up, his brow was furrowed, his mouth stretched into a tight line. Either he was an award-winning actor all of a sudden, or he really was struggling with this.

"Like I said, I never wanted to hurt you. From the moment we met, all I wanted in the world was to make you smile. When you left for San Francisco—"

"When you pushed me away and made me go. Without you."

"Right. When I made you go without me, it was the hardest thing I ever did. What I really wanted was to take you in my arms and kiss you and hear you tell me that everything was going to be okay." Drawing in a breath, he held it for a moment, then he seemed to completely deflate. "Because I knew it wasn't, and that it never would be again."

Tilting her head, she frowned. "What the hell are you talking about?"

"Just after graduation, we found out my dad was sick." He slid his hands down her arms, staring as he ran his thumbs over her knuckles. "We found out that he was dying."

Her heart dropped into her gut and tears pricked her eyes. "Oh, Jay."

He sighed. "Pancreatic cancer that had already metastasized by the time we even knew it was there. He didn't have long, less than a year, and we were devastated."

"I wish I had known." Charlotte wound her fingers through his. "I would have stayed, I would have—"

He looked up at the ceiling, his laugh jagged and painful to her ears. "That's exactly why I didn't tell you. I knew you'd stay. You'd stay, you'd comfort me and my mom, be my rock and my saving grace. Until you realized what you'd given up for me."

"You don't know that." Her face flushed even as her fingertips turned to ice.

"Yes, I do. There was no way I was going to be the reason you didn't go after your dreams." He smiled that crooked smile that always made her swoon, but this time it only made her heart ache. "You earned that scholarship, and you deserved the chance to see it through and spend your life doing what you were meant to, what you love. If you had stayed with me, it wouldn't have taken long for you to resent me for keeping you here. Things would have ended no matter what. At least this way, you got a chance at a life you were meant to live."

He unwound their fingers and jammed his hands into his pockets with a sad smile and a furrowed brow. "He ended up holding on for almost another year, the stubborn bastard, and I'm glad I had the time with him. But you didn't need to go through all of that. Not for me."

Words failed her at his confession, and she stared with her mouth open. She couldn't believe he'd gone through all of that, needing to be there for his mother without having someone there for him to lean on. Her heart fractured a little more at the pain she knew he went through, but then she growled and shoved his chest with both hands.

"You're such an asshole!" His eyes opened wide, surprise clear as day. "You're selfish and stupid and an asshole!"

"What? Do you know how hard it was for me to send you away?"

Her hands balled into fists at her sides, and she glared at him, snarling through clenched teeth. "That. Exactly that. Who the hell did you think you were to send me away? Since when did *you* get to make decisions for me? I loved your dad too, you know. And you robbed me of getting to say goodbye to him." She spun away and back again, fury and hurt flooding through her in equal measures. "And to think, all this time, I was convinced that I had done something wrong. For years, I beat myself up because I thought you didn't want me anymore, didn't love me."

Tears filled her eyes, and her chest heaved with the effort of trying to hold them back. Jason was watching her, his expression unreadable as he chewed at his bottom lip, but she refused to give him the satisfaction of seeing her cry. Never. Again.

He sucked in a deep breath and looked up at the ceiling again, as though trying to gather his strength. When his eyes locked on hers again, the tenderness and yearning shining through caught her breath. "I thought it was the right thing to do Charlotte, and I have regretted that decision every minute of every day since then. You are at the root of everything good in my life, and no matter what happens after tonight, my heart will always belong to you. Always."

Blinking slowly, Charlotte couldn't move, could barely breathe. The corners of his mouth curved as he trailed the backs of his fingers down her cheek, before cupping her chin and leaning close to brush his lips over hers.

"I love you. After all this time, you are still the only one I could ever want." His hands fell to his sides, and he shrugged with a heavy sigh. "No matter what else you might think of me, Charlotte, just know that I never stopped loving you, not for one minute."

Then he took a few steps backwards, keeping his eyes on hers, before turning and walking out of the Jackalope.

THIRTY
JASON

Trudging into his house, Jason dropped his keys on the table and closed the door behind him. He didn't bother turning on any lights. He just wanted to sit in the dark and lick his wounds while he tried to figure out what to do next.

With a bottle of beer dangling between his fingers, he padded to the living room on bare feet before he lowered himself to the couch and dropped his head to his chest. Damn, that had been hard. The look on her face when she'd found out about Chancellor had cut straight through him, leaving him in pieces. Did he regret lying to her, keeping things from her? Of course. But if it had kept her safe in any way, it was worth it.

Chancellor was no joke, and whatever he was up to, he was willing to hurt people to get what he wanted. He'd already intimidated Jed and had Charlotte run off the road, not even trying to hide that it was him. Jason's blood boiled when he thought of that smug piece of shit smiling at her while he threatened her life.

And there was no way he was going to get away with it.

Jed moved the file from his desk, just as Jason knew he would. Most likely he carried it with him in his briefcase, which went with him everywhere. Thankfully, though, Jay had managed to snap a few pictures with his cell before Jed caught him. And even then, he had the foresight to slide a handful of the pages off the desk and into the back of his waistband. It wasn't enough—wasn't nearly enough for a clear answer, but it was a start.

And maybe it was enough to buy him time to talk his uncle into helping him take Chancellor down.

With a list of the properties already purchased, Jason had driven around the county, trying to figure out what Chancellor was doing. Every property sat vacant, no one going in or coming out, grass and weeds overgrown, each one looking like its own ghost town.

Men like Gerard Chancellor didn't do anything that wouldn't make money. All of the operations purchased had been successful at one point, could be profitable again with a little help. So why wasn't Chancellor doing anything with them? Jason was missing something, he knew it.

Tomorrow, he'd dive back into the papers he'd taken and see if he could make rhyme or reason out of any of it. Then he'd have leverage against Chancellor and an opportunity to get his uncle out of trouble and even get a chance to explain everything to Charlotte and hope she'd understand.

He took a long pull from the bottle and let his head fall back on the couch. God, he hated lying to her. The coldness in her eyes as she looked at him, as though he was something she needed to scrape off her boot, had burned in his gut for weeks. She'd been reluctant to let him close to her from the start and fuck it all if she hadn't been right. He'd ruined her faith in him, her trust in anything he had to say, but once this was all sorted out, he'd spend the rest of his life trying to earn it back. Even if she'd never open her heart to him again, he needed her to understand why he did what he did.

Headlights flashed through his curtains and the sound of a car skidding across the gravel made Jason sit up at attention. Had Chancellor already sent someone to stop him from looking any further into his business dealings? No way. The only way he'd know anything was if Jed had given him up. And his uncle would never do that.

Right?

A car door slammed, launching Jason to his feet, and then his front door flew open and shut, revealing a seething Charlotte Trevino in his entryway. Her cheeks were flushed, waves of her hair swirling around her face, her hands fisted in the skirt of her dress. Christ, she was stunning.

"You don't just do that."

Tilting his head, he narrowed his eyes. "Do what?"

She stalked into the room, eyes blazing and chin trembling. "You don't just say all that to a person, tell them you love them, and then leave." One fat tear rolled down her cheek. "You don't *do* that."

A wave of relief flowed through him, and he set his beer on the table. "Charlotte…" He reached for her, but she shook her head, holding up a hand to keep him where he was.

"Why? Why would you drop all of that on me, say such beautiful bullshit and then walk away?" Her voice caught in her throat, and he closed the distance between them. "You know it doesn't change anything. I still hate you, Jason Archer."

Stopping in front of her he buried his hands in her thick, wild hair and nodded. "I know, Char. I know you do."

As his thumbs smoothed away the tears on her cheeks, she swayed into him, her eyes drifting closed. Then they flew open and locked on his. Her face lifted, and her lips parted slightly as she murmured, "I really hate you."

Nothing he'd ever seen in his life could hold a candle to the heartbreaking beauty of this woman, so vulnerable before him. He was afraid to move, afraid she'd pull away or disappear, but then she slid her palms up his chest and surged forward, capturing his lips. And he was lost.

There was nothing gentle about this kiss. It was passionate

and brutal as she slipped her tongue past his lips. When he sucked it deeper into his mouth, she moaned and set his blood on fire.

Yanking at his shirt, she untucked it and slid her hands under the edge, scraping her nails down the skin of his back. In one quick move, he ripped the shirt off over his head before cupping the back of her head and deepening the kiss until they were both gasping for air.

Then she pushed his hands away before guiding them down, and down, pressing them against the bare skin of her thighs and guiding them up under her skirt.

"If you don't put your hands on my skin in about three seconds, we're going to have a real problem." She bit his bottom lip before sucking on it, and he groaned into her mouth.

He didn't need to be told twice. Dragging his fingers up the softness of her thighs, he bent his head and kissed down the slope of her neck. When he slipped the strap of her dress off her shoulder, she wriggled the top down to her waist, his breath escaped in one long rush. Cupping her breast, he stroked his thumb back and forth over the nipple pressing his palm between her shoulder blades until she arched her back with a gasp. Then he closed his mouth around her, licking and biting while she whimpered and squirmed.

Shifting slightly, he lifted one of her legs over his hip, giving him better access to the hot center between her legs. When his fingers skimmed over the wet panel of her panties he thought he was going to combust. He slipped a finger inside the leg, pulling the fabric tight and rubbing it against her, making her shudder. "God, Charlotte." Rolling his palm over her hard nipple, his hand shifted between her slick folds, and he could barely breathe. "You are so fucking wet."

She pressed against his hand, using it exactly how she wanted, setting the pace and angling her hips. The sound that came from the back of her throat sent shocks of heat straight to his cock and he growled against her neck.

"Do you have any idea how hot that is? Tell me what you want, Charlotte." She arched against him, and he pressed a little harder, moved a little faster.

"That. Exactly that." She rolled herself against his hand, her breath coming in short bursts. "Holy hell, that feels so good."

Their lips crashed together again, and she deftly worked the buttons of his jeans, pushing them down past his hips. When her hands wrapped around him, her thumb brushing over the tip, his knees nearly buckled.

She wrapped both hands around him again, stroking firmly, and he sucked air in through his teeth. Her touch was electric and felt so damn good he wasn't sure he'd outlast her. Moving his fingers against her, she met his speed, rubbing her thumb over the head with every caress and he groaned against her neck.

"Do you have any idea what I want to do to you right here, right now?" He pushed a finger inside her, and she whimpered, so he pushed in another, making her tremble. "You're driving me wild. I can't think of anything but feeling you come against my hand, then being inside you and making you come again and again."

"Yes, oh god, yes." Her head fell back as he pushed her closer, his fingers moving fast then slowing, the changing pace making her pant and buck against him. She was close, so close, and he knew it wouldn't take much to push her over the edge, but he wasn't done with her quite yet. Every whimper sent a renewed jolt of desire down his spine, and he needed more of her, needed all of her. He slipped her dress down her curves until it pooled on the floor at her feet. The sight of her stripped down to just her underwear, flushed and trying to catch her breath was everything he ever wanted. He could spend all night touching this woman, worshiping her body, and never want to stop.

Lifting her hair off her shoulder, he pressed a kiss to her collarbone before leading her to the couch. He laid her back gently then settled between her legs with a devilish grin. Leaning forward, he sucked one nipple into his mouth, then paid the other the same attention. Goosebumps skittered over her heated skin as he kissed his way lower and lower. She drew her fingers through his hair, sucking in a breath when he nipped at the sensitive skin of her inner thigh.

He chuckled as he kissed along the leg of her panties, then scraped his teeth over the wet fabric, making her arch into him. Then he pushed the panel to the side and moaned.

"God, I love that I can do this to you." He lapped at her with the flat of his tongue before circling her most sensitive parts, making her cry out. Using his fingernails, he drew the rest of her clothing down and off before using his palms to gently press her thighs flat. He sighed, sucking and licking until she was trembling beneath him. "Every noise you make is better than the last. I could do this all night."

"Don't you dare!" She pressed and rolled against his mouth, every breath a gasp and a whimper. Placing his hand under her hips, he lifted just enough to close his lips around her at a different angle, the suction making her buck and cry out. *More.* He still needed more, couldn't get enough. When he slid a finger inside her, pressing up before pulling out and returning with two fingers, she tightened her grip on his hair and cried out. "Jason!"

Without releasing her as she bucked and panted, he rode out her orgasm, wanting to push her so far beyond pleasure that coherent thought completely escaped her. "Holy shit." Her body continued to twitch even after he pulled away, and he was sure he was smiling at her like a lunatic.

"You are just so proud of yourself, aren't you?"

"Oh yes, I am."

"As you should be." She laughed, trying to slow her breathing. "Well done."

He crawled onto the couch and pulled her against his chest. "Thank you. Honestly, I think that was some of my best work."

Wriggling out of his embrace, she smirked. "Oh, we're not done yet. Turnabout is fair play."

She dragged her fingers down his thighs, lowering herself between his knees. When she closed her lips around him, everything else disappeared.

The heat of her mouth, the swirl of her tongue, the pressure of her hand around his shaft, drove him toward the edge of sanity. And just when he thought he couldn't take anymore, she'd shift or pull away for a moment and then the shock of cool air made him suck in a breath. Then her mouth was on him again and all rational thought left him.

Finally, when he thought he was going to burst into flames, he pulled her from her knees, kissing her with a ferocity he'd never felt before. She climbed onto his lap, straddling his hips, and smiled down at him. Framing her face, he smoothed her hair back so he could see the heat in her amber eyes as he entered her.

Throwing her head back, she rocked her hips and moaned. She was so warm and wet and tight around him, he groaned and dug his fingertips into her hips, trying to slow her motion. "You're going to be the death of me, Charlotte Rose."

She arched back, bracing herself on his knees while keeping her eyes on his. Breathing heavy with her tongue pressed hard against her top lip, she had never looked so sexy as she did taking charge, taking what she wanted and giving him all he could ever want.

Only Charlotte could make him lose all control, and he gladly surrendered it to her. Her movements sped up and she leaned forward, pressing her forehead to his and gripping the back of his neck. Thrusting up to meet her every move, there was no way he could hold out any longer.

"Charlotte…" His voice sounded gruff and strangled to his own ears. "Charlotte I can't—" Every muscle tensed, and all the air left his lungs in one long groan even as she gasped and shuddered, tightening and pulsing all around him.

They clutched at each other, but neither seemed to want to stop touching the other. God, she was amazing. He didn't think he could give up hearing the little noises she gasped out with every shift in position. And whether she stopped touching him or not, he knew he was really and truly lost to this woman. He whispered against her smooth skin, "You are unbelievably perfect."

When she kissed him, it was slow and deep, the swipe of her tongue languid and delicious. He dug his fingertips into her hips, holding her against him, and she scraped her nails down his back. Would he ever get enough of her?

As though reading his mind, she opened those warm amber eyes and smiled up at him. "I don't have anywhere else to be. Wanna go for round two?"

THIRTY-ONE
CHARLOTTE

O pening her eyes slowly, Charlotte stretched in the hazy light filling the room. Then she turned her head, and her stomach got all fizzy and bubbled joy up through her chest. Jason was lying next to her, head laying on his arm, and his crooked smile shot straight between her legs. Again.

Damn.

"Good morning." With one finger, he moved her hair off her cheek before tracing the column of her throat. "God, you're stunning."

Her body was still warm and heavy from sleep but his gaze on her woke up every cell, humming across her skin. "Good morning, yourself."

He raised up on one elbow and hovered over her, eyes searching her face before he brushed his lips over hers, warm and soft. "While I would love to keep you in my bed, naked and warm and *mine,* we would likely waste away to nothing because we'd forget to eat for days."

Now his mouth was on her jaw, teeth nibbling along her chin, his hand splayed over her hip. Good lord, he was going to be the death of her. With a quick push and roll, she had him on his back and she straddled his hips. "Speak for yourself. As

221

much as I'd love to let you worship my body, I've never been one to skip a meal."

His throaty laugh vibrated all the way through her, making her smile. "Noted. But you'd better move before things get out of hand. Again."

Wrapping both hands around her waist, he lifted her off him and rolled away and off the edge of the bed. God, his bare form was enough to make her mouth water. And the way he moved around the room rooted her in place, unable to drag her eyes away.

He drew his jeans up his legs before dragging a t-shirt over his head. Then he lifted an eyebrow and stalked toward her. "I am absolutely on board with you walking around my house in the gorgeous skin god gave you, but if you change your mind, your panties are by the door. And you are welcome to put on any of my shirts." He kissed her forehead and strode out of the room, calling over his shoulder, "Or not. But I can't be held responsible for what happens next."

Tugging a Zac Brown Band tee over her head and retrieving her panties from where they'd been discarded the night before, Charlotte followed him to the kitchen where the scent of hot coffee was already hanging in the air. She perched on one of his barstools and watched him drift around the kitchen, whipping up what she was sure would end up as the most delicious omelet she'd ever tasted.

He paused his chopping and looked up at her, his brows drawn together. "Suppose we should talk? I wanted to protect you from all of this, but that's not fair to you."

"Want me to chop while you talk?"

Feigning shock, he clutched at his chest and stumbled backward. "Charlotte, you wound me! This is my kitchen, my safe space, and you are my guest." Then he winked and resumed preparations. "I really don't know where to start. Maybe you could just ask me questions."

"Okay. I guess start at the beginning? How did Jed get tangled up with Chancellor?"

He snorted. "Good question. He said he made an investment that should have been a sure thing but then wasn't. He lost a lot of money, to the point that he was going to lose the firm."

She reached for a slice of bell pepper before Jason shooed her away, making her laugh. "And then Gerard Chancellor just *happened* to show up with the answer to his problem."

"Exactly. I've never seen Jed like this. He's hardly eating, he's not sleeping, he's drinking at all hours." Dropping the vegetables in a line down the center of the egg mixture in the pan, he sighed. "He's being secretive, too. Normally we talk about every client, about everything, to be honest. And now he's barely talking to me."

"I'm sorry, Jay." Chewing her lip, she tried to order her thoughts. "So, why does Chancellor want all these properties so badly? I don't understand why he's here, in this small community in the first place. With his money and influence he could do whatever he's doing anywhere, closer to a bigger metropolis. So why Zearing?"

They were both quiet for a moment, Charlotte rolling possibilities around her mind. "Land anywhere in Texas is valuable, so it's not that it's any cheaper here than it is outside of San Antonio."

"We don't have any more or better natural resources, either. Our connection to the power grid is stable but not better than anywhere else." Jason removed the pan from the burner and slid the omelet onto a plate, grabbing two forks and settling on the stool next to her.

His eyes slid over her bare legs and all the places the t-shirt hugged her curves and Charlotte blushed. He'd seen her naked—hell he'd had his hands and mouth on more of her body than was visible, and yet his gaze burned on her skin. He cleared his throat and leaned in to kiss her cheek. "No one else should ever wear that shirt. And you shouldn't wear anything else."

"Don't get distracted."

"You're very distracting."

When he leaned toward her, she kissed him until she felt like her bones were soft and she could just mold herself against him. Then she pulled back and shook her head. "If we go down that road again, we're done for. Now eat."

Dishes cleaned and put away, Charlotte and Jason sat on the couch with the papers spread out before them. "What do you make of all this? I'm not sure what I'm looking at here."

"I don't think that whatever he's doing out on those farms has anything to do with farming."

She frowned. "What makes you say that?"

"No one is living there, no supplies are going in, no product coming out. They are all abandoned. But why?"

He sat back and scratched his chin, and Charlotte tucked her legs underneath her on the couch. "Who would we even talk to about this? Who might know what this means?"

"Not sure." Jason ran his hands through his hair and blew out a breath. "I'd ask Jed, but...well."

"Should we talk to my dad? Maybe he'd have some ideas?"

Shaking his head, Jason frowned. "I don't know that I want them involved. Not yet," he added quickly when Charlotte opened her mouth to protest. "Shit. Maybe we can talk to them about it like it's a client looking into an investment in the area. We don't tell them it has anything to do with Chancellor. This is my problem, and I want to figure out what's going on before anyone else gets hurt."

She framed his face in her hands, and pulled him in for a long, lingering kiss. When it ended, he grinned and cupped her cheek, tracing the curve of her bottom lip with his thumb. "What was that for?"

"Just for being so careful with the people around you.

You're trying to get Jed out of an impossible situation, you're trying to keep me and my family safe, you're trying to get a fair shake for the people of this community." Standing and pulling him with her, she raised her eyebrows and walked backwards toward his bedroom. "Your chivalry is an incredible turn-on."

Something caught her attention in the window behind Jason and Charlotte stopped. "Were you expecting someone?"

From what she could see, there was a big black truck in the yard, two dark figures circling around it. She and Jason approached the window, and he pulled back a corner of the curtain. An icy coldness tore through Charlotte's body. She knew that truck. That was the one that chased her, that drove her off the road. And now it was here.

They dropped a big bundle onto the ground and then jumped in and sped away. Jason turned to Charlotte and grabbed her shoulder. "Stay here. I mean it." Then he opened the door a crack to get a better look at whatever was left in his yard, and she felt him tense before he threw the door wide and bolted over the threshold.

"Jed!"

THIRTY-TWO
JASON

Jason's teeth ground together as he dabbed at the cuts and scrapes covering Jed's arms. Dirty, beaten, and bleeding, his uncle hadn't said more than a handful of words since Jay nearly dragged him into the house.

With a clean, wet rag, Charlotte dashed back into the kitchen and wiped some of the grime and dried blood from Jed's face. He winced and she jumped back. "Oh, I'm so sorry!"

He eased the rag from her fingers and patted her hand with a smile. "Don't you worry about me, darlin'. It's all right."

"What the actual hell, Jed." Jesus, Jason couldn't seem to unclench his jaw. He was pissed, sure, but not at his uncle. Not really. It was more that he was worried, that he felt guilty, that he wanted to find the assholes who did this and hurt them the same.

"Look kid, I should have seen it coming." He dabbed at his cracked lip and shook his head. "I mean, when you get in bed with crooks and goons, some shit's bound to go down."

Jason flinched. This was his fault. Everyone around him was in danger, and things were only going to get worse if he kept digging. Who would be next? They already went after Charlotte without any damage, thank god. But Mitch? His mom? No way he'd let that happen.

"I still think we should get you to a hospital. You may have some busted ribs under there."

"No." Jed's answer was quick and short. "No hospital. They just ask questions, and I can't give them the answers. I'll be fine."

Charlotte handed him a bottle of water and perched on a stool next to him, her eyes narrowed, and her mouth pressed into a thin line. "Just tell us what happened."

Looking from Charlotte to Jason, Jed's face relaxed into a broad smile. Until it stretched the split in his lip, at least. Then he waved a hand between them. "This is nice, this is a good thing, here. I'm happy for you two kids."

"Me too, but don't try to distract us, old man. How'd they get a hold of you?"

He shrugged. "They just grabbed me from behind the office. I was walking out to my car and about halfway across the lot, this truck screamed up and I was blindsided. They pulled me into the cab and one guy started punching my gut before we were even out on the street."

"Do you know where they took you? What did they want?"

Jason slapped his hand on the kitchen counter before raking it through his hair. He knew what they wanted. He knew why they grabbed Jed and didn't come after him.

"They wanted to send me a message." The words were quiet and forced out of his throat. "Chancellor's a grade-A dick, but he knows that if he comes after me, I'll just dig deeper. But by hurting you, and running Char off the road—"

"What?" Jed sat up and looked at Charlotte with his eyes wide and his mouth open. "Are you hurt? Why am I just now hearing about this?"

She patted his hand and smiled. "I'm fine. No harm done."

But the memory of that night made guilt rise up in Jason's throat, burning like acid. If he had just told Charlotte from the beginning, she wouldn't have had to go through that.

As though reading his mind she turned to him with a pointed look. "Don't. Once again, you couldn't have done anything to stop it or to protect me. This isn't on you, Jay."

"It is. I started snooping around and asking questions. I pushed you to renovate the barn, encouraged you to basically tell him to fuck off."

Charlotte's sudden laughter surprised him and both he and Jed stared at her.

"Have you met me, Jason Archer? You didn't push me to do anything. I wanted to." Her lips curved into a wicked grin. "And you can bet your sweet ass that the first time I met that sleaze he was not a fan of mine."

"When was that?"

"A day or two after I got here."

His jaw dropped. "Charlotte…what happened?"

"Oh, you know. I'm sure you can imagine how condescending he was." She scowled. "I let him know exactly how that was going to fly with me."

Well, shit. Once again, Jason was reminded how amazing this woman was. "Let me guess: he called you sweetheart or darlin'?"

"Little filly." She snorted. "He learned his mistake pretty damn quick. Now he calls me little rattlesnake. And he's going to find out just how apt a description that is."

While his heart swelled with love for this spitfire sitting across from him, Jason's stomach also twisted painfully with fear. "No. You can't. I'll back off. I can't take the chance of losing you." He looked at his uncle. "Either of you."

As he watched, Jed's face twisted into a mask of anger. "Fuck that." He stood and threw the rag at the kitchen sink and turned back to Jason with a ferocity he hadn't seen in months. "The thing about assholes like Chancellor is that they keep getting away with everything. There are no consequences because they have money and can buy their way out of any trouble, can pay people to look the other way. Letting him get away with shit for so long only makes things worse."

He paced the room, tucking his shirt into his torn dress slacks before stopping in front of Jason. "You know I love ya, right kid?" Jason nodded. Even if Jed hadn't told him, the look in the older man's eyes spoke volumes. "Because of Gerard Chancellor convincing me that I'd be ruined if I didn't do what he said, I've done things I'm not proud of. Things that I'll have to live with for the rest of my life. I refuse to let him drag you down, too."

These two people were Jason's family. Two of the three people who meant everything to him. They were strong and kind and their courage lodged a stone in the middle of his throat that made it hard to swallow. Charlotte stood with her hands on her hips, determination shining from every pore.

Jed was thumbing through the papers on the coffee table, chuckling as he dug down deeper. "You sneaky little shit. I knew that folder seemed lighter." He winked at Jason, pride beaming from his face. "I'm in. We're gonna nail that dick to the wall."

THIRTY-THREE
CHARLOTTE

The breeze coming from across the field was sweet and a little cool, hinting at rain that was sorely needed. Charlotte tucked her hair behind her ear and frowned. "Do you think we need any other beverage options? I mean, we'll have water and a few coke options, two red wines, two white, and some craft beer. Do you think we should—"

"Charlotte." Jason pressed his thumb into the bottom of her foot, rubbing with a delicious pressure that had her nearly purring. "This is going to be perfect. You have thought of everything from the drinks to the music to the most comfortable chairs. You even had me work up some vegetarian food options." He rolled his eyes but grinned. "In Texas."

She laughed. "Hey, not everyone eats meat, not even here." Then her brow furrowed, and she pressed her teeth into her bottom lip. "I just need this to work. Everything is riding on this open house, every*one* is counting on me to make it work."

There it was. The knot that had been tightening in her stomach for the last week squeezed and twisted. Every night had her tossing and turning, going over every detail again and again until the sun came up and she'd barely closed her eyes.

Well, every night except the ones she spent with Jason. When she looked up, he was watching her with a raised eyebrow and a soft smile. And butterflies erupted, loosening that knot and allowing her shoulders to ease away from her ears. How long would he have that effect on her? How long would just the gaze of those midnight-blue eyes smooth her rough edges and make her giddy like a teenager?

Forever. Forever would be good.

"Charlotte, you promised me you'd take today to just relax." Both hands moved over her feet and up over her ankles in firm, easy circles. "You have done everything, you have thought of everything. You have planned the perfect party and there won't be a single person there who won't see how hard-working, thoughtful, and meticulous you are. It's going to be amazing."

With a little push, he started the swing moving again. They were less than a week away from the Open House and Char-lotte's nerves were beyond frayed. And yet, having Jason there with her made it a little easier to breathe. He sat on one end of the swing and she on the other with her feet in his lap. It had been a compromise, and she was doing a very poor job of sticking to her end of it. Jason was trying to get her to take a day off, to put everything down and walk away just for a few hours. But she couldn't stop going over the lists, checking and double-checking that everything for the party was ready.

Everything was riding on this. Everything.

"Yeah, but what if—"

"It won't."

"You don't know that." She chewed on the corner of her mouth. "I need to be ready for anything. I could—"

"Charlotte Rose, if you don't put that tablet down, I will be forced to take drastic action." Her heart thumped at the wicked gleam in his eye as he pulled gently on her legs, inching her closer to him. "Now that I think about it, please push me. I'd really love to distract you with my hands, and my lips, and…"

When he turned his face inward and nipped at her inner thigh, she squirmed and giggled. "You know Bran and my dad are just out checking the fence. They should be back in about five minutes."

"Well then, I have five minutes, don't I?" He pulled her onto his lap and buried his face against the curve of her neck, breathing deeply. "Why do you always smell so good? Like wildflowers and oranges and sunshine. I can't get enough."

"Good." She framed his face with her hands and lowered her lips to his.

The sound of an engine coming up the driveway interrupted them, making Charlotte jump up. Her pulse surged, beating in her fingertips, and she tensed. Was it Chancellor coming to make more threats? Or some of his goons, coming to make good on those threats? The vehicle was drawing closer, the engine getting louder, and she was about to leap out of her skin.

"It's okay." Jason laid a hand on her arm and stepped next to her. The truck finally came into view, and she let out a shaky breath. Then her brow furrowed.

The black SUV coming up the driveway was a surprise. But when two men in Kevlar vests stepped out and walked their way, she could barely believe her eyes. She reached for Jason's hand and gave it a squeeze before they stood at the top of the steps, side by side.

"Hi, can I help you?" She stepped forward and tucked her hands in the pockets of her shorts.

"I'm DEA Agent Gomez and this is Agent Fisk. We're looking for Charlotte Trevino?"

The warmth from Jason's hand on her shoulder as he stepped up behind her was a comfort and kept her from letting panic crawl up her throat. "I'm Charlotte. This is Jason Archer. How can we help you?"

The two men exchanged a glance, and Agent Fisk cocked his head. "Any relation to Jed Archer?"

She felt him stiffen behind her and caught the quick intake of breath before he answered. "My uncle. What's this about?"

"Mr Archer, Ms Trevino, we were contacted by Jed Archer a week ago with some serious allegations about a local businessman. We're following up on those allegations and wanted to ask you a few questions."

"Yes, of course. Come on inside." Finally! Relief flooded her chest as Charlotte led them inside. There was a light at the end of this dark tunnel she'd been crawling through since she returned to Texas. Thankfully, Jed had called Jason that morning and let him know that he was staying with his new girlfriend in Seguin. So at least they knew he was safe.

Seated around the kitchen table, she and Jason listened to Gomez and Fisk lay out what they knew and what they suspected.

"You see, we've been watching Chancellor for a while, ever since he had some business dealings with members of the Mexican Gulf cartel." Agent Gomez rubbed the bridge of his nose. "We became aware of some strange activity, large property purchases made but then nothing else. No license applications, no utilities utilized, no new business filings."

Agent Fisk sat up and locked on Charlotte's face. "We believe that Gerard Chancellor is working with the Gulf cartel, setting up a smuggling route to move product from Mexico across the border and farther north through connected private properties. He's been forcing landowners to sell so he had a clear path. And your family, Ms Trevino, has disrupted his plan."

The blood drained from Charlotte's face. Mexican cartels? She'd grown up in southern Texas, it wasn't like she was unaware of them. But knowing that they were looking at and trying to use her little town made her skin crawl. "How does owning these properties help?"

"Drug mules will smuggle product across the border in the most remote locations, across the most dangerous terrain, carrying only a backpack. Then they need a safe place to stash their load until it can be picked up and distributed." Agent Gomez rubbed the back of his neck. "One after another, the mules leave their packs in abandoned buildings, barns, houses, until there's enough for a distribution pick up."

Agent Gomez leaned forward. "We believe having the properties all connected makes it safer or easier for the mules to come farther north since they won't be spotted by anyone moving from private property to private property."

"What can we do?" Jason leaned his elbows on the table. "If there is a way to put Chancellor behind bars for good, we are all in."

Gomez cleared his throat. "We appreciate that, we really do. And we welcome your assistance. But you need to look at this realistically."

"What do you mean?" Charlotte frowned. "It sounds like you're gathering evidence, that you know what he's doing and are planning on stopping him."

"We are." Fisk shifted in his seat. "People like Gerard Chancellor, men with money and influence, men who control the lives of others and don't care who gets hurt as long as they get rich, rarely see any real jail time."

The corners of her mouth turned down and Charlotte sat back in her chair. "Shit. He pays his way out."

The agent nodded. "Correct. We are working on weeding out the crooked law enforcement officers, lawyers, judges, even legislators who take his money and that of other criminals in trafficking, but there are a lot of powerful people getting rich, so they fight back."

"I see." She did, but she didn't. Of course, for some people, power was all that mattered. Power and money and the ability to control others were gospel. It was just hard to understand that kind of thinking. Charlotte chewed on her lip and tapped her fingers on the table. "Okay, so what can we do? Why are you here if Chancellor is just going to get away with what he's doing?"

"Agent Gomez and I aren't saying he won't face consequences, or that we aren't going to stop him." Agent Fisk wrapped his hands around the collar of his vest and leaned back. "We have an operation in the works, and we will stop him. He'll likely wriggle out of the justice system and move on somewhere else, but he'll be on radar."

"We are here to just make sure you're aware that he is a dangerous man." The DEA agent's earnest expression made Charlotte's blood run cold. "We haven't heard anything specific but just know that he knows that Jed has talked to us and that we're closing in on him. And an animal is most dangerous when it's backed into a corner."

Standing, Agent Fisk offered a business card to Charlotte then to Jason, shaking each of their hands. "Just watch your backs. If anything seems off, seems out of place, trust your instincts and call us."

The truck disappeared around the curve in the driveway, leaving Charlotte at the bottom of the porch steps, Jason's fingers tangled with hers. It still didn't stop the trembling, but it helped. "Well, that happened."

He grunted, then gave her hand a squeeze. "You okay?"

Pulling in a shaky breath she nodded. "I guess I'm not surprised. We knew what he was and what he was capable of. It's a relief to know that someone's trying to stop him, though."

The Gator appeared over the crest of the hill, Brandon and Arthur heading their way, and Charlotte's chest grew tight. "Shit. I suppose I can't keep putting this off."

"We." Wrapping an arm around her shoulders, Jason pulled her against his side and rested his chin on the top of her head. "You're not in this alone, and you don't have to handle this alone."

She looked up at Jason, gratitude and love washing through her. *This man.* As long as he was by her side, she knew she could make it through anything. "Thank you."

He kissed the tip of her nose and laughed. "Don't thank me yet."

THIRTY-FOUR
JASON

P erfect.

That was the only word Jason had to describe that night. *Perfect.*

The Open House went off without a hitch, and there was no doubt in his mind that Charlotte had made it all happen. From the moment the first guest arrived to the taillights of the last hired server disappearing in the dark, she had been a shining star and the driving force.

And he was so stupidly lost in love with her.

Standing in front of the house with the Trevinos and Dr. Angus, Jason couldn't stop smiling. It had been the same all night. Watching Charlotte move through the crowd, welcoming everyone, answering questions, giving tours, had kept him on cloud nine. He hadn't been able to tear his eyes away. Her hair was pinned up in a loose twist, curled tendrils waving around her face, and she was the picture of elegance in a pair of flowy pants and a sleeveless blouse. Even now, after hours of entertaining and selling her idea, she was simply glowing.

He tried not to glare at the rest of the people around them, anxious to get her back to his place where he could pamper her and worship her and keep her in his arms all night. Wouldn't they ever stop talking?

"At least five planners took my number and already texted me about upcoming weddings for Texas Drawl performances." Brandon shook his head in disbelief. "And not only that, but one of them has a connection to a label that is looking for our sound. The guys could hardly believe it. Hell, *I* hardly believe it, myself."

"You deserve it, Bran." Dr. Angus smiled at him from next to Arthur, snuggled under his arm. "It was only a matter of time before your hard work paid off."

"See?" Arthur puffed his chest. "I told you there was nothing to be worried about. There were no boogeymen, no villains bursting in to ruin the night. It was an overreaction, nothing more. We won!"

"I can't believe we pulled this off." Charlotte's voice was thick with emotion and Jason looked down, surprised to see tears shining on her cheeks.

"I can." He pulled her against his chest and buried his face in her soft, warm curls. "There is nothing that can withstand the will of Charlotte Trevino. With you at the helm, there was no way this *wouldn't* be a raging success."

Everyone around them cheered and echoed his sentiments. Then she pressed her lips to the side of his neck, sending goosebumps skittering over his skin.

"Thank you," she whispered.

Jason dipped his head and brushed his mouth over the shell of her ear. "Let's get out of here and you can thank me by letting me make love with you all night, any and every way you want me to."

The shiver he felt run through her started a fire low in his gut and he needed to get them out of there. Now.

Dr. Angus yawned, setting off a chain reaction around the little group, and they all laughed.

"Okay, everyone needs to get to bed. Sleep, relax, celebrate." Charlotte's smile was bright even in the dark of the late hour. "I need to go down and turn off lights, make sure everyone is gone, and lock up."

"I can do it, if you want," Brandon chimed in. "You've done everything else."

But she just shook her head and laughed. "Have you met me, Bran? You know I need to go see for myself. It'll take me ten minutes."

"Want me to come with you?" Jason rested his hand on the small of her back, and she rolled her eyes.

"I can manage. Why don't you go get the truck." Pushing up on her toes, she brushed her lips over his and lowered her voice. "I'll be right back. Then you better get me home and naked. Fast."

She walked backwards with one eyebrow raised, and he couldn't stop smiling. Watching her make her way down the hill, waiting until she disappeared through the barn door, he couldn't believe how lucky he was. Why the hell this smart, passionate, stubborn, beautiful woman chose him, he'd never know.

He just knew that he would spend the rest of his life making sure he deserved her.

A little breeze ran up the hill, ruffling his hair, and he turned into it. What was that smell? Something pungent and oily, like a motor overheating. The rest of the group had just moved to go their separate ways when Jason turned his gaze to the barn just as a flash of light near the barn's entrance caught Jason's attention. A second later, he heard the first *boom*. Jason took one step in the direction of the barn, still trying to figure out what the noise was, when he saw the flashes and heard the booms of the second and third blasts.

Several more explosions sounded in quick succession, yellow flames licking up the outer walls before Jason had taken more than two steps. With a roar and blast of heat, the side of the barn facing them was a wall of fire.

"Charlotte!"

He took off at a sprint, panic pushing him forward. He was vaguely aware of Brandon's voice behind him, but his brain didn't register anything but the need to get there, to get to Charlotte, to make sure she was okay. More *booms* followed, explosions chasing one after another around the perimeter of the barn, the glow of the blaze climbing higher and higher.

This wasn't happening. This was a nightmare, nothing more, and he'd wake up drenched in sweat with Char lying next to him any second now. It couldn't be real. Fuck! Why was it so far away? Every step should be cutting the distance, but somehow the barn wasn't any closer. All he could hear was the pounding of his heart in his ears, beating in time with his silent prayer, *Be alive, be alive, be alive.*

Almost there now, it felt like he was inhaling broken glass, his throat raw and burning. "Charlotte!" The smoke was thick now, making him cough, and he couldn't see into the building anywhere. Hysteria clawed into his chest and despite the inferno in front of him, the searing heat burning his skin, he made a run for the entrance, calling her name.

He had to find her, she needed him, he had to save her. But before he could make a move to leap over the flames, he was grabbed from behind and spun around and away from the building.

"What are you doing, man?" Brandon had one arm wrapped firmly around his chest, holding him back. "You can't go in there!"

"Charlotte! Let go of me, Bran, she's in there! She's just inside and she needs me, I have to—"

"You can't, Jay!" Brandon's voice broke, but Jason continued to struggle and pull against his grip. "Stop fighting me! You can't go in there; you won't come out alive!"

A sob ripped out of Jason's throat. "But she's in there, she's still in there! I have to find her. I need to get her out!"

Suddenly, a horrible groan and creak sounded all around them, sounding like the earth itself was splitting in two.

"*Run!*" Brandon hauled Jason off his feet, shoving him back up the hill as fast as they could move. But when the structure came down with a resounding rumble of thunder, the flames reached out for them, scorching the grass halfway up the hill.

The two men stumbled and collapsed in a gasping heap on the ground. Jason jumped up and fisted his hands in his hair as he stared at the enormous pyre where a barn had been just a minute ago.

Falling to his knees, Jason couldn't breathe. He was aware of people moving around him, a woman's scream, the sound of sirens in the distance. But there was no air in his lungs, no pounding of his heart. His stomach shrank, twisted, expanded and contracted until he was forced forward onto his hands and he threw up everything. Even when he was empty, he retched and heaved, finally falling back onto his heels, gasping for air.

Not real, this cannot be real. He repeated it over and over in his head, refusing to believe what was right before his eyes. She went into the building, but did she come out? Maybe he just didn't see her. Pressing his fists against his eyes, he shook his head.

Wake up! You have to wake up!

He had to be dreaming because there was no way he could exist in a world that didn't include Charlotte.

———

The fire was still smoking, the crew still putting out hotspots several hours later. Jason, Brandon, and Arthur were all standing in the yard too stunned and heartbroken to speak.

He'd seen Charlotte go into the barn, had been looking at the building as it caught fire, but Jason never saw her leave. *He never saw her leave.* The fire burned too hot for him to get close, but damn it he tried. Brandon had to hold him back, had to try to convince him it was too dangerous and that they wouldn't do any good for her by getting themselves hurt, too. Instead, they took turns calling and texting her phone, praying to the gods and the universe and anyone listening to just let her pick up.

"Charlotte, it's Jay. I need you to call me immediately. Or text me. Or—just let me know you're okay."

"Damn it, Char, pick up the god damned phone!" His voice broke and he choked back a sob. "We are all here, we're all scared to death—where are you? Please Charlotte. Please call me back."

The phone rang and rang, and he left message after message until her mailbox was full. Then he started texting. Frantically, at first. But as time went by, as the trucks showed up and they got started on subduing the fire, as his phone didn't ring or chime or do anything in his hand, the texts became less panicked and more hopeless.

Charlotte. Please, please, please come find me. I won't be mad that you haven't answered. I won't care, just come home.

I need you, Char. Please don't leave me. I can't BE without you.

He swallowed the lump in his throat and turned away from the smoldering barn. If he thought about her last moments, he didn't think he could keep breathing. Already his chest was full of boulders and his feet made of lead. She was gone. Charlotte was gone.

Arthur and Brandon held each other, crying together and trying to offer comfort while their worlds had collapsed. Again. Jason knew this wasn't his place. He knew he didn't belong there with them. This was her family, the people she belonged to. Who was he?

Just the man who loved her.

After he'd given his statements, barely able to choke out the words, feeling numb from head to toe, he snuck away as quietly as he could. The headlights swept around the curves in the road, muscle memory the only thing navigating his drive. His body remembered where to go even if he saw nothing, felt nothing.

He parked the truck in front of his house, shutting off the headlights and turning off the ignition. In the dark of the cab, he put his head on the steering wheel and wept.

She was gone. The one woman he couldn't stop thinking about, the one woman who knew him better than he did himself, the one woman he'd loved from the moment he'd met her was gone. What was he supposed to do now? How could he get out of bed tomorrow and the next day and the next, knowing that he'd never see her or hold her again?

What was the point?

Dragging his hands down his face, he took a deep breath and got out of the truck. What was he going to tell his mom? Would she even understand that Charlotte was dead? He couldn't imagine how she'd react. Or how painful it would be for him every single time she asked him where she was or when she'd be coming by again.

Bracing himself on the hood of his truck, he had to stop and catch his breath. Even outside in the cool Texas night air, there was no oxygen, and he felt like he was suffocating.

When he felt like his lungs were moving again, he trudged toward the front door, kicking the mat back into place where it had folded over on itself. Just get inside, he told himself. Get through the front door, lock it behind you, and then think about what comes next.

He stepped inside, tossing his keys into the bowl next to the door. With barely any strength left in him, he floundered for the light switch. The same switch he'd hit his whole life, as a child, as a teen sneaking in after hours, as an adult stumbling through after too many drinks. But now he couldn't find it. The world was different now.

Light finally flooded the room and he rubbed his eyes against the sudden brightness. He took a few shuffling steps further into the house before he looked around to let his eyes adjust.

"I didn't know where else to go."

He jumped at the unexpected voice coming from his kitchen, and when he looked again, his knees went soft. "Charlotte?"

Sitting on a kitchen stool, a towel wrapped around her forearm, she stared up at him with her golden eyes wide and terrified. There was soot and dirt and blood smeared over her, her hair was tangled, and he could see clearly where her tears had cleaned streaks down her cheeks.

She stood, wobbling a little, and he heard her voice catch in her throat. "I didn't know where else to go, Jay. I was so scared. There was someone else there, I saw them outside, they were dousing the walls with gas or kerosene, I don't know—" her voice broke, but then the words started flowing out of her like she'd explode if she didn't set them loose. "Then the explosions, Jay. I didn't know what to do, I didn't know how many there were, or where they were coming from. I ducked under a table, and they just kept coming. And then they stopped, and it was so silent for just a second and then... there was this enormous *whoosh,* and all the air was sucked out of the room and there was fire and...I don't know how I got out, not really. The doors were blocked, I could barely see across the room, the smoke was so thick. But I didn't panic. You would've been proud of me." Her voice broke again, and she pressed her fingertips to her lips, eyes wide. "I crawled along the floor and then there was broken glass under my hands. I climbed through the window and then I was outside, and I could breathe. God, I was so scared. I didn't know if they were still out there, if they were watching me, and I just needed to get away. So I ran and I crossed the whole ranch, just running and running and then I was here." She paused, blinking at him before holding up the kitchen towel she was clutching. "I'm sorry about your towel."

Jason stared at her, trying to remember how to breathe in and out. Was he hallucinating? Had his grief overtaken his mind to show him what he wanted more than anything? She was holding one of his kitchen towels out to him, a big slash of blood soaked into it, but he barely registered it. Her bottom lip trembled as she watched him, and he realized he didn't care. Didn't care if she was real or a figment of his imagination, she was there.

One foot in front of the other, he approached her, not blinking, not looking away for fear that she'd disappear. Tears were pooling along the lower curve of her eyes, and her breath was coming faster as he got closer. Tentatively he reached for her, pressing his palm against her warm, damp cheek, stroking her hair, just taking her in and letting himself believe it was her.

Because it *was* her. Charlotte. She was here, alive, warm and real and *here*.

"Jason."

It was a plea and an apology, and it was so low he almost didn't hear it. Cupping her face in his hands, he brushed his lips over hers. *Warm.* He pulled her against his chest and kissed her again, slowly, in case she was nothing more than a mirage and any sudden movement would make her vanish.

His heart would disintegrate.

She curled into him, her mouth soft and sweet even through the smell of smoke that clung to her. There was no rush, no need to hurry or to take this moment any farther than right now. Charlotte was in his arms. She was alive, she was safe. And he wouldn't let her go again.

When he pulled back to see her face, he felt a surge of relief that nearly knocked him off his feet. Still holding her in his arms, he lowered them to the couch, pulling her into his lap, needing to keep as much contact between them as possible. But at least now his blood was moving again, his heart was still beating, and he could think a little more clearly.

"Where are you hurt?"

SHARON L. CLARK

She shook her head a little, then held up her arm. There was a long, angry gash running up her forearm, but it was barely bleeding anymore. "I think I cut myself on the window when I climbed out. I don't know if the blast broke it or if it was me, but I didn't realize it until I was here, dripping blood on your kitchen floor." She blinked at him. "Sorry."

The absurdity of her concern about the mess made him laugh. Then the laugh turned into a sob, and he crushed her to him again. "I don't give a flying fuck about that towel. You're here. You're alive. Messes get cleaned up, wounds can be stitched back together." Settling her on the couch, he ducked into the kitchen for a wet towel and then started wiping the grime from her face. From her precious face. He kissed her tenderly again for what felt like the thousandth time, but it still wasn't enough. It took him several tries before he was able to choke any sound from his throat. "I thought...Jesus Charlotte, I thought I'd lost you."

With her arms around his neck, she nestled against him, her voice thick with tears. "For a minute I thought you did, too."

They stayed like that for a few minutes, just breathing and holding onto each other. If he had any say in the matter, he'd stay like this, with her, all night. All week, all year. Suddenly she tensed and let out a gasp.

"What? What's wrong?"

"My dad! Brandon!" She slid off his lap and sat next to him, her eyes pinched at the edges. "Do they think I'm dead, too?"

"Shit." He jumped up and searched for his cell. "Shit fuck god damn it. They do, Charlotte. We all did. The fire wasn't out yet when I left and the chief just said he'd let me know when he knew anything more."

"I don't know where my phone is, I don't remember the last time I had it and then I got here, and you don't have a landline, and I didn't know what else to do so I just sat here in the dark and waited. But oh my god, I have to let them know that I'm okay!"

What did he do with his phone? "Yes, we do and we will. They were destroyed—we all were—when we thought…well you know what we thought." He finally found it on the floor in the entryway and handed it to Charlotte. "Go ahead and call them, I'll make us something to eat, get some water for you. Let me know when you've talked to them."

He turned to slip into the kitchen to give her some privacy, but she called out to him.

"Jay?"

"Yeah?"

She chewed the inside of her cheek as she dialed with shaky hands. "Please don't leave me. I don't want to be alone."

His heart fell like a stone into his feet at the tremor in her voice, but he just nodded and sat back down. After she hit send, she paced the room, crying and trying to explain what happened and reassuring them that she was all right.

"No. No, Bran, you don't need to come get me. If you guys thought I was dead then he does, too. And I need to figure out what to do next. I'm safe as long as he thinks I'm dead." She listened for a moment, her eyes twitching to Jason as she nodded. "Mhm. I know. I'll tell him. I love you guys."

She disconnected the call and handed the phone back to him, keeping her eyes on his. There was no way he was going to look away, not tonight. He tossed the phone onto the couch and ran the backs of his fingers down her cheek. Closing her eyes, she leaned into his touch and wrapped her hand around his wrist.

"I need you, Jason." She opened her eyes, moving his hand to her waist and burying her fingers in the front of his shirt. "Please, I need you to hold me, to touch me. Make me forget tonight for at least a little while. Remind me that I'm alive and that you love me and that everything will be okay."

A single tear rolled down her cheek and he rolled his thumb over her cheek, trying to erase the fear it represented. "Charlotte…" He should just let her sleep, put her in his bed and stay on the couch. But he couldn't stop touching her.

With her hand wound through his hair, she pulled his face to hers. "Please." Her lips were soft and warm when she kissed him, and when her tongue traced his bottom lip, he couldn't resist any longer.

He cradled her head in one hand, the other against her low back, pressing, pulling, holding her closer, he needed her closer, impossibly close. She whimpered in the back of her throat and every nerve ending came to life. Angling her head just a fraction gave him better access to her lips, to her mouth, to her tongue and he didn't think he could breathe if he stopped kissing her.

Sweeping an arm behind her knees and wrapping the other across her back, he lifted her into his arms and walked toward the bedroom. No matter what else happened, he was going to make her feel safe and whole. She would fall asleep knowing that she was loved–that *he* loved her–and that he'd never let her be afraid or feel alone or lost ever again.

———

The last time Jason had sat on this porch swing, Charlotte had been with him, her bare feet in his lap, the breeze blowing her bangs into her eyes. The peace of that moment swept through him and the corner of his mouth lifted.

God that seemed like a lifetime ago. The reality was that only a week had passed and everything was different. Arthur was on the other end of the swing, Brandon standing on the top step with one shoulder against the beam.

His eyes were drawn time and again to the blackened mass at the bottom of the hill, the spot that had been Charlotte's dream, her triumph. And there was nothing recognizable there.

"Are you sure he's coming?"

They heard an engine coming up the driveway, tires churning over the dirt path before a white pickup truck emerged from the line of trees like Moby Dick crashing through the surface of the ocean.

Eyes narrowed, Bran descended the steps while Jason and Arthur stood behind him. When Gerard Chancellor climbed down from the cab of his gaudy white dually, Arthur laid a hand on Jason's arm.

If he hadn't, he'd already be across the yard with his hands around the man's throat.

Chancellor strolled toward them, shaking his head, and stopped halfway between the truck and Brandon. Then he clucked his tongue and turned the corners of his mouth down into what Jason could only assume was supposed to be a frown.

"Ah, such a tragedy." He looked each man in the eye one at a time. "May I offer my sincere condolences on the loss of your daughter, your sister, and your...paramour."

The bones in Jason's hands nearly creaked from how tightly he was clenching his fists. *What a smug piece of shit.* Despite the plan laid out here, he really wanted to just pummel the life out of him.

"Has there been any progress in the investigation? Was the fire chief able to determine the cause of this horrendous accident?"

"Yep." Brandon pushed his hands into his pockets and cocked his head. "Turns out it was no accident. The investigators found evidence of a pipe bomb." Chancellor's eyes narrowed. "Several, in fact."

"Is that so?"

"Oh yeah. I think they counted thirteen? Maybe as many as twenty." Jason moved to the other side of the porch and leaned his elbows on the top rail. "See, they recovered pieces of multiple small travel alarm clocks and 9-volt batteries at fairly even intervals around the perimeter."

Arthur stepped forward now. "They believe an accelerant was used on the outside of the barn, too. Kerosene, they're pretty sure. These old barns go up fast on their own, but someone wanted it to go up *really* fast."

"You're saying this was arson?" Chancellor held very still, only moving his eyes from one man to another. "Why on earth would someone want to hurt that sweet little lady?"

Now Brandon crossed his arms over his chest. "You know, we were asking ourselves the very same question."

"Did you know she was almost run off the road a little over a month ago?" Jason watched the old man very carefully, waiting for some kind of tell, some kind of indication that he knew he was well and truly screwed.

When Chancellor didn't respond, Jason continued. "Oh yeah. Some big black truck terrified her on a lonely stretch of highway just outside of town. Come to think of it, I believe she said you came by shortly after and asked if she was okay." He looked at Arthur and Brandon. "Is that what you guys remember, too? She did say *Gerard* Chancellor, didn't she?"

The other men nodded their assent, and the smarmy bastard actually scoffed.

"So what, then? Are you trying to say that I was the one who tried to kill her? I was nowhere near the area on that night." He lifted his chin in challenge and scowled. "Besides, what possible motive would someone like me have to cause harm to someone like her?"

Bingo. "Oh, I think you have quite a few reasons. Billions, in fact."

"You're being ridiculous." Chancellor huffed and waved a dismissive hand at Jason. "Now, I believe these gentlemen had something they wanted to discuss with me, and I don't believe it involves you. So do scurry off now, won't you?"

Jason stayed exactly where he was and shook his head. "Nope, I'm good. I think I'll stay."

The old man reached inside his suit coat and produced a folded bundle of papers which he held out to Brandon. "Now, this is a very generous, very reasonable offer for this property. Of course, it was much higher before the barn tragically burned down. But you'll see that it's more than enough for you to retire comfortably, Arthur. And for young Brandon here to chase his dreams of stardom."

Bran looked at the papers like they were covered in shit and took a step back away from them. "Oh, no. I think you misunderstand. We didn't ask you here to sell the ranch."

"Don't be so stubborn. This piece of land has been an albatross around your neck for the better part of a year now, and with the *accident*—" Jason's rage burned in his chest at the emphasis on the word. "—that befell fair Charlotte, I would think you'd be anxious to walk away from here. It's time to be rid of this nightmare before another senseless tragedy befalls this family."

If he noticed the way Arthur, Brandon and Jason all stiffened at his words, he didn't show it. He actually moved closer, holding out the papers once more. "Just make the deal, take the money, and go off to lick your wounds. Start all over far from here and the painful memory of Charlotte's demise."

The door behind Jason opened and closed, and he was so glad he'd kept his eyes locked on Chancellor. Watching the color leach from his face and his eyes almost bug out of his head was a sight he wouldn't have missed for the world.

"I believe my brother said he wasn't interested."

Jason turned to watch her emerge from the shadowy overhang of the porch and it didn't matter that he got to see her when he woke every morning or before drifting off to sleep every night, she still sent a thrill of joy through his veins.

And judging by the shock on Chancellor's face, it sent a jolt of fear through his.

THIRTY-FIVE
CHARLOTTE

It didn't take long for Chancellor to recover his composure, and Charlotte wasn't surprised. This man was practiced at the art of deception. She locked her gaze on his and watched the wheels turning as his lips spread into a poisonous smile.

"Well, well, if it isn't the little rattlesnake. I am so *relieved* to learn that you are, indeed, alive." He braced both hands on the head of his cane and pulled his shoulders back. The look he leveled on her could only be described as loathing. "Welcome back from the dead, Ms. Trevino."

"Save it. This is a horse ranch, remember, and we are already full up on shit." His eyes narrowed slightly, and she smiled sweetly. Oh, he was going to make the next ten minutes so very satisfying.

"You know, none of us could figure out what you were doing out here in Zearing, in the middle of nowhere. Sure, San Antonio is a short drive away, but what could we possibly have to offer someone such as yourself?"

He sniffed. "I saw an opportunity to expand some of my interests, and this little community was struggling. It was as good a place as any to get into the business of horses and farm production."

She pointed at him. "Yes, you wanted to expand your interests. That part I believe wholeheartedly. It's just everything else you said that was utter garbage."

"Now you look here, missy. I don't know who you think you are to talk to me like that, but you will sorely regret it."

The bluster only made Charlotte's smile broader. "No. I don't think I will. But thanks for your concern."

She turned to Jason, and he winked, making her stomach erupt in butterflies. Seamlessly, he stepped up and continued for her.

"You see, it took us a while to put it all together, but we got there eventually. My uncle was instrumental in gathering all the pieces, and he's very sorry he couldn't be here to see this."

Chancellor's mustache was vibrating with rage at this point, and he raked his eyes over each of them. "I don't know what kind of game you all are playing here, but I am a very busy man, and I don't have time to screw around with it."

He turned to go back to his truck when his phone started ringing and pinging with notifications. With a start, he pulled it from his pocket and swore under his breath before accepting the call.

"What do you want? Why are you—" His voice cut off suddenly and he froze. After listening silently for a couple beats, he spun around and stared, blotches of angry red creeping up his neck. He ended the call, but it started ringing again before he had the chance to even lower the phone. Glancing at the number, he became as still as stone.

"There's no need to answer that one. I'm pretty sure it's going to be the same as the last. So will the one after that and the one after that." Without looking away, Charlotte walked down the steps, planting her feet in the dirt just out of Chancellor's reach. "If I'm not mistaken, that was one of your flunkies on the phone, right? Calling in a panic to let you know that there are DEA agents swarming the property, right?"

The door to the house opened again, and Charlotte nearly burst into laughter as rage and disbelief flooded his face. Agents Fisk and Gomez walked past her on either side approaching the old man with the handcuffs already out.

"Gerard Chancellor, you are under arrest for drug trafficking and aiding and abetting known international felons. You have the right to remain silent."

"You *bitch!*"

Charlotte laughed. "Apparently, that's not one you're going to exercise."

"You have no idea what kind of a shit storm you have just unleashed on yourself." Chancellor's lips curved up on either side, spittle flying from them as he raged. "These assholes will place me under arrest for now, but we both know that I'll be out before dinner. None of these charges will stick, my lawyers will make sure I don't spend a single day in jail. And then you and I will see each other again, little rattlesnake. You can count on that."

"I have no doubt that you're right. But there's something you're not considering that will throw a bit of a wrench into your plans."

The hatred rolling off of him was almost palpable, and he sneered. "Oh really? And what, pray tell, am I not considering?"

"How many sites did you have set up here, Chancellor?" Brandon stepped around his sister. "At least four or five just through Zearing, right? And then how many other drop sites do you have scattered across Texas, each one moving millions of dollars of cocaine, if I'm not mistaken?"

Now Arthur stood on the steps, scratching his chin. "Those phone calls were from your men, telling you that your properties and all the drugs were seized by the DEA simultaneously. Those men are also being arrested as we speak, and you can bet your ass they're gonna start singing as soon as they're offered a deal."

Realization opened Chancellor's eyes wide, and he swallowed hard.

"So, by dinner, on the timeline you mentioned, these nice men are going to have the locations of all of your installations, and they will seize everything they contain, as well." Jason looked so happy when he glanced at Charlotte that she had to cover her mouth so she didn't burst into laughter. He tapped a finger to his chin as he continued. "How much money will you lose because of this? Millions? Billions? But the thing is, that isn't actually your money, is it?"

Chancellor's head was already shaking, his mouth opening and closing without any sound coming out. "No. You can't do this to me. You wouldn't."

"We aren't doing anything to you. This is all your own doing and it's a bed you're going to have to lie in now." Charlotte paused, the sheer terror in his eyes giving her pause for a second.

But just for a second.

"You're right that you won't spend any time in jail, but you may want to reconsider that option. Because everyone here knows you'll probably live longer there than you will on your own. You know that too, don't you? You know that word is already spreading, and your bosses are finding out what's happened and how much money they just lost because of you."

The old man looked at her once more as Agent Fisk guided him into the back of the patrol car that had arrived. She refused to look away and shrugged before the door shut.

"I imagine they'll want a word with you."

CHARLOTTE
EPILOGUE

"This is so much more than I expected, Mitch. You have outdone yourself."

Charlotte stepped back and looped her arm through her friend's and leaned her head on his shoulder. "It's perfect."

He chuckled and kissed the top of her head. "Think nothing of it, m'lady. You have had a wacky year, what with rebuilding the barn and holding events without walls, managing all of it with grace. Besides, when I'm enlisted to help with a surprise birthday party you can bet your ass I'm all in."

"He doesn't know anything does he?" Charlotte chewed her lip. "If Jed gets him here and he isn't surprised, I'm coming for you."

"Me?" Mitch was all smiles as he backed away and she laughed.

Looking around the space, though, the butterflies took flight, and she pressed a hand to her stomach to stop them. Nearly everyone who had helped with renovation the first time around had once again volunteered their time, talents, and supplies to build it from the foundation this time. And they were all gathered here waiting for the guest of honor to arrive.

"Charlotte Rose, have you eaten anything at all today?" Arthur and Dr Angus wandered over, hand-in-hand, and the kind woman who looked at her dad with stars in her eyes leveled her with an accusatory scowl.

"I've nibbled."

"Mhm. That's what I thought." She nodded and Brandon appeared out of nowhere with a plate of food that he nearly shoved into her hands.

"Hey! That's for the party!"

"There won't be a party if the hostess passes out first. Just eat and quit being a pain in my ass." The words were delivered with a wink and were full of nothing but brotherly love.

She lurked around the edges of the building and watched all the activity around her while she ate. Yes, she'd held events here without walls, nothing but the exposed beams holding up the roof while people pledged their lives to each other. No one who had wanted to hold ceremonies there before the fire had batted an eye after it, either.

But now, a little more than a year since there had been nothing but burnt rubble where she was standing, there was a nearly complete barn, with walls and running water and electricity. Weekends were already booked for the next several months and Charlotte was so grateful for everything and everyone who had stuck by her.

Especially Jason.

She had spent the last two months planning and sneaking around behind his back to pull this surprise together. It wasn't nearly sufficient to show him how much he meant to her, but it was a start. Expressing that kind of love and admiration wasn't possible.

Mitch burst through the door and whistled. "They're coming!"

"Everyone hide! Dad, hit the lights, will you?" She crouched behind the beam closest to the door and held her breath. There was still shuffling going on behind her as everyone got ready, but it settled down long before she heard Jed's voice drawing nearer.

"You know, I swear Brandon said he left that toolbox on the porch. But he probably left it down here."

"If you say so." Jason's voice followed the sound of the door opening and closing and then the lights burst to life and Charlotte burst from her hiding spot.

"SURPRISE!" But hers was the only voice that bounced from the rafters.

Jason stood a few feet away, his hands in his pockets and looking as handsome as she'd ever seen him. What he didn't look, however, was surprised. "Hey."

Well, shit. "You guys!" She turned to see what all the other guests were doing, why they hadn't jumped out when she did, and she froze.

Every guest was emerging slowly from their hiding spots. And every one of them held a single yellow rose.

"What's going on?"

One by one, they approached and kissed her cheek, handing her their roses until she could hardly hold them all. When everyone had filed past, Jason was at her side, easing the gorgeous blooms and their heady scent from her arms.

"Let me take those." Passing them to Mitch, Jason turned back and kissed her cheek. "Hi."

Her stomach leapt, her mouth suddenly dry. "You already said that."

"Right, I did." He laughed and raked a hand through his hair. "You'd think I'd have this planned out a little better, wouldn't you?"

"Planning the flowers without me knowing was pretty damn good." Charlotte squeaked out as Jason took both her hands. "But this was supposed to be for you."

"It *is* for me." He took a deep breath and lifted her hands to his mouth. Even though his breath was warm, the touch of his lips on her knuckles sent goosebumps skittering up her arms.

"When I saw you in Mitch's store last year, I thought I was dreaming. But when you challenged me and called me out with the first words you'd said to me in eight years I knew I was looking at the real deal. And every day since then, I've been so grateful that you're here that I can't believe I wasted so much time without you."

Tears pricked the backs of her eyes and Charlotte couldn't take in a full breath. "Jason…"

"From the first time you smiled at me across the football field, to the night I held you after you lost your mom, every time you pushed me to follow my dreams and demanded that I see my strengths, especially when you refused to let me get away with any kind of bullshit, I fell a little more in love with you."

She tried to swallow, but there was something in the way. Tears blurred her vision until she blinked and set them free. Cupping her cheek, Jason brushed them away with his thumb, giving her a smile that melted her insides and made her knees shake.

"Charlotte Rose, you are the best part of me. I never thought I could feel so complete until you, and I never knew what love really was until you. There is so much I lost by not spending every minute of every day making you smile, arguing with you, kissing you. And I won't ever make that mistake again."

Her heart battered her ribs, swelling so big that she thought it might burst. When he pulled a small box from his pocket and held it out to her, she choked out a sob.

"Open it," he whispered.

Inside was a ring of white gold, delicate swirls of tiny sapphires twisting up the sides and surrounding a pear-shaped diamond.

"This is my mom's ring." The tears were falling freely now, and she turned her face up to Jason's.

There was no way Charlotte could believe that anyone, anywhere, at any point in time had felt as much love as she felt looking into his midnight-blue eyes. "It is. And if you wear it, I swear to you that I will cook the most amazing dinners just for you, I'll take you dancing and teach you my secret chili recipe. If you let me, I will fight with you every day for the rest of your life as long as I get to make up with you after. You'll never know another day doubting that you are cherished, and that you make my life better just by existing."

Laying a finger on his lips, Charlotte laughed. "Will you please just ask me so I can say yes?"

His lips curved under her touch and he wrapped his arms around her.

"Charlotte Rose Trevino, wanna marry me?"

Laughing, her head dropped back, and she shouted to the ceiling, the feelings inside her suddenly too big and too powerful. "YES!" She looked into his eyes and whispered it again.

"Yes, Jason James Archer. I wanna marry you."

He kissed her then, the sound of whistles and whoops barely registering as she melted into his embrace. She clung to him, wanting forever with him to start immediately, yesterday, if possible.

The party slid into full swing all around them, but neither of them even noticed. "So you kinda like me, huh?" He nodded and she kissed him again, saying, "Good," against his lips.

He framed her face with his hands, and she couldn't believe that she'd get to see that smile, the one he saved just for her, for the rest of her life.

"Welcome home, Charlotte."

THE END

THANK YOU FOR READING

———

Did you enjoy this book?

We invite you to leave a review at your favorite book site, such as Goodreads, Amazon, Barnes & Noble, etc.

DID YOU KNOW THAT LEAVING A REVIEW...

- Helps other readers find books they may enjoy.
- Gives you a chance to let your voice be heard.
- Gives authors recognition for their hard work.
- Doesn't have to be long. A sentence or two about why you liked the book will do.

ACKNOWLEDGMENTS

I always dreamed but never believed that I'd have a book published, and yet here I am with TWO out in the world! How and why I've been this lucky, I'll never know. But I know for sure I didn't get here alone.

Thank you to my agent Amy Brewer and the team at Metamorphosis Literary Agency for keeping the party going and helping me continue to chase my dream.

Thank you to Nancy and Caroline and everyone at Melange Books. Your belief in me and your gorgeous book covers are more than I could have asked for.

Thank you to Sophie Mitchell for sharing your extensive knowledge about horses and horse training.

Thank you to Tim for answering my questions, not laughing at me, and setting me straight on how things work out in the real world.

Thank you to the crews in the Cops and Writers and Authors Fire/Rescue Groups on Facebook. I promise that knowledge will only be used fictionally.

Thank you again to my mom and to my sisters for having my back and checking in and showing up, and I love you all. And special thanks to Wendy; you're an awesome book pimp and the best hype-woman around!

Thank you to Jamie, Stephanie, and Sarah. How'd I get to be so lucky to have you in my life? Writing and laughing with you keeps me (relatively) sane, and I know I can always count on you for encouragement, affection, and acceptance of all my wackiness. Writing connected us, friendship keeps us together, and I appreciate and love you more than you know.

Thank you to Maddie, Simon, and Garrett: you continue to impress and amaze me all the time. Knowing you believe in me means the world to me, and I'm so proud to be your mom.

Thank you, Andrew, for continuing to have my back, for encouraging and supporting and promoting me every chance you get. I'd have talked myself out of this long ago without you. I love you.

 Sharon L. Clark is a romantic suspense author hailing from Des Moines, Iowa, where she never outgrew her enormous imagination and continues to feed both her hopeless-romantic heart and her villain-wannabe brain.

An avid reader from a very young age, Sharon still enjoys living vicariously through the heroines in adventure novels, falling in love again and again through romances, and getting the tar scared out of her now and again. After attending the University of Northern Iowa Sharon met her husband, Andrew, and together they have raised three pretty cool humans and a handful of dogs. It wasn't until she was nearly an empty-nester that she allowed herself to explore and share the stories running around inside her head: the good, the bad, and the bizarre.

I'll Call You Home is the second novel in her "Enderlin Calling" series. You can check out her short stories and other musings on her website at SharonLClark.com or see what she's up to on her other social channels:

SharonLClark.com

facebook.com/SharonLClarkAuthor
x.com/sharclark36
instagram.com/sharclark40
linkedin.com/in/sharonlclarkauthor

ALSO BY SHARON L. CLARK

WITH SATIN ROMANCE

Enderlin Calling Series

I'll Call You Mine

I'll Call You Home